DAVE WARNER

DOUBLE EXXXPRESSO

fi

For Pitch

In memory of 'Son'o'Marty'

and the hope of a few more winners before the last race.

SOMETIME NOT LONG BEFORE FACEBOOK

It wasn't the first time Father Paul Monaghan had snagged his cassock on that splinter. Like everything else in his church, the confessional boxes had seen better days, those being back around 1969, the year of his ordination. Vibrant times, he thought wistfully. Anti-war songs on the radio, golf on the moon, soap on a rope, and TV shows like *F Troop*, funny shows but with real satire kids would watch on the old black and white Pye. Now it was all My Space and Foxtel ...

'Father?'

A plaintive voice emanating from the other side. Not from the heavenly realm, from behind the curtain of the confessional box. Daydreaming, professional hazard. Touching back down to reality in the here and now: August 2005.

'Three Hail Marys and an Our Father, Angelina.'

He'd long given up pretending he didn't know who the penitent was behind the thin cloth. Like footballers, they had habitual weaknesses: even if you couldn't recognise a voice, you could tell by the sins. Angelina's was spite and gossip, so even though he'd tuned out, he had a good idea of what her transgressions had been. He heard her leave the box, hoped there'd be no more custom. Out here on the periphery of the Perth metro area—where shopping centres consisted of a row of single-level brick shops and where you had to daily sweep gumnuts from your driveway—his clientele was largely of Italian descent: market gardeners, winegrowers, earthworks operators. A small parish, but the older Italians were devout—and time-consuming—especially when there was so much to do and so little money to do it. Collections were down every month while the school repair bill was ballooning.

Often the priest found himself wishing he was back at the prison tending lost souls who really needed his support. Not that his scorecard there had been anything to write home about. A few he'd managed to pull through to some kind of spiritual optimism. Many he had failed. That could be very hard to take. His drinking had grown heavier there, in synch with his moods. He suspected that's why the bishop had moved him on.

One thing, though: you never would have copped a splinter in the prison confessional box. They'd had a budget. He'd try to remember to sand down that shelf, ask Maria, his most dedicated volunteer, if she could mend his sleeve. Was a time he could sew it himself, but sixty was closing in as fast as his eyesight was receding. Young people didn't sew these days. And they certainly didn't come to mass, let alone confession.

Well, looked like that was it for the day. Good. Just beginning to rise when he heard the door of the confessional box swing open. New customer, a man, given the noise and bulk.

'Agh,' the penitent moaning, like kneeling was an effort. Older guy, out of shape. 'Forgive me, Father. Been a while since I confessed.'

Italian accent. Enzo? Yes, he could smell the hay and a trace of horse manure. Unusual. Enzo would accompany his wife to mass most Sundays, but the horse trainer rarely made it to confession.

Paul waiting for more. Enzo stalled, the silence hanging between them. With no admission of sin yet from his visitor, Monaghan prompted.

'How can I be of help?'

'Father, I need absolution for something I haven't done yet.'

'Some act you are planning on doing but haven't yet?'

'Yes. Not like killing anybody but ... yeah.'

'I'm afraid, Enzo, that I can't forgive you if you're planning to go ahead with this. The right course of action would be to avoid any wrongdoing in the first place.'

'It's a bit late for that.'

Which led to an obvious deduction. 'So, you have sinned?'

'Kind of, but not really. See, I have a horse that is going to win a race but ... well, not on its merits.'

'Are you planning on drugging the horse?'

Paul took a dim view of animal abuse.

'No ... I can't say. Trust me, the horse is fine. If I pull out now it would disappoint the wrong kind of people to disappoint.'

'But if you don't pull out, you will be disappointing your God.'

'Which is why I'm asking forgiveness. His punishment won't be as swift as theirs.'

Paul Monaghan's years around criminals had left him with an understanding of the dark currents that could drown a decent man. He was also acutely aware that very few criminal enterprises succeeded—if this was indeed criminal.

'You realise, Enzo, that the best laid plans of mice and men can go astray.'

'What do you mean, Father?'

'Your horse might not win.'

'Oh no, it'll win. You'd be mad not to have a few bob on it yourself: Hysterical, this Saturday, the last at Belmont. It'll be at least twelve to one.'

'I urge you to refrain from your planned course of action. Please find some time to communicate with God and let Him show you the right path.'

'Thanks, Father. I know you mean well, but it's too late. I'll say a few Hail Marys anyway. You never know, do you?'

Going through the quotes for a new school toilet block while munching on a toasted-cheese sandwich, Paul felt despair creeping into his bones like a virus. Not because the giant slabs of no-frills cheddar he was forced to buy to meet budget became hard and tasteless within forty-eight hours of opening: such privations he could live with. This was about money.

Sixty thousand the cheapest quote, and the parish savings account only in credit by five thousand seven hundred and thirty-six dollars. He needed a certifiable loaves-and-fishes miracle.

All clergy, Paul knew, went through a crisis of faith at some point. He felt himself on the verge of one now. If God wanted His word to be spread to a new generation, the school needed pupils, and what parents would send their kids to a school where the toilets never worked, and the sewer pipes were perpetually broken?

'Why don't you send me some miracle?' Muttering as he stared at the neat drawings.

'*I already did, arsehole.*'

Paul's head snapped up. That was real, right? Surely God doesn't speak like a yobbo. Tracing the voice to his open window, Paul getting up, shuffling over, looking out to the car park next door. Two blokes arguing over a car space. The car park was supposed to be for the exclusive use of church patrons, but with the welfare office next door, it was always full during the week. The only time there were empty bays was during the weekend mass. The antagonists parted with fingers pointing.

In prison somebody would be on the floor by now with a sharpened toothbrush sticking out of their guts. Small mercies. Paul lumbered to the electric kettle, tested the volume of water, shaking it—hearing the slosh. Enough for a cup. He kept the level in the kettle low to save on electricity.

I already did, arsehole.

In the act of clicking on the kettle, it was as if he simultaneously activated some dormant billboard in his brain that buzzed and flickered and flashed: *Maybe God Has Already Sent That Miracle.* Was it pure coincidence that the exchange in the car park seemed to answer his demand for divine intervention?

He'd asked the Almighty for help, but too obsessed with his torn cassock, the toilet block and the gross cheese, perhaps he'd ignored the response. Was he a pilot lost in cloud, unable to see spread out below his doubter's wings a solution as large and obvious as the MCG?

Enzo Rapanaro, who never came to confession, had materialised and told him that he had a horse that was going to win on Saturday at odds of at least twelve to one, which by Paul's calculations meant that, if the parish savings were invested, the money for the toilet block would be forthcoming, with more than a little left over.

A genuine loaves-and-fishes miracle.

2

'Being woken at three in the morning by a guy in a balaclava pointing a sawn-off shotgun at you, saying you have forty-eight hours to get out of town, seemed a career setback at the time. In retrospect it was the best thing that ever happened to me.'

The man doing the talking would have described himself as being six-foot one. He'd grown up with imperial and no way was that going to change now. Between sentences he would stop, take a sip from the very small espresso cup, one of a set he'd bought specially for the industrial unit's coffee machine, itself a twin to the one at the house on Broadbeach. Wishing he was there now, in his robe, gazing out over the ocean.

The man he was talking to was hanging from the hook where a heavy punching bag usually marked the exact dead centre of the unit. The man hanging was naked, his bound wrists looped over the hook, a thin gag tied around his mouth. There were tears staining his high cheekbones. His name was Marcus.

The big man, who wore a royal blue Armani shirt, was sitting on an old armchair with springs coming out the seat. 'What I find fascinating,' he said, 'is the way lives intersect at any given moment. Two distinct pasts come together to create a new history. I find that a mind-trip, like they used to say.' The Armani man was involved in a variety of commercial ventures. One of which was a daily invitation-only business-meets-pleasure cruise, where for five thousand dollars businessmen could cruise the Brisbane River in a luxury yacht that provided sightseeing opportunities of an exotic nature. Regrettably, Marcus, who collected patrons' fees, had found the temptation of ready cash exceeded his duty to, and fear of, his employer. It wouldn't do.

While that was the immediate reason that they found themselves sharing this moment of time, that hadn't been what the big guy had been referring to.

'What I'm saying, Marcus, is that these steps go way, way back.'

Giving the nod to a big Islander standing off to the side of the bag, a former pro boxer named Tongan George, who'd just taken a breather on account of it was damn hot in this tin box in Nerang. He'd already taken off his prized Broncos official merchandise shirt, yet sweat still dripped off his pecs onto the concrete floor. The nod signalled his breather was over. Tongan George brought his right fist back and drove it into Marcus's side, making him yelp through his gag.

That made the fourth guy in the room look up from where he'd been lying in a bean bag, eyes closed. Kieran was slimmer and younger than the boxer, and he was white, with twisted lips above a long jawline. Like George, he was on the big guy's payroll. He'd done the legwork to find Marcus and bring him here, so technically his job was done, but Kieran enjoyed watching pain being dealt out.

The Armani guy started talking again. 'You may wonder how I came to get the name Vinyl Lionel. Way back in 1971, when your mother was probably a schoolgirl dancing around to David Cassidy, I was a young man invariably wearing an Aston Villa shirt, driving his Mini-Minor through the streets of South London. I followed Villa because in those days Palace and Charlton were hopeless, and Millwall ...'

Nodding for George to lay in another punch, this one a left to the kidneys.

'... Well, I wasn't a psycho.'

George obliged. Marcus whimpered.

'In the back of my Mini on any given day would be a hundred vinyl LPs, bootleg recordings, the kind of bands whose gigs would be advertised in the back pages of *Melody Maker*: Hawkwind at the Surrey Rooms, Caravan and Genesis at the

Starlight down Crawley way, Supertramp at the Temple in Soho.' A golden age, Lionel inwardly grinning at the memories: knitted vests, pint of Watneys, cheap petrol. 'The bootleg industry—albums that were released by people who didn't have the licence to release those albums—was thriving, and I, by good fortune, a little business acumen, and a sizeable quantity of sheer bullshit, carved a niche in it for myself.'

Tongan George looked over to see if he should go again, but Lionel gave him a *not yet* signal, partially because he didn't want Marcus dying on him, also because he was enjoying telling his story. Kieran had gone back to lying there with his eyes shut, switching off between punches. Lionel figuring the story bored Kieran, him being the sort who would be riveted if it involved torturing a cat. Unfortunately, Kierans were a necessary evil in Lionel's empire.

'My career started when, I, as an enterprising young fellow of twenty-one, suggested to my local record store proprietor ...' Lionel conjuring him now, a resettled Scot, all beard and loon pants, '... that we get into the burgeoning bootleg market ourselves. He organised to borrow a tape recorder from a jazz muso customer, and I hauled my arse to Brunel University and recorded Blodwyn Pig—exactly the kind of band that I knew would generate demand. That was the acumen—the good fortune was that the band's official album didn't sound much better than my bootleg.'

Now Lionel gave the nod, and George drove a right into the dangling man's stomach. Marcus wailed loudly, but Lionel wasn't worried about noise. Even if Marcus were to spit out his gag and scream, it would simply blend with the whine of power drills, the rasp of grinders and the hiss of compressors from the other units.

'I went solo. Soon I was paying Dutch, French and German kids to bootleg Deep Purple or whoever. A cheap pressing plant in Antwerp punched out the vinyl and hey presto, I was supplying the UK and Europe. Trouble was, the quality of my finished product was generally shit and customers became wary. Meanwhile, I was shifting a decent amount of product here.

And believe me, Marcus, if there was one thing I had always hankered after it was surf and sun. So, I invested in a trip to Australia, wound up in Melbourne and hooked up with a go-go dancer, Jackie. Amazing legs and arse.'

George, who hadn't heard this part before, was taking an interest, so Lionel was half-addressing him as well as Marcus.

'Things went belly-up with Jackie but I couldn't find it in my heart to go back to London.'

Porkpies, flat ale, things he'd loved once no longer held any charm.

'Soggy. That's how London felt. For a while I ran the operation from Melbourne, but it was getting tougher to dodge the record companies. And then the final blow: I was ousted in a coup by my Dutch assistant, the little cunt.' Although by then, in his heart, Lionel really didn't give a toss. He'd seen the writing on the wall and it spelled *The End*.

'But I'd made valuable contacts in the music industry, and next thing you know, I'm supplying product far more lucrative than vinyl. Heroin was on the up and I rode it to the roof. Unfortunately, up there you are highly visible. Hence the shotgun and what I thought of as banishment to the Gold Coast.'

George gesturing, should he go again? Why not?

Lionel waited for the smack of fist against flesh before continuing.

'I couldn't have been more wrong. Southern Queensland was the land of opportunity.' Smiling even now at the memory of those early days, large profits and abundant real estate in which to invest them. 'Now I was the one pointing the shotgun and giving orders.' He stood up from the chair. His turn. 'Okay, Marcus, let's give George a break.'

Kieran sat up expectantly like a dog who'd just heard the treats packet rustle.

'At this moment, Marcus, you may think you're hurting, but believe me, it is nothing compared to the wound I feel at your perfidy.'

Lionel casting eyes over a variety of tools spread across the bench. Any of these—pliers, hammers, saws—could be gainfully employed, but Lionel eschewed such grandiose statements for the simple. His hand hovered over the more mundane kitchenalia.

'This, I think. The humble cheese-grater will do nicely to indicate to you, Marcus, the kind of pain I feel.'

A snigger from Kieran's direction. The man on the hook wriggling on cue, muffled yelps behind his gag. Lionel headed over to the record player, flicked through the albums, pausing on Atomic Rooster at Waltham Forest Tech, one of his very first bootleg releases, taking him back to bottles of Newcastle Brown, the hum of amplifiers, platform soles. The recording was shit but Palmer and Crane's virtuosity was still evident. Plus, it was very loud.

'Kieran?' Holding the album out. Kieran off the beanbag knowing the drill, carefully removing the vinyl disc from the dust cover.

'A record, Marcus, like a relationship, must be looked after. You abuse it, it might scratch you back.'

Kieran placed the stylus down carefully, as he'd been tutored. The music boomed out of the big speakers—heavy motherfuckers, half a tree in those. Lionel picked up the cheese-grater.

'Like me to do that, boss?' Kieran eager to volunteer for this part of the show.

'Thank you, Kieran, but it's important the proprietor keep his hand in.'

Lionel walked to the dangling, wriggling Marcus and gave a hard rake down the swinging torso. Any screams were lost in the swirl of the Vince Crane keyboards.

3

Joe Harris crouched down behind dumpsters out the back of the Satay Dream Malaysian restaurant. He could feel his heart pounding the way it had when he was eleven years old and Micky Lester was hunting the playground for him. To be honest, it wasn't as if it'd been an unfamiliar sensation in the twenty-six years since either. Often, these situations didn't end well, but tonight hadn't been a complete disaster. It was some kind of miracle that he'd evaded Pendle's boys. Okay, so he was forty-six thousand in the hole and that was before the clock on overdue payments had even started ticking. If he had any sort of instinct for self-preservation he'd have melted into the greasy newsprint on the footpath, become invisible. But he hadn't done that, had he?

Avoiding his flat had been a pretty shrewd move, he thought, giving himself a pat on the back. But even a habitual self-deceiver like Joe was forced to admit that showing his face at the Apostrophe was a misstep. Yes, it was the only bar that still allowed him credit, and he needed a calming drink more than the standups there needed punchlines, but you had to be a dumbarse to ignore the fact that it was one of the first places Pendle's muscle would look.

The rope the bookmaker had offered Harris had finally run out. What had begun three weeks ago as a mere eighteen-hundred-dollar debt—after Joe had inevitably emerged on the wrong end of a photo finish—had quickly spiralled. Before the most recent debacle, he and the bookmaker had sat on wobbly bentwoods in a mirrored saloon bar in Northbridge, Pendle carefully measuring his Somac.

'With medication, it's important to develop a routine. I keep mine with me. Apparently, it's not stress that gives you ulcers, did you know that?'

Joe in fact had no idea of that whatsoever, but Pendle ploughed straight on. 'All these years my wife telling me I should give up bookmaking because it was making me sick, and it turns out that has nothing to do with it. It is bacteria in your stomach that's the culprit. A local Perth guy discovered that. They're giving him the Nobel Prize. That makes me proud, Joe. A guy from our little city is changing the world. That, and Herb Elliot, they are the things that make me proudest to be West Australian. Do you know that?'

Joe did now. Frankly, he couldn't care less about Pendle's ulcer or the Nobel Prize. He faked a half-smile.

Carefully putting away the Somac, Pendle asked, 'What would you say makes you most proud of our hometown?'

Nothing made Joe proud of anything. He'd been born in New Zealand and come here when he was five, so the whole hometown thing was moot. But right now, he needed to suck up. He tried to think. What made him most proud of this little city, the most isolated city in the world, perched between the Indian Ocean and the desert like a hot pie on the tips of a frail old man's fingers?

'I'd have to say Pure Steel. Or maybe Mount Eden.'

The bookie pursed his lips, like the answer disappointed.

'A couple of pacers? Granted, they were outstanding animals, Joe, but you need to broaden your horizon beyond the scope of form-guides.'

The bookmaker had been slouching slightly, but now he sat up.

'As to your request ... Joe, if I give you the ten-grand credit and Jingoism comes through at four to one, by the time you wipe your debt you will be up four grand. Most of that you will lose in the additional commission I will deduct for the privilege of allowing you to bet with me when you are clearly insolvent.'

'But I'll be square.'

Where could he get a cigarette? Joe's head had been on a swivel. His nerves were shot. He didn't have time for a forensic analysis of the self-evident.

'Focus, Joe. I will only say this once. If the horse does not come through, you will owe me forty-six thousand bucks, and payment in full will be due within thirty minutes of the event. Do you understand?'

D'uh. 'Yes, Dominic, I understand.'

'Do you also understand that if you default, I shall inflict severe physical damage upon you, damage that will likely cost you as much in medical expenses to repair as the outstanding debt?'

Joe certainly did understand that. It was a myth that bookies never beat up debtors because they wanted them fit to earn the money back. With a huge waterfront property in leafy Applecross, Dominic Pendle had more money than he needed. He demanded accountability and respect. He demanded a pound of flesh in lieu of payment.

The wizened guy in the wheelchair selling footy programs outside of Subiaco Oval was testament. Not so many years back he'd run the catering company that sold the hotdogs inside the ground, but he was a bad gambler and had stiffed Pendle. Joe wasn't sure of the amount. He hoped it was a lot more than forty-six thousand, because life in a wheelchair had to be worth a lot more than that.

Pendle sipped his tincture, grimaced. 'This is not a bet, it is a covenant. Are we clear?'

'We are.'

'I don't get pleasure from inflicting pain, but pain will be demanded because betting is a noble profession, Joe—like boxing. You step into the ring with me there is no climbing out until one of us hits the canvas. You can step away now and be reasonably confident of still being able to walk your daughter down the aisle at some future time. However, increase this debt ...'

Pendle flipped his chunky palms as if to say, 'Do I really need to spell it out?'

An image of the wizened guy in the wheelchair clambered back into Joe's brain. But he quickly expelled it. He absolutely knew this horse was going to win. Joe had used his last hundred to get a university maths guy to run it through the department's supercomputer. At the weights, four to one was a steal.

'I understand.' Joe wasn't going to be cowed by Pendle. He stared right back into the man's cold eyes.

'Very well.'

Pendle pushed away the glass that had held his medication.

'If you win your wager, Joe, thus returning to me the forty grand, I intend to donate it to medical research. If you lose, and default on your debt, I will be donating something else of yours to medical research.'

Pendle's eyes twinkled, and for a moment Joe's stomach burned like he was the one with the ulcer. This time he was going to emerge a winner. They could give him the Nobel Prize for punting.

'The computer program deduced the correct odds were even money. That doesn't make it a certainty to win.'

Henry, the computer programmer, was trying to suck up the beer Joe Harris had bought him as an anticipatory thank you gift. This was difficult because Joe was shaking him by the shoulders. They were in the public bar at Belmont Racecourse, and the smell of fried onions from the hamburger grill was making Joe want to puke, although, to be honest, his guts were churning anyway. He had just seen his life flashing before him like the brown mare that had come charging down the outside to beat Jingoism by a long neck. As much as Joe would have loved to wring *Henry's* scrawny neck, he had retained a flake of reason. Survival trumped revenge.

In just twenty-seven minutes Pendle's goons would be looking for him, Joe having made the mistake of strutting past the bookmaker's stand earlier and saluting him. History had taught him that when it was time to run, one must not hesitate. He dropped his grip on the computer nerd and fled.

The trouble was: where exactly should he run to? His flat was too obvious; he couldn't afford the petrol to make it to the country in his battered Corolla; and his last-resort squat in Highgate was being developed by that private school cokehead Oscar Cornelius, who had already ruined every dimly-lit jarrah blokes' bar in Perth by turning them into light, airy budgie-cages where the clang of cutlery and the shriek of hysterical young women on their third woody chardonnay made quiet contemplation impossible.

Joe had a conundrum: he desperately needed to think. To think he needed a drink. And the only place he'd get one would be the Apostrophe.

It might have been okay if he hadn't stayed for the second whisky. After the first, something of a plan had materialised, nothing solid, flimsy like a spirit rising at a séance. Joe thinking he could stow away on one of the Rottnest ferries and hide out on the island, thirty minutes off the coast of Perth. It was winter; it wouldn't be that crowded. He could break into a vacant bungalow or befriend some boaties, maybe even crash with them. They were rich and careless with their wallets, potential pickings. Then he had the second whisky and that left him dreamily remembering that hot afternoon in Rome, the purchase of the jacket he happened to be wearing this very minute, the aroma of fried garlic mingling with Zeen's perfume.

He and Zeen had been a great team. No one could plan a con like him, and nobody could pull it off like Zeen. And the sex had been great too. They might have still been together if she hadn't thrown her hand in with that loser Boski. She was just pissed off with Joe because he'd double-crossed her on a big gold score, but bridges could have been mended. Instead, he'd wound up with a fractured skull from some Thai kickboxing dude who mistook him for Boski.

Fucken Boski. Now he reflected on it, Joe's decline traced right back to when that guy intersected his life. Joe's life was bifurcated. First there was BB—before Boski—when he'd been riding high. And then AB—after Boski—this haunted, miserable life spent trying to extricate himself from the gutter.

As Joe mused on this—he might even have muttered 'AB' aloud—he'd felt a substantial weight on his shoulder. A sideways glance identified the meaty hand of Missouri, Pendle's main enforcer, named for the battleship. Missouri was accompanied by a younger, thinner thug.

'Come on, Harris,' Missouri said. 'Dominic is waiting.'

Joe had tried to wriggle away, but found his arms were being held the way a jilted lover holds a grudge. Resistance being futile, he'd slid off his stool and allowed Missouri and his apprentice to guide him inexorably towards the exit, both in a real and symbolic sense. It gave him no solace to imagine what good his body parts might do for others when Pendle donated or on-sold them on the black market.

Then fate intervened.

A group of drunk and disgruntled Dockers supporters—the Fremantle Dockers had just lost their footy game to cross-town rivals West Coast—stumbled into the bar, directly in the path of the exiting trio.

Joe didn't hesitate. 'I don't care what you say, dickhead,' he shouted at his captors, 'Pav is twice the player Cousins is.' This a reference to Fremantle's best guy being better than West Coast's. Then he let out a howl, as if Missouri had broken his arm.

Invoking the name of the Dockers' most decorated player had immediately borne fruit, the Fremantle lads bristling at this treatment of a fellow Dockers fan.

'Leave him be.' The widest of the Dockers boys had a beard, big shoulders and a shape that suggested a high take-away component in his diet.

'Stay out of it, fellas.' Missouri trying to keep it calm in public.

Which is when Joe had turned and bitten Missouri's assistant on the ear, getting him just what he wanted. Slowed by the whisky, Joe had caught a hard left on his cheek, even though he'd predicted it coming. But it had been worth it. The five Dockers guys piling in on Missouri and associate allowing Joe to extricate himself and make it out the back door and down the street.

For something like thirty-six hours now, Joe had been a fugi-
tive, ceaselessly moving around the city, trying to find somebody who'd loan him escape money. Doors had slammed in
his face, but he'd forced himself to keep moving, taking only
brief breaks: a few hours in a small boat up on the slipway near
North Fremantle, an hour in a Cannington cinema while a Bol-
lywood movie ran, a short snooze beneath the ferns of Queens
Park. The promise of salvation from an old punter pal who lived
Leederville way had alas turned to dust when it transpired that
he was in the early stages of dementia.

Like a dying animal, Joe had kept moving in ever decreasing
circles, until finally his legs had gone from under him—and that
was how he'd found himself here, under a thin mist of sambal
and soy behind the dumpsters, a few blocks from where he'd
started. Joe's elation at escaping from Missouri had collapsed,
the way you saw some Cairo apartment block pancaking on
a news highlight. All was now dust. He'd been free thirty-six
hours and had only made things worse for himself.

He needed cash, but he owed everybody. Nobody owed him,
nobody gave a damn. Except ... would *she*?

Would Zeen help him in his hour of need?

Against: he had once traded her to a guy whose next move
was going to be burying her in a hole somewhere near Kalgoorlie. Fortunately for Zeen, she'd escaped.

For: Hmm. Only one positive came to mind. He could offer
to get out of Zeen's life once and for all. Okay, they hadn't com-
municated for five years, although he'd spied on her, knew the
café she lived above, the Honda Civic she drove. If she believed
that she had such a great thing going with Boski and that dumb
prison-themed café of his—what was it called again? Café Inside. What a fucking lame name. If she felt that life was working out for her, she wouldn't want him anywhere near her. She
would give him money to disappear, and Joe would be only too
eager to oblige.

4

A silver Mercedes sports with a blue personalised plate, CORN 001, had completely parked Zeen in. Her first instinct was to put down the two boxes of croissants she'd just picked up from the bakery, pull out her nail clippers and scratch the duco, like back in year nine she'd done to Johnny Hielman's copy of his beloved 'Breakfast in America' after she'd caught him two-timing her with that slut Tracy Carpenter. She would have done it, even knew what she'd etch into the Merc's body—PISSEDOFF 2— when a couple of women emerged from the hairdresser's opposite, plonked themselves by their cars and started yakking. What was going on in these people's lives, that they had time not just to go to the hairdresser, but then stand around talking? Time was a luxury Zeen did not possess. Today especially.

She was late already. There had been a long queue at the bakery and Rick needed the croissants right now. If she abandoned the car and ran, she could be at the café in under ten minutes, deliver the pastries, pick up a screwdriver—which would do a far better job than the nail clippers—and return. If this arsehole was still blocking her, she would get to work on vandalising the car. Unfortunately, ahead of a meeting with the bank, Zeen was dressed in heels, white linen jacket and pencil skirt. Not ideal for a sprint. Reluctantly she started walking, throwing one final scowl over her shoulder as she left the car park back onto the street, the Mercedes still squatting like a lump of bright silver dogshit.

Sandy, the ageing ex-con Rick paid a few bucks to help out, was sweeping outside the café as she came clip-clopping down the footpath. One of those wiry guys with corded arms, gave the impression some time back aways drugs or alcohol had been a demon. Looked like he'd wrested control back. For now.

'Whoa, Missus. Careful!'

It irked, Sandy calling her missus. Though it had been five years since fate had thrown her and Rick together, they weren't married. 'Missus' conjured pill-box hats, cooking aprons, pumpkin scones and department store elevators, not how Zeen saw herself. Sandy was close to sixty, though, and it was the vocab of his era, so she cut him more slack than she would have Boski. According to Rick, Sandy was a good old bloke who'd spent years inside for something in which he'd played only a minor part. Sure, they all said that, except sometimes it was true.

Take Rick. He'd been banged up for minding a dope crop, copped a magistrate on the warpath against drugs, and then had his unreasonable sentence extended after resorting to violence to save the life of another inmate, a bent cop who'd been marked for payback.

Since he'd got out, Rick had never been in trouble. Café Inside, prison-themed with bunks and cell-bars and those much loved 'lockdowns'—two-for-one deals when the siren went off—had been his dream while he'd been in jail. Soon as he'd got out, he'd thrown everything into it. Thanks to his ex, Marietta, fleecing his bank account, the concept had nearly been stillborn.

He'd borrowed money from a shylock, and during some hairy moments Rick and Zeen had been thrown together, for a time each trying to best the other. She'd tried to resist joining forces, but in the end, they partnered up in all kinds of ways that worked.

Not only had Boski got his café, it was going off. They were raking in the coin. They'd also started a coffee import business, Zeen's baby, hence the high-heels and linen jacket to impress the bank today. Everybody wanted coffee and Zeen could supply it. It was time to expand.

'Let me help.'

Sandy had begun to look frail lately, but despite her objections he carried the boxes inside, where she found Rick in parlay with Goose, his best pal from his prison time. A long pretzel,

Goose kept a room in Zeen and Rick's place—a four-bedroom apartment above the shop. These days he spent a lot of time 'up north' where his predilection for explosives earned him a fortune blowing up shit for mining companies.

Rick did a double take when he saw Zeen coming in from the front of the café, and not the rear where they had car spaces. She anticipated his query.

'Some arsehole parked me in at the bakery. If it's still there when I go back, I'm going to scratch the shit out of his Mercedes sports.'

'Don't you have a bank meeting?'

Rick was so transparent when he was trying to derail her dishonourable intentions. Sweet, but she could look after herself.

'Give me two minutes on that duco, it'll make a junkie's arm look pretty.'

'You didn't see the driver?'

'No. The numberplate was Corn One.'

'That'll be Oscar Cornelius.' Goose saying it with real authority, leaning back on his elbows.

'I've heard that name.' Rick's brows furrowed.

Zeen said, 'Isn't he the guy who did up the Globe in Murray Street?'

'He's got lots of pubs,' said Goose, sipping a double-shot like a bird taking seed from a foreign hand.

'His old man is Tiny Cornelius, the iron-ore guy.'

Everybody in Western Australia knew Tiny Cornelius, a prospector who'd located a huge iron-ore deposit in the Pilbara desert back in the fifties. The company had long gone public, but Cornelius was still a major shareholder and one of the richest men in the country.

'Daddy's boy? He's probably never done a day's work in his life,' said Zeen, hoping the car would still be there to receive her ministrations.

'They don't get on,' said Goose, once more the oracle, finishing his coffee in a gulp.

Rick gestured at his empty cup, and Goose nodded and laid the story down for them as Rick poured a fresh one.

'Oscar was always in trouble at school. The old man had to keep donating libraries and swimming pools to stop them kicking him out. Fat lot of good it did. Oscar flunked out of uni. Used his pocket money to buy into the old Hawthorn Arms but lost the lot and Tiny had to bail him out. Same with his next three pubs. Then he cracked it with the Globe and hasn't looked back. But he never so much as thanked the old man, let alone paid him back, so Tiny's grooming the sister to take over the mining company.'

Rick was curious. Goose didn't exactly mingle with the rich western suburbs crowd that ruled this city. Him coming out with all this was like Hopalong Cassidy on a mobile phone. It didn't fit.

'And you know this how?'

'My boss was in with Tiny in the early days. We talk about loads of shit. Not much else to do out in the desert, except talk and count stars.'

'Well, this is fascinating, fellas, but I have to leave, and I need a screwdriver.'

Rick tried to block Zeen's access to the toolbox under the sink, but she dropped her spiky heel onto his sneaker and applied warning pressure through the thin layer.

'Don't worry, I'll wear gloves,' she joked as she extricated the screwdriver, removed the threat from his foot and kissed him on the cheek.

You could never tame a woman like Zeen. Rick had known that from the time their paths first crossed, when he'd been forced into a hare-brained scheme after his ex-wife had made off with his savings. Their introduction had been across the barrel of her gun, and things had become competitive from there, but he'd won out and eventually wooed her. True, he almost needed to blackmail her into the coffee business, but she was happy to have that excuse, he could feel it even before they kissed that first time. There would never be another woman for him. He loved her, she him. That didn't mean it was easy going.

'Any luck, Cornelius will be gone,' said Goose.

Rick hoped so, but he never got to reply. Three customers jangled in, one after the other. Rick had staff but liked doing the mornings himself, making sure the Milano —the Ferrari of coffee-making machinery, boasting a built-in jukebox as well as making espresso to die for—was cleaned and sparkling, the croissants fresh and the newspapers ready. Rick had just seen off the last of his customers with a large flat-white takeaway when a voice boomed from behind.

'Good morning, fellas.'

So often during Rick's time in prison, that voice had been the only thing that was human and warm. Everything else was metallic, tubular. Cold. Rick wasn't exactly certain what a brogue was, but it always seemed to be applied to Irish accents. Father Paul Monaghan—he insisted on being called Paul—had a light-toned one.

'Morning, Father.' Goose waved a hand and then extended his bony fingers for a shake.

'Just Paul, Goose.'

Paul was in civvies, a neat check shirt, business not flannel, tucked behind a smart leather belt, like a guy who runs the computer repair shop. His hair was mostly silver now, but what wasn't was jet black, a decent mop of it too. He had a good-looking face—square jaw, healthy—though the lines were getting deeper. Most people would put him around fifty-five and they'd be a little short.

'Long black?'

Rick made a habit of remembering every customer's preference. Of course, it was easier with the priest: they'd shared many a cup of instant in prison.

'How's the parish treating you?'

Last time he'd been in, Paul had opened up, told Rick he was finding it difficult to settle back into the more regular duties of running a parish, where there was more administration than salvation.

'Well enough,' he answered. 'But there's little money about and the organist has never heard of Rick Wakeman.'

The men chuckling at their private joke about the prison organist, a busted drug courier who Paul had dubbed 'Rick Wakeman' because of his penchant for flourishes. Maybe he wasn't in Wakeman's class, but he'd sure rocked 'Amazing Grace'. It had been a depressing day when his time was up. The warders had joked they might plant something on him to keep him in longer.

Rick handed Paul his coffee. The priest proffered a five-dollar note. Rick waved it away.

'So, what brings you into town?'

Paul's eyes slid over to Sandy at the far end of the room.

'I think he's one of the few people I truly bring solace to. I have to seek your advice on something. Perhaps we could talk after?'

Rick said sure. Paul took his coffee and headed in Sandy's direction.

'What advice could you give him?' Goose amused.

Rick miffed. Why wouldn't he have something to offer the priest?

'Maybe he's thinking of buying an espresso machine for the parish.'

'Or,' Goose snapping his fingers, 'I had this TV series idea about a priest who starts growing dope to sustain his poor Mexican village. Then the cartel gets wind of it and come to wipe them all out, but the priest hires a group of loser mercenaries to fight the cartel.'

'Like *The Magnificent Seven*?'

'A little, but there's a twist. One of the mercenaries is a hot ex-stripper and she falls for the priest and vice-versa. So, he's torn between leaving the priesthood and his people or going with her.'

'Sounds terrific,' said Rick, 'but Paul would never do anything illegal.'

Paul thought Sandy had deteriorated since his last visit just a month ago, his clothes hanging more loosely, his skin a shade greyer.

'How are you doing?'

Asking quietly, the two men down by the special group cell known as the Tank, reportedly in high demand for hen's nights and other private functions. Paul had to give it to Rick Boski: he made an excellent coffee.

'They're saying I've got six to eighteen months, best they can tell.'

Sandy dropped his wet rag into the bucket at his feet, pulled out a cigarette pack and pointed outside. 'You mind?'

'I don't mind, but it can't be good for you.'

'A few days in the big scheme of things ... it can't matter.'

Paul drained his coffee and followed Sandy outside.

The back of the shop was a concrete apron bordered by the back wall of the café and its neighbouring shops, but open to the laneway where a high gate was propped open. There were bays for four cars. It was chilly in the shade, but where the outside steps led up to the apartment, there was a wedge of bright and surprisingly warm sun.

Sandy perched on a low step. Paul hadn't smoked since he was a teenager, but when Sandy lit up it reminded him of his dad and his uncle. Christ, they'd never stopped smoking. Even on Carrowmore beach on holidays they'd be at it, while in the same wheezing breath they extolled the restorative quality of sun, sea and open air.

In prison, Paul had found Sandy Hearne to be one who always took seriously the spiritual dimension of his life—if not so much as a guide on how to live it, as how to come to terms with it. Their discussions were generally reflective and philosophical. Sandy liked to be reassured that remorse could make up for his past deeds. He was the kind of man you didn't want to let down, even if you doubted yourself.

Looking off into the distance, Sandy blew a long stream of smoke, loosed a deep sigh.

Paul said, 'What's troubling you, Alexander?' It was not so much a ploy as a habit of the clergyman's—to slip in the formal Christian name of one of his sheep when he felt that a more serious tone was demanded.

'I've been in trouble my whole life, you know that. Or at least the first forty years. Since I've been out, this last time, I've not put a foot wrong. But earlier, I did a lot of wrong things. I can honestly say that most of the time I don't recognise the man who did them, but I know it was me. The old me.'

Nothing but a nod, to acknowledge he was listening, was required of Paul here.

'You know I never killed that fella in that TAB holdup.'

Of course he knew. Sandy mentioned it every time they caught up. Like it was something the priest might forget.

'You wouldn't name names. That's why you took the brunt of it.'

'You didn't do that—help the cops. Well, *I* didn't.' Sandy drew on his cigarette.

'I expected to be looked after—by the fellow who did it. That was a long stretch I copped. I lost my chance of ever finding a woman, marrying, having kids. It's not just the time itself, you understand—I mean, maybe I could have lived in the desert for seventeen years and still had something when I left it, something that made me feel worthwhile, human. But not prison.'

Paul knew exactly what he was talking about. He'd felt that

same alienation from the real world in his eleven years as a chaplain.

'Thing is,' said Sandy, squashing out his smoke on the rusted handrail, 'I thought I'd at least be comfortable this time of my life. Expected to be looked after for staying staunch. The bloke I took the rap for went on to bigger and better things. From a crook's point of view, anyway. He wasn't struggling. He was rich. So, when I came out and found him and asked him what he had for me, he offered me a job selling drugs. That was what he had for me.'

'It made you angry.'

'It still makes me angry. It smoulders in me. If I was to pass him in the street I would throw him under a bus.'

And if it wasn't outside but say in a gents in a pub, Sandy had something ready: a blank plastic card, like a credit card, bottom edge honed to razor sharpness, sitting there in his wallet. Cops could pat you down, never even notice it.

'See, what I'm saying, Father, try as I might to ignore it, the old me is still there. I don't want it to be. I don't want that in my soul when I die, but it is.'

'It's understandable you're bitter.'

'Is there something you can do to wipe that out. Like with confession?'

'You haven't done anything. We're talking hypotheticals.'

'My old Christian Brothers taught me there was no difference between thought and action. It was just the same.'

'Personally, I don't agree. We're human. We might imagine doing something, but that's not the same as going through with it. In fact, not going through with it, even though you've lusted after that satisfaction, is laudatory.'

'But I *would* go through with it. It's just the opportunity never presented. So, can you help me?'

And for the second time in a few days, Paul found himself being asked to absolve an action that had not taken place.

'What I can do is pray with you.'

As the two men bowed their heads, Paul found himself fingering the roll of notes in his pocket. Every cent from the parish savings. It was the right course of action, wasn't it? Surely having Enzo call in on him like that was just like God telling Moses to go and gather the bread from the desert. Paul was no more than an instrument of God's will.

5

From what Joe Harris could divine, Zeen was not at the café. No sign of her car in the space out the back. He'd just have to wait. It was cold in the shadows, and there was a nice strip of sunlight by the back stairs, but he'd be exposed. He couldn't risk Boski discovering him. Dumpsters had become his friend and there were two big ones in the shade, with some milk crates alongside. He wedged himself in there and waited. A guy he'd seen here before, some kind of yardman—an ex-con, you could tell—came out and started chatting to an older guy who might have been his parole officer. Joe couldn't be sure what they were talking about: their heads bowed, almost touching, careful, for a long few minutes, as the better-dressed guy—maybe it was actually his fence—whispered. Some illegal shit. Joe knew better than anyone: you could never trust an ex-con. Finally, the jailbird headed back inside, and before Joe could reconsider his situation, Boski emerged from the café, swinging more empty milk crates.

The older guy sidled over.

'How's he doing?' asked Boski.

'Struggling with a few things.'

'His health isn't good, but he won't talk to us about it.'

'He's a proud man, doesn't want to burden anyone.'

'So, you mentioned you need some advice?' Boski said. 'Buying a coffee machine?'

Joe didn't dare raise his head over the dumpsters, so he couldn't see them now, but he could picture their faces from the exchange. The other guy chuckled.

'You never know. No, I need to place a wager on a horse: last race Belmont, Saturday.'

'You've never bet on the Melbourne Cup?'

'The odd bet. It's not that. I know how to walk into a TAB. This is a bit different. And I mustn't be seen to be associated with the bet ...'

Nothing made Joe's blood pump faster than secretive conflabs and punting. This was getting interesting.

'... and it's a lot more than I'm used to putting on. Eight thousand dollars.'

Boski sounding surprised. 'That's an awful lot to bet.'

'I know. But the horse can't lose.'

'I've heard that before,' said Boski.

So had Joe.

'Enzo Rapanaro, the trainer, is absolutely certain. I mean ... like it's a done deal.'

'The race is fixed?'

Exactly what Joe was thinking. But Rapanaro was a joke trainer with just a couple of broken-down old nags. How would he have the resources to fix anything?

'To be frank, I'm hoping it is. Yes, I know, that's a terrible thing for a man of the cloth to say. But for once I want to do some real good, and I think—I think the Lord may have sent this opportunity to me.'

'Are you sure?'

Boski sounding heavy with doubt. Joe wanting to call out, 'Of course he's sure!' So the guy turns out be some kind of priest, he's human, everybody on the planet wants to bet on a sure thing.

'I look at people like Sandy there, and I think God wouldn't be happy at the position they find themselves in: no money, no future. Our parish school needs a toilet, a photocopier and whiteboards. The parents don't have the cash. This could change that. I can't go into detail, but I feel certain that God directed this opportunity my way. The odds are currently fifteen to one. Apparently, they're higher if you bet earlier.'

'That's because if the horse doesn't start, you do your dough. And Paul—at those odds, the bookies are saying it has virtually no chance.'

'What is a man's calculation against the will of God? Enzo has no doubt Hysterical will win. I know Enzo. The horse is going to win.'

'All right. You give me the money, and I'll get Goose to put the bet on. He's across this stuff a lot more than me.'

Joe picking up a hint of resignation in Boski's voice.

The two men retreated into the café, but Joe didn't move for a long time. He had needed a miracle, and the Lord had provided.

But he also needed money. That, the Lord had *not* provided. Not yet.

Joe started flicking through his brain, wondering who might stake him five grand. Answer—absolutely no one. But perhaps he was getting ahead of himself. Enzo Rapanaro was a hack who trained hacks. He'd be lucky if he managed ten winners in a year. Even if Rapanaro was using a jigger—a battery under the saddle was old-school, which fitted with a guy his age—or, more likely, doping it up, could you rely on Hysterical to win?

Not from its form, though it was lightly raced, injuries keeping it off the track until it was a four-year-old. Since then, it'd only had a handful of starts, a second in a country race. So, the jockeys must be in on it, paid off to ensure it wins—a boat race. That would take serious money, surely more than Rapanaro could stump up. From memory he owned Hysterical, but he must have somebody with money funding the scam.

The trainer was clearly craftier than Joe had given him credit for, keeping its true ability under wraps, waiting for the right opportunity. It wasn't unheard of that a low-profile trainer lucked onto a decent horse—though usually they'd let the horse run on its merits every chance they got, needing the money as soon as possible.

Joe knew his breeding, every horse on every course slotted into his brain. Hysterical was by Jokes On Me out of Traffic.

The sire was a joke all right, but the dam had thrown a couple of decent winners. All the same, Joe couldn't rid himself of the feeling that he was missing something.

He tried to remember where Rapanaro had his stables. Gin Gin? No, Helena Valley, in the foothills, half an hour by car. Not too far to hitch, get a first-hand look at the horse. Did he dare risk getting out in the open?

What choice did he have? If Pendle's goons picked him up, Joe could use what he knew as a lever. And if Pendle didn't pick him up and everything about Hysterical checked out ....

Oh boy, he'd come at Pendle with both barrels, and sit that fat bastard right back down on the bones of his arse. Give him a whole tub of Somac worth of stomach upsets.

Perth could throw in some stinker winter's days, where cold rain slashed like the blades of a thresher. This wasn't one of them. It was overcast with a light wind, no smell of rain. By the time Joe climbed out of the Hilux—he'd hitched with a fella carting some bathroom tiles up to his daughter's place—the day had warmed to a tick over twenty degrees. Joe had chanced a call to an old punter mate, Tractor, who had once lost a leg to diabetes and a nice house to the bookmakers. Tractor had made ends meet carting hay to properties and he was able to give Joe directions to Rapanaro's, but only after he promised to pay him the sixty bucks he owed Tractor from three years back.

Joe didn't know exactly where Rapanaro's property was located, but Joe Harris was a simple man. Look for horses in a paddock, see if you recognise any. Thirty minutes later he was standing in the middle of a paddock with Hysterical. Every race day he made a point of studying all the horses in the mounting yard, committing them to memory. A brown mare, Hysterical had a good rump and strong hind legs, but Makybe Diva she wasn't. He was starting to regret his trek. It had been time consuming and dangerous, and he'd really learned nothing except this horse looked like it was double-figure odds for good reason.

It was hot now, and he needed a drink before he headed back, whichever direction that might be. There was always a tap at stables, so Joe headed that way. The place was deserted. He drank his fill, keeping an ear out for company, but apart from a horse kicking up in the stables, it was quiet. He started past the stable door and peered into the gloom, spied the troublemaker at the far end covered in a horse blanket.

'Will you shut the fuck up? A man needs his peace.'

The horse reared and whinnied as if it didn't like his attitude. Fine, he didn't like the horse's either. He was about to turn away, but his eyes, accustomed now to the interior light, found the horse's eye, and the white blaze on the forehead that looked remarkably like ...

Joe advanced on the horse like a Nebraska farmer who'd just found a flying saucer squatting in his field, magnetically drawn, his own free will abandoned.

It was a mare. And it wasn't just the blaze on its forehead: in every visible mark, this horse was the doppelganger of Hysterical, out there in the paddock.

His heart boomed. He no longer chastised himself for coming out here; he congratulated himself. He had sensed there had to be more. Now he knew why Rapanaro had been so confident about Hysterical winning.

There were two horses that looked identical—and this one, he was damn sure, was a winner.

6

Lionel stood in front of his spacious built-in wardrobe, debating whether he really needed to take a suit. Surely, a couple of jacket and tie combos would do the trick? After the unpleasantness of the previous day, where he'd been pulled away from Broadbeach to the depressing unit in Nerang—having to toss a favourite shirt in the bin because of unsightly blood flecks—today had been a dream. A swim in the surf, a coffee on his balcony, and now confirmation that the Brisbane River cruise *sans* Marcus had been fully booked. A familiar number illuminated Lionel's phone. Penny, his travel agent.

'Penny.'

'I have your flights as requested. Two business and three economy to Perth, all under separate names and bookings.'

You couldn't be too careful.

'The car will be ready at the airport and accommodation is at the casino, apart from Mr Langer who is at a motel near the airport as requested.'

'Appreciate that, Penny. Thank you.'

He was—to use an apt expression in the circumstances—champing at the bit to be there in person to see his carefully planned project reach culmination.

A decade after arriving in Surfers, Lionel had found that land deals, protection rackets and construction-industry rorts could make him even more money than drugs. His tentacles continued to edge into more exotic crevices. His illegal casinos had flourished until the government decided it wanted a piece of the action, but the racing game: that, in his opinion, could never be regulated. And, thanks to the electronic super-highway, he could bring his considerable weight to bear on race results all over the country, as well as New Zealand.

Because he had no need to regularly score from his racing exploits—his other interests brought in plenty of cash—Lionel could afford to be patient while his turf ambitions came slowly to the boil.

And this latest one, it was a pearl.

The racing game was the best. Lionel had run breeding scams, had horses and dogs doped, jockeys bribed, you name it, but the idea of a ring-in appealed like no other. It had been four months back when Arnold, one of his smart young fellas tasked with coming up with racing 'opportunities', had sat across from Lionel on his patio and excitedly told him he might have found something. Arnold had been in the pub enjoying a burger and beer, watching the races from Northam in Western Australia, when he'd spied a mare going into the barriers.

'I was absolutely certain it was Double Volley.'

Double Volley was a smart galloper purchased in Singapore they'd brought to Queensland to make a first-up killing, but the mare had gotten ill. A year on, she still hadn't raced, although in secret she was trialling the house down.

'I mean, the mare wasn't just a lookalike, it was *identical*.' Arnold had pulled out two photos from a cardboard folder and slid them across. Each showed a horse. Lionel couldn't detect any difference between them.

'Two different horses?' Looking extra hard for a discrepancy.

'Yep.'

'What's the other horse like?'

'Not very good. Name of Hysterical. Provincial place chance, double-figure odds in a metro race.'

'And you're thinking ...? No, wait ...' Lionel felt the smile already creeping over his face, like it was ahead of his brain. 'We swap them.'

That was exactly what Arnold had been thinking. Hysterical was owned and trained by a battler. Perfect. As for Double

Volley, its ownership was quietly transferred to a group of elderly patients in a Brisbane nursing home. That way Lionel could mask his involvement. He would happily give any winning stake money to the geriatric 'syndicate'. Ten grand or so meant nothing to him. It might buy them cataract surgery or something. This way he could feel he was really benefitting the community.

Who he wouldn't be benefitting was bookies. He would hit SPs in every state, a hundred grand at fifteen to one. That was a worthwhile score.

It hadn't been too hard to bring the WA trainer, some Italian fella, around to the scheme. The imperative for silence had been impressed upon him. Double Volley had been trained up and freighted to Perth incognito. It now resided at the trainer's property and was cherry ripe to win.

Lionel hadn't been to WA for a long time, but he was already savouring the thought of being there in person when the horse won. Not that he would back the horse over there. The odds needed to stay long right up until they jumped. This was going to be one of his life's most memorable moments.

When Zeen had taken the screwdriver—despite Rick's protestations—she had turned back at the door for one last glimpse of him before she started her day. Not infrequently she asked herself if she'd have fallen for him if she'd met him at a friend's barbecue, instead of in the desert at the end of her gun barrel. She might have; she might not. His blue eyes—they were likely to get most women in—and back then he had a sexy James Dean quiff going. He was only average height and looked like he'd never spent a day in the gym, which he hadn't. Thing with Rick was his heart. A woman could underestimate just how valuable that was: to be loved by a good man. She loved him more deeply now than that sharp blowtorch spark at the start, but if they ever did get married, she would not want to take his name. 'Boski' sounded squashed, conjured women in peasant scarves working in frozen fields.

Rick needn't have worried about her vandalising the Mercedes. By the time she got back to the bakery and her marooned car, CORN 001 had gone. She headed off to her bank meeting deeply disappointed, the screwdriver nestling unused in the console where she kept her coffee cup. But as she parked her Civic behind the café, any lingering disappointment was swamped by euphoria. The reception she'd been given at the bank had been overwhelmingly positive, and without requiring her to rouse any of her sexual charisma from its slumber.

Her personal banker turned out to be a woman her age—Nicole—who was turned on by Zeen's accounts, not her body. The steep upward slant of the coffee import profit chart had Nicole breathless.

'You're doubling your turnover every six months!' Nicole tapping her biro on the photocopied accounts, as if Zeen herself might somehow have missed this detail.

'That's right. People used to smoke and drink alcohol, now it's coffee. It's a fraction of the cost, and it's not taxed. Cafés can set up with a single machine, and women like us can meet and chat without sticking to the carpet and having some drunk hassle us. It's like when TV aerials started to appear on the roofs of every street in every suburb. This is just the beginning, you know?'

Nicole was sold. Overdraft doubled. Like that!

Zeen opened the car door and stepped out, walking on cloud.

Then that cloud was ripped apart and she felt herself plunging. The reason was the skinny guy who'd just emerged from behind the bins.

'Hey, Zeen—'

Joe fucking Harris. Looking like shit. On some guys a little stubble could be sexy; on Harris it made him look like a derro who'd been sleeping in cat litter. And he was giving off a gar-bagey odour too, so maybe he *had* been.

'Whatever it is, Joe, the answer is no.'

'I'm in the shit.'

'Tell someone who cares.'

'I mean it. I owe Pendle fifty.'

'Not my problem.'

'No—but it could be your opportunity.'

Oh shit. There was nothing more frightening than a Joe Harris opportunity. Was a time she'd been seduced by the fun of it all: the scams, the cons. But she dressed and slept a whole lot better now, without Joe Harris in her life. Plus, she was in love with Boski.

'I just need five grand, that's all, till Saturday. Sunday, I'll pay you back six. That's twenty per cent interest, for like three days.'

Five years and nothing had changed except his teeth needed more work.

'Would this opportunity have four legs, by any chance?'

He pulled a face, like she'd just insulted him. Which of course she had.

'Actually, it has eight legs, Zeen. Eight! Listen, this isn't some tip I got in the gents. This is the real deal. I just need five thou. I can pay you, pay Pendle, get myself a little bank to start over.'

'Absolutely not.'

'Five grand and I am out of your life for good. I promise I will never bother you again.'

Tempting. 'How about you never bother me again, and we skip the money part.'

Harris got in close, seized her wrist, pulled her to him. The refuse smell even worse up close.

'Remember Fine Cotton?'

What Australian punter didn't? The most infamous horse racing scandal of the last fifty years. Fine Cotton was a ring-in—a horse with little chance, replaced by another a couple of classes above. All of Australia knew about it, most before the race, and consequently it went south, even though the ring-in won the race.

'Are you saying—?'

Harris nodded vigorously.

'That's exactly what I'm saying.'

'Fine Cotton didn't have a happy ending. People wound up in jail.'

'You owe me, Zeen.'

'How do you figure?'

Harris removed the cap he was wearing, greasy, Ryobi badged. Zeen presumed it had been filched from a tradie's ute, the window left down for the dog. He turned so the back of his head faced Zeen, then parted the hair with his fingers. A scar ran across his skull.

'This is why you owe me. A fractured skull.'

He turned and faced her again.

Zeen snorted. 'Which you got after giving me up so you could make off with our money.'

'Because I thought you were double-crossing me. Come on, let bygones be bygones. Five grand and I'm nowhere.'

Zeen reaching into her car, grabbing the screwdriver still sitting on her dash, pressing it against his throat.

'Joe, we are done. Over. Kaput. I was going to use this on Oscar Cornelius's Mercedes, but I think I'd get even more satisfaction using it on you.'

Harris jammed the cap back on his head.

'I thought you'd appreciate me thinking of you,' he said indignantly. 'One last score, keep us friends, end on a high note. But no, you want enmity. Your choice, Zeen.'

Someone was opening the rear door of the café.

Joe shook his head, sighed. 'You had the chance of a final goodbye, Zeen, but you blew it. *Au revoir.*'

Joe Harris was merely a shoe disappearing around the corner when Rick emerged with more crates.

'Who was that?'

'Some loser wanting a handout.'

'You can be uncharitable,' said Rick.

She sure could, especially to Joe Harris.

'How did the bank go?' Rick kissed her on the lips before he settled the milk crates.

'Very, very well.'

'And the other business?' Nodding at the screwdriver still in her fist.

'On hold. But I'm keeping this handy.'

Her day had been sailing along merrily until Joe Harris poured a bucket of slime over it. Five years. She thought she was rid of him. With luck Pendle would arrange that.

She pulled herself up. No, she didn't want him dead, just so scared he had to move permanently interstate.

She would have liked to talk to Rick about it, but she didn't want him to think she was even remotely interested in Harris's plans. Rick would have nothing to do with that kind of chicanery, and it was bound to end in disaster. But she had to admit, just for a minute there, she had felt that zing, that adrenaline buzz she used to get from the prospect of working a new con.

Fine Cotton, eh? The secret with a ring-in, like any con involving a swap, was that you had to keep the pool of those in the know very, very small. If Joe Harris knew about it, it was already too big.

7

You had to give it to the Italians: they might not be able to keep a government longer than it took to snort a line of this most excellent coke he had acquired, but Oscar Cornelius could not fault their pastries. Or men's fashion, he conceded, stretching his legs out on his desk to properly admire the soft leather sandals he'd picked up on his recent holiday along Lake Garda. The thing about Perth was, even in winter you could get a cracking warm day. You go walking around in sneakers, your feet sweat; these babies, on the other hand, let the air in.

Air was one of Oscar's main priorities. He liked space. Look at his office: half the top floor of the old Globe Hotel, his flagship business. The rest of the floor comprised two large apartments. One he kept for himself, so he didn't have to drive all the way out to the house in Scarborough after a big night in town. The second was a guest apartment. Say someone like Bono was in town visiting, he could use it. Not that Bono had stayed there yet, but it was available if he wanted to.

There were monitors all around the office so you could check Bloomberg or sports if you needed; a big original Caltex sign from a servo out Williams way; a pool table, natch, and the usual office shit of filing cabinets and benches. Where you work should be a fun place—that was one of Oscar's business principles. Thinking maybe he should acquire some of those *Seven Steps To* books that you see on the bookshelves behind tycoons when they're interviewed on TV.

Oscar licked every last pastry flake from his fingertips. It was the third cannoli he'd finished off, and he still had three more to go plus some other pastry thing looked like a shell filled with custard. Last night's numbers were excellent at all five of his venues. Fremantle was a bit soft, but that was Freo for you, too many hippy types and old farts who spent all night sitting on a single schooner.

There was a soft knock on his door.

'Yes?' he called. From where he sat with his back to the window it was ten metres to the door. Space, see, that was the thing, but it could be hard on your voice after a big night. The door opened and Maya poked in her gorgeous head, blonde ringlets, cute heart-shaped mouth. She looked absolutely fuckable balancing on her high heels in that short skirt, but he'd been doing his best not to go there. You really shouldn't screw the staff, that was one valuable lesson the old man had bestowed on him. Though if you followed his example, you could fuck waitresses and women who ran art galleries, ditching the mother of your children soon as they left school. No, sexy as Maya was, flawed as his old man could be, Oscar was with him on the shitting-in-your-own-nest issue. Besides, things were going pretty good with Lucy.

'The bouncer guy is here.' Maya leaned forward as she whispered it. She really was hot.

'What's his name again?'

'Tony.'

'Show him in.'

The guy was shorter than he imagined, with bronzed skin and a moustache, clearly Asian. He was wearing a collared shirt, but his shoulders were broad like a rugby half-back's, so the shirt was stretched to the max over the guy's biceps. Maya discreetly closed the door.

'Have a seat, mate. Tony, right?'

'Yeah.'

He sat. Dude looked nervous.

'What was your fighting name again?'

'Thaiphoon Tony.'

'That's right,' Oscar remembering now, like Hulk Hogan, the catchy same-letter names favoured by fighters. 'Kickboxing?'

'Yeah.'

'That would be like cricket to you, I guess. I mean you grow up with it.'

'I suppose.'

'You like cricket?'

'Not much.'

'Me either. You don't fight these days? Not in a ring, I mean.'

Oscar smiled, so Tony would know he was being clever, referring to his role as a doorman. You could never be sure Asians got the joke. They were always so serious. But Tony smiled.

'Not for a couple of years.'

'I hear you've been doing good work for us.'

'I'm trying.'

'Well, not just trying but succeeding. Ben told me about the bikies at Z Bar.'

Bikies were a hazard of running any bar or nightclub in Perth. Most club owners rolled over and paid the protection money they demanded in return for providing 'security'. Trouble with that was, before long, your so-called doormen were letting in their drug-dealing mates. Oscar didn't want drugs being dealt in his venue. Up here, sure, consume to your heart's content, but while Liquor and Gaming could be paid to turn away for the price of a new flatscreen, those drug squad guys were either zealots or expensive. Thing was, though, soon as you refused the bikies, they'd test you out, start a fracas or two. When he opened the Globe, Oscar had hired some ex-SAS guys as security. They could handle themselves okay. The bikies were wary of them. There weren't enough SAS dudes for his expanding roster of venues, but this guy Tony had put two troublemakers out of action without fuss. His guys said he flipped them like he was dealing cards.

'So,' Oscar pulled his feet off the desk and leaned forward. 'You know Ben, my bodyguard? He's restricting himself to day duties, kid on the way and all that. I need a night-time driver and bodyguard. Mostly I like to drive myself, but there are times when that's not viable. Double the money you're getting now.

Starting tomorrow. You in?'

Oscar assuming the guy would jump at it. But he was unmoved.

'Is there any particular threat to you?'

Oscar could think of a few. Angry females who blamed him for dumping them, mainly. 'No. Precautionary.'

'I don't have to carry a gun or anything?'

'Shit, no! My line of business you can make enemies without even knowing. Some guy gets tossed out of a bar and holds a grudge. Or dudes try and big-note themselves by coming on all aggro. That kind of thing. I need someone alert, watch my arse.'

Thaiphoon Tony nodded, cool like. Oscar found it impressive, the guy acting as if he was the one doing Oscar the favour. It did miff him a bit, though, because for a little Asian dude this had to be the opportunity of a lifetime. The moment dragged on like one of those plays with no music. And then just as Oscar was about to ask if there was a problem, his new bodyguard shot out a hand and they shook. Guy had a grip that could break necks.

'D'you like cannoli?

Shit. After the hand squeeze Oscar could barely lift the little white cardboard box to offer it.

'I'm good, Mr Cornelius.'

Addressing him respectfully, not something you expected these days. They stood and Oscar let him out.

'Thanks, Tony. Maya will give you all the details.'

As he closed the door, Oscar decided this had already been a productive day. Perhaps he should go to the gym, get in shape like Tony there? On the other hand, in his position he didn't need to do that shit, he could just hire guys like Tony. He used his intact left hand to select another cannoli.

Why couldn't her parents have given her a more exotic, interesting first name?

Liz.

Flat and dull as a canteen tray. No zing. A fucking no-effort, brainless choice. Even the longer form, E–liz–a–beth. What did anyone think of when they heard that name?

What she imagined: a sourpuss librarian, glasses perched on the end of a long nose for suspicious, gossipy eyes to squint through; a mature woman travelling by herself in the dining car—conservative, grey-haired, studying a tourist handbook with photos of marble sculptures, a lonely, companionless sherry perched on her table.

When you were staking out a place, your mind had time to roam free, and in Liz's case, roaming free meant it got bogged down in this shit. Her rank didn't help matters. In fact, it made everything worse. 'Detective Inspector' sounded authoritative, but when you added 'Liz Atwood' people conjured Margaret Thatcher.

Liz had just turned thirty-five, celebrating at the same local Chinese restaurant where she'd had her seventeenth: Mum, Dad, her old school pal Genevieve—yeah, *she* got the name to die for—and two of the women from her D division netball team. So, eighteen years on, the space she occupied in the world was still a void. Aliens could abduct her and the only impact would be a mystified waiter standing there with a spare fried ice-cream.

She was certain that so much of this failure to make an impression came from the handicap of that fucking name. You could see the shock on people's faces when they met her for the first time. Elizabeth was a museum name, the Queen's name for crying out loud, and she'd hated it as far back as she could remember. Melissa or Lucy or even Sarah would have been so much better.

She glanced over at the apartment block she had under surveillance, wondering if Joe Harris had split town, leaving his crappy Corolla here out front.

Then she drifted straight back to the trench of self-reflection in which she'd been mired these last forty-five minutes. Starting with that name. Okay, Liz Hurley made it work, but she was a bit older, and glamourous.

Atwood checked herself out in the rear-vision mirror. Not glamorous, not exotic, but she was confident she was reasonably attractive. Her nose was on the small side but cute, and her ears were good. Her mouth, well, more generous lips wouldn't hurt—hers seemed to have been allocated during rations. Her eyes were good, not Liz-Hurley sexy, but they had spark.

Thank God it wasn't any warmer. Stakeouts in the heat were the pits. This city in summer, air-con was a necessity, but of course you couldn't just sit there with the engine running. Today, though, was pleasant. Mind you, there were a hundred places she'd rather be.

Maybe she was wasting her time. Her barman snitch at the Apostrophe had told her about Saturday night, the guy called Missouri and another of Dominic Pendle's heavies grabbing Joe Harris, and then Harris making a run for it. When she'd first started at L&G five years back, Joe Harris had been on their radar. A con-artist and pickpocket working with a woman named Zeen, Harris had always stayed just out of reach. The town's largest bookmaker, Pendle, was a marlin—difficult to hook and, with his powerful friends running interference, even harder to land.

She knew Pendle rigged races, among other things, he'd also been involved in a breeding scam, but she'd never yet managed to get anything on him to stick. The stories of his payback on defaulting debtors were legion, but the victims could never be made to talk. She was working on the theory that a scared Harris might cooperate, help her set Pendle up. Or, failing that, that she might catch Missouri and his cronies in the act of beating the crap out of Harris.

She'd been here five hours now. Pendle's boys had swung by twice, one staying with the car and one heading inside to check the flat—or at very least the meter box—for signs of occupation. Not Missouri, lower-level flunkeys. Both times the guy emerging shaking his head.

Unlikely Harris would be stupid enough to come here. Okay, he'd gone to the Apostrophe, but no way would he return there. He would want to run, but he clearly needed money, and who would loan it to him? He must have burnt every acquaintance.

She pulled herself up. Her mind had kicked over to one of her ex-lovers, Dazza. No matter they were through with one another, whenever Dazza got himself into trouble, she'd find him standing on her doorstep. Got Liz thinking now: needy men. What about that woman, Zeen? Last Atwood had heard, she was shacked up with an ex-crim. Par for the course. Guy had been jailed on a drugs charge, Rick somebody-or-other. She made a call on her new mobile.

'Bender, it's me.'

Bender was ex-drug squad, now working as a salesman in reticulation.

'Hardwood. What's up?'

The old nickname they'd given her. She wasn't sure if it was because she was tough and unrelenting, or because she turned blokes on. Either way she didn't mind.

'Guy named Rick, got done for minding a dope crop out Gin Gin. Intersected with a grifter by the name of Zeen.'

'Zeen, real name Roísín O'Neil, but people misheard the name, and she became "Zeen". Now *she* was hard to forget. Made Liz Hurley look like Margaret Thatcher.'

Did he just say ...?

'Rick Boski. That's the lucky prick.'

'They still together?'

'I sure hope not. A man can dream.'

She let it go. Men were stupid. Full stop.

'Know where I can find Boski?'

'Owns a café in William Street or thereabouts. Prison theme.'

Gods were smiling. That was close by.

'Thanks.'

'How're your lawns looking?'

Touting for business. Not caring it was obvious.

'I'm in a townhouse in Maylands. A beach towel would about cover the grass.'

'I'm thinking a water feature might be what you need. I'd be happy to slip over. Do a free quote.'

And the way he said it, he had more in mind than plastic hoses. Bender wasn't exactly her type. A big solid beer drinker. Divorced, though, which was a plus. And he was never gross.

'I'll keep it in mind.'

'Please do.'

On rare occasions things just panned out. Two stops in William Street to ask for directions and she was rolling towards Boski's café in her car, when who should emerge up the side lane but Joe Harris. As usual he looked furtive, like he hadn't shaved either. He was wearing a cap, hunching his shoulders, but she'd recognise those skinny legs anywhere. She parked the car and followed on foot.

It was clear that Harris was worried about being grabbed again. He tried to keep himself camouflaged as he scooted over the Horseshoe Bridge towards the city. Atwood thinking he must be heading for a train, but he passed the railway station. Then when he hit Wellington Street, bus paradise, she figured that to be his destination. But no, he crossed the street and darted up a laneway, crossed again and entered the Globe Hotel.

She gave it a beat and followed. The old workingman's pub was now hipster. Young women with fresh hairdos and wearing dresses that made Liz's wardrobe look like Vinnies' bargains, gossiping, sipping wine in glass goblets the size of a bidet; men in business shirts chuckling over some shared secret.

Décor-wise the pub had clearly been given the Oscar Cornelius make-over: playing on the pub's name, a vast seafarer map adorned the wall behind the bar, the lazy Susans were bisected globes, with plates set on top of the southern hemisphere. She edged towards the wide jarrah staircase, saw Harris in conversation with a young woman wearing a short skirt and expensive blouse. Blonde curls.

She'd bet anything her name wasn't Liz. Before she could get close enough to eavesdrop, Harris and the woman started up the stairs. The woman clipped a little red rope and chain back across the steps to make it clear the public wasn't allowed in this private area.

Liz stopped a passing waiter. He gave her a look like she might be applying for kitchenhand.

'What's up there?'

'That's Mr Cornelius's office. Do you need a table?'

As if he was expecting 'No' for an answer. He gave a smug smile when she said she was fine. For a long minute she stood there trying puzzle out what she'd seen.

So, Joe Harris is in trouble with Dominic Pendle. He goes to his former squeeze, Zeen, and next thing he's here. Why would a trendy rich kid like Cornelius be meeting Harris? The drug squad, she knew, had more than a passing interest in Cornelius. Bender had confided that they'd intercepted calls from local footballers talking about the blow they were getting courtesy of the good Oscar. The little pricks should have been busted but footballers were too popular, and Oscar's old man had too much juice, so the drug squad was just sitting on it. Atwood had a suspicion that some of her L&G colleagues were getting under-the-table payments to turn a blind eye to underage drinkers and overcrowding. Every time she'd been to one of Oscar's venues they were choc-a-block with kids on X.

She decided on a 'watch-this-space' approach. She would love to bring down Harris, and Pendle would be a coup. Oscar Cornelius would provide a nice bonus, the spoiled brat of a billionaire who partied with Melissas, Sarahs and Beckies. Yeah. She'd show them all what Hardwood could deliver.

8

Sometimes life provided in a roundabout way. His back to the wall, Joe had gone begging to Zeen to help him get out of Dodge, and now thanks to a bent clergyman he was privy to a huge potential score. But life can be frustrating: redemption at your fingertips, but will anyone give you a boost to grab it? No, people are too petty, too mean, or in Joe's case, had memories that were too fresh. He'd called every one of his old associates, painting the picture of blue skies and an indolent life, only to be snubbed. Here was Van Gogh presenting them with a masterpiece, but they were too ignorant to see it. Not a single taker. Two threatened him and one sounded so eager that Joe was suspicious he was trying to set him up for Pendle.

In desperation he'd returned to Zeen's, and this time he'd managed to pitch direct.

That she'd refused to join him had cut to the quick. She was not the woman he remembered. But even as her rejection slashed him like a Stanley trimmer, the solution had been delivered, and by Zeen herself. She'd told him she was going to fuck up Oscar Cornelius's car. It only hit Joe as he turned up the laneway from the café back towards William Street. And then *whoomph*, there it was.

It must have been six years back. He and Zeen were in the desert town of Kalgoorlie for Diggers and Dealers, the conference where miners and stockbrokers wound up as untidy as the open-cut pits they were hawking. It was the best place to filch wallets, gatecrash parties, run cons. Mind you, when you were talking the mining game, the room was full of conmen and women who'd made a squillion more than he and Zeen ever would—faking results, ramping stocks, you name it.

In one of the after-hours two-up games, Joe had seen this young guy who was down to his last twenty bucks ride his luck on tails, doubling his money and then reinvesting it all on every throw, finally pulling out with two and a half grand in his hand. He'd asked who the guy was, and they'd told him it was the Cornelius kid.

'Old man's the richest prick in Australia. Born lucky.'

But next day at the races, Oscar's luck ran out. Joe watched as he put the entire stake on a two-to-one favourite, only to see it beaten into third. Thing was, even as the kid handed his cash over to Dominic Pendle's bagman, Joe knew he'd never stood a chance. Pendle had bought off the jockey—a little piece of information Zeen had come by in a late-night steam-bath with the horseman. Joe had a trunk full of examples of such race-track perfidy, and up till now it had been just one more piece of junk cluttering his brain. But now, when you rubbed off the patina, it shone.

Joe had been certain before he even stepped into the Globe that he would get an audience with the kid, who he'd never officially met, and who of course was a kid no longer but a businessman in his own right.

'Tell Mr Cornelius,' he'd said to the sexy assistant, 'that on Saturday I will be placing this amount of money in his hand.' He'd handed her a folded paper napkin, on which he had written $200,000. Naturally, he had been invited upstairs. Joe knew from that time in Kalgoorlie that Oscar Cornelius was the kind of bloke who didn't mind taking a chance.

So now here he was in this spacious room with a pool table and an honest-to-goodness petrol sign, sitting in a chair looked straight out of *Get Smart*. Only this chair was brand new and was likely worth more than Joe's Corolla. Cornelius sat across the desk from him, wearing a blousy white shirt, top button undone. He leaned over, holding Joe's serviette in front of him, the number facing out, like a driver at the airport waiting for a client just off the plane.

'Two minutes, Joe,' he said. 'I'm a busy man.'

Which of course was BS, but Joe rode it.

'We've never met, but I remember you from the two-up game at the Diggers and Dealers about six years ago.'

Cornelius sat back, disarmed, a grin on his face.

'You remember that?'

'You hit seven tails in a row and then you cashed out. If you'd have stayed for one more, you would have doubled your money.'

'It came up tails again?'

'It did, but quitting when you were ahead was a move told me you weren't just some lucky young dickhead.'

'That's what a lot of people in Perth think.'

'You're not *that* lucky.' Joe was feeling good now. He *knew* this guy, had shared countless beers with other Oscars at racecourses and pubs. 'Unfortunately, you lost it all the next day at the track.'

Cornelius tried to hide his frown but didn't succeed. Sort of guy enjoyed someone talking about his successes a lot more than his failures.

'What you didn't know was that the race was fixed.'

He had Cornelius hooked now.

'Oscar,' using his first name, getting familiar, risking it, 'there is nothing more soul-destroying than discovering you've been on the wrong end of a con.' He paused, 'And nothing more fulfilling than being on the right end. My two minutes are nearly up, so let me lay it out. A horse is going to win at Belmont on Saturday. I know this for a fact. If you put twenty thousand on, as of an hour ago, you win three hundred grand. Of which I would like a third.'

Joe sitting back, job done. Cornelius regarded him carefully.

'How can you know "for a fact"?'

'Fortune allowed me to come into possession of some confidential information. I then followed up with empirical evidence.'

'What evidence?'

'Before I disclose that, I'd like an indication of your interest.'

'What's to say you're not conning me?'

'What would be in it for me? I've got nothing against you. I'm not a bookmaker. In fact, bookmakers are the reason I'm forced to seek a financial partner. I have no connection to any other horse in the race, so there's no value in me getting odds for another horse. If I had the funds, I would not need to make this visit. I asked myself, "Who might hear me out?" I saw you in Kalgoorlie. I know you've got the balls. And the money. Twenty grand is nothing to you.'

Cornelius began twiddling the pen on his desk.

'You're wrong. Twenty grand means a great deal to me. I need specifics.'

It was a risk from here on. Everything he told Cornelius made Joe more expendable.

'I somewhat fortuitously came by some information about a scam, wasn't sure what exactly. I went to the trainer's property and found a horse hidden in the barn that is identical to the horse that is entered. A ring-in. That is what I uncovered.'

'How do we know the ring-in will win?'

'We don't. What I can tell you is that the trainer is certain it will win.'

'This trainer is a friend?'

'No. Never met him. Which is good for us, because there's absolutely nothing to connect us to the ring-in.' Slipping that 'us' in there delicately, like they were already a team.

'This could get dangerous?'

'It could. Especially as I've left out the best part.'

'What's the best part?'

Joe was practically dancing inside now. He'd known those would be the next words out of Cornelius's mouth.

'The bookie who took your money back in Kalgoorlie, the one who fixed the race, was Dominic Pendle. I think we should pay him back in spades. But he can be a very dangerous man to cross.'

Joe could tell Cornelius was liking it even more now.

'What's the name of the horse?'

'I don't want to tell you that. Where all ring-ins come unstuck is that too many people know. Look at Fine Cotton.'

'Yes, but you just said you didn't set this deal up. People might've already talked. You don't know, right?'

'If they had already talked, the price in the pre-markets wouldn't still be fifteen to one.'

'You expect me to entrust you with twenty-grand?'

Joe held up his hands. 'No way. I provide the information. You put the bet on and pay me my share when you win.'

'Who's to say I won't rip you off?'

'Why would you? You still make two hundred and I might prove useful sometime in the future.'

'But then Pendle comes knocking on my door.' Cornelius ticking off a point with a fat forefinger.

'Hopefully not.'

Cornelius already shaking his head. 'No. I'm not scared of Pendle, but it's not good for business. I'd rather you put the bet on. Then you pay me my winnings. If you don't, I come looking for you. Trust me, Joe, I can be every bit as scary as Dominic Pendle.'

Not being in a position to refuse, Joe said, 'That's up to you, but the race is seventy-two hours away, and that's a lot of cash to keep on me. My place is currently being redecorated.'

Cornelius chuckled. 'You mean your face is in danger of being redecorated?'

Lying was always Joe's first instinct, but instead he just opened his hands in a 'you got me' gesture.

Cornelius said, 'I don't see the problem. Put the bet on pre-market with Pendle, give me the ticket, then even if you get roughed up, the money is still safe.'

Harris didn't like the idea of putting money on early and said so. 'It will create too much suspicion.'

'But whoever is behind this switch might go early and take the price.'

'I don't think so. This smells like pros. They won't go till the day of the race for the same reason. I wouldn't be surprised they even put a bit of money on other horses to keep the smoke-screen. I don't know for sure, but I'm thinking this ring-in is based out of the Eastern States, or even overseas. The local end of it wouldn't have the financial muscle. They probably won't even back the horse here.'

'What do you mean?'

Clearly Cornelius was something of an ingenue in the betting game, especially starting price—or SP—betting.

'When you back with an SP bookie, you don't get odds right off like you do on course, you get whatever odds the horse starts at on the track. To score maximum, the people behind this scam will keep the odds of the horse long by not putting money on it on the track here. They'll put their money on with illegal starting-price bookies all around the country—probably only half an hour before the race—because if the SPs know they're going to be hit, they'll organise somebody to dash to the course here and put a shitload of cash on ...'

'Which would force down the starting price, reducing their payout.'

'You're not just a pretty face, Oscar.' Cornelius struggling to suppress the smile on his fleshy lips, Joe seeing the flattery was working. Enjoying being mentor now, extending the guy's education. 'You also mustn't go too soon, because if a bookie like Pendle gets a whiff of this, he might buy off the jockeys—or, when the race is over, if he loses, let the stewards know something was off. So, we don't go early, we keep our powder dry. But then, as I say, if you want me to get the bet on or organise for the bet to go on via a third party, I need to get lost somewhere for a day or two.'

'Forgive me, Joe, but I am averse to letting my money out of my sight. How about this: you can stay here for the next couple of nights. I have a spare room down the hall. I call it the Bono room.'

'He stayed here?'

'Not yet. Then, Saturday, you take the money and put it on. I'll have one of my guys keep an eye on you until you collect. Just to ensure I'm protected, you understand.'

'Comes with the territory.' Staying here would be perfect. No way was Missouri going to find him up here.

Cornelius said, 'But I think twenty is too small a bet. Why don't we go fifty?'

This enthusiasm made Joe nervous. He shook his head.

'Pendle won't take more than twenty. He'll smell a rat. Twenty is the max. Maybe spread another five to ten through the rest of the bookies, but Pendle is the only one that counts in this town.'

'What about these starting-price bookies in other cities?'

'They won't take any decent bet with someone they don't know. Trust me on this.'

Apparently, Cornelius did. 'You need to get a bag, clothes?' he asked.

'Better I don't.'

'Okay, I'll get Maya to show you to your room and pick up a couple of shirts and pants for you. We'll deduct it from your winnings. Fair enough?'

Joe Harris thought it was just bonza.

'And—' said Cornelius, '—we'll get those clothes laundered. They stink.'

9

'Father Monaghan's money is on.' Goose waving a slip of paper, handing it over to Rick. It was near seven at night and there wouldn't be a lot more trade from here on, but there was still plenty to do. That was the trouble with owning a café. Every day and night there was something—washing dishes, mopping floors, fixing broken tables. Rick was always way more exhausted at night than he'd been in prison. He had established a great business, sure, but Zeen's import business was where the real money was. Even this late, she was still out signing up new clients.

Goose, helping himself to one of the little shortbread cookies Rick kept in a jar by the till, said, 'I went to Dominic Pendle. He's really the only bookie who could handle a bet that size. They gave me one hundred grand to eight, so it averaged out at twelve-and-a-half to one.'

'Didn't make a fuss?'

'Didn't blink. Of course, it was over the phone, and it wasn't him personally, I don't think—sounded too young—but the buck stops with Pendle. He has mining guys putting thirty grand on a race.'

Rick put the betting slip under the cash-register tray for when Paul came. He offered Goose proper food, but Goose was heading for the airport. He shook a few more of the cookies into his long thin palm.

'I've got a couple of days near Newman. Well, when I say near Newman, I mean nearer there than any other town, but really, we're talking lonely desert.'

'So I can't reach you?'

'Only way is a satellite phone. You'd have more chance of speaking to me if I was in the spirit world.'

They said their goodbyes with hand signals, Rick wiping down the Milano in readiness for the new day. No sooner had Goose gone out the front door than Zeen came in the back. Even after a hard day on the hustings she looked good and smelled better. Rick put his arms out, pulled her to him, and they kissed. He wanted to race her upstairs that minute, controlled himself, pulling back, getting a little distance so he could admire that face he never grew tired of.

'How did it go?'

'Twelve more clients, including the Carnival chain. They have seven outlets. It was almost the perfect day, the bank gives us the loan, everyone loves the pitch. I'm starving.'

Rick had already set aside her favourite mushroom risotto. He told his young assistant, Jess, to look after things, then set Zeen up at her preferred table, just outside the sliding jail-bar booth. He put a quarter of a lemon on the side, the way she liked it, and a small dish of grated parmesan, which his Italian mentor Mrs Androcelli had told him was not a condiment any self-respecting Italian would add, but which Zeen loved. Immediately taking to the risotto like a backhoe in soft ground. 'You make this, or Adrian?' she managed between forkfuls.

'Me. I let Adrian do the curry and the chicken.'

'It's good. What are you staring at?'

'You. Just to remind myself this is real.'

She liked that, leaned over, kissed him again.

Rick picked up on what she'd said before.

'So why wasn't it perfect? The day.'

She rolled her eyes.

'I didn't want to tell you earlier. When I got back from the bank, Joe was waiting out back.'

'Harris?'

She nodded as she chewed. Joe Harris was a grade-A scumbag. A noxious weed. And Zeen's ex-partner in a couple of different ways. Fortunately, he hadn't been seen nor heard of for a few years.

'What did he want?'

'What do you think he wanted?'

Her body? That was what Rick was wanting this second.

'Money,' she snapped. 'The usual: he has a sure thing in some race, and if I loan him the money, I'll never see him again.' Pointing the prongs of the fork at Rick. 'That part of it was tempting.'

'Is he still living up Bulwer Street?'

'I didn't ask, but I can't see him ever moving. His aunt owns the flat and lets him have it for practically nothing.' She stopped eating and narrowed her eyes like she was a radiographer looking at a scan. 'You're not jealous?'

You bet he was.

'Course not.'

She reached over and grabbed him behind the neck, used her thumb to massage the back of his skull.

'I like it that you're jealous.'

He didn't reply, let her think she'd won that round. He had a plan, though.

When Zeen had finished her meal and gone up to shower, Rick told her he'd clean up and then join her. Instead, he locked up quickly, waited till he heard the shower running and snuck into their bedroom. In the third drawer on their dresser was an old biscuit tin in which they kept a variety of crap—the valve for a footy pump, duplicates of car keys, some freebie passes to nightclubs that had long gone out of business, and some broken necklaces that Zeen had never gotten around to getting fixed.

And a key to Harris's apartment that for some reason she had never given back.

It had been a sore point with Rick, wondering why you wouldn't toss that thing first chance you had, but it had been lying in there for five years now. Was it backup in case things didn't work out with him and Zeen? He couldn't believe she would ever contemplate Harris again, either as a lover or a partner, but he'd never raised the key with her.

Now, after all this time, it might finally prove useful. Rick knew where Harris lived. He was going to pay him a visit and tell him to steer clear of Zeen once and for all.

It was only a five-minute drive to the small apartment building, quite a nice one if the outside was anything to go by, had a bit of an LA feel about it—white with those bubbly looking walls and a Mexican-style arch leading to a front door, a couple of low palm trees guarding the front. There were no lights showing in Harris's flat, but maybe he just wasn't advertising the fact he was home. Rick got out of the car, walked up the short path and entered the front doorway.

Inside, the building wasn't special in any way. A low side lamp up on the wall threw just enough light to see. There was a wooden staircase leading up to the second floor, where Harris's flat faced the street. Rick could hear muffled TV from the lower flats, but otherwise there was nothing. He scooted up creaky stairs, turned right, put his ear to Harris's door. No sound inside. He rapped on the door. No response. Well, if Harris wasn't in, Rick reckoned he may as well take a look around.

He took the key from his pocket, wondering if Harris might have changed the lock. Nope, the bastard was too cheap. The key turned easily.

Rick stepped into the apartment and closed the door. It was airless, wouldn't want to be here in summer, no sign of a ceiling fan or aircon. Not wishing to risk a light in the loungeroom, he moved on down the hallway. First stop, a minimalist bathroom in need of a clean. A narrow rectangular window. Rick hung a damp towel from the rack across it and clicked on the light, satisfied the towel would block it showing from outside. Shower stall a fungal hazard; tubes of toothpaste and other stuff tossed carelessly on the ledge above a stained basin.

He exited the bathroom, turned off the light, returned the towel, the smell of unwashed clothes and sheets a deterrent to advancing to the bedroom, but one he steeled himself to overcome. There was no window, so he clicked on the bedside lamp to reveal a tangle of sheets, clothes tossed willy-nilly. The drawers in the bedside dresser held a few lottery tickets, triple-A batteries, some discount pizza vouchers. Starting to realise by then he hadn't thought this through at all. Should he leave a note? *Stay Away From Zeen.*

Nah, sounded pathetic. He could write it on the walls in marker pen; except he didn't have one. That wasn't his go anyway. He would confront Harris face to face, but leaving stupid messages felt weak, pissy, something Harris might do.

Oh well, Harris would keep. Best he got back before Zeen asked where he'd been. If he told her the truth she would mock him. Oh so gently, sure, but that would gall.

Rick retraced his steps and left the apartment. He made sure the door was locked, dropped the key back in his pocket, but then thought he should have left it in there. Turning back towards the stairs when—*wham!*—something hard as concrete struck him in the solar plexus, dropped him to his knees. He fought for breath, saw shapes in shadows.

'Mr Pendle wants your company, fucker.'

The voice was young, coarse, like you might hear from up on a roof while tiles were tossed into a skip below, and right now Rick was one of those broken tiles. He felt arms gather him from either side and drag him down the stairs, his feet clattering across the edge of the steps.

'You really shouldn't have hung around, Harris,' said another voice, a bit deeper.

Rick still couldn't breathe. Looking out for a passerby, a saviour, but likely all he'd be able to manage would be a gurgle. He was dragged up the road just beyond his car and thrown into the back seat of a Commodore, one of his assailants joining him. The other got behind the wheel and started up.

About three minutes into the ride, Rick managed to gasp, 'Not Harris.'

'Nice try, you fucking moron.' The higher voice, the one beside him in the back. 'You just happen to find the key to his flat?'

Rick shut up after that. He knew where he was being taken: to the bookie, Pendle. He'd sort it out there. A fair chance Harris hadn't paid a debt.

The car headed east. It smelled of cigarette smoke and leaky petrol. After about ten minutes it turned off into a complex of low-rise industrial units, brick walls, tin roofs. Nobody about this time of night. The car stopped out the front of a unit and Rick was dragged out again. He could see the men better now. The one next to him low-twenties, muscled, wearing a short-sleeved Kmart shirt. The driver around the same age, his hair short, his tee-shirt worn under a satin jacket. A garage roller-door was down, they bypassed that, knocked on a narrow wooden door.

The door opened and he was shoved in. The unit was almost bare: cement floor, cheap mats, a water cooler, some verge-collection furniture and what might have been boating or fishing gear off to the side. A bloke already inside—mid-to-late forties and big—sports jacket over a tee shirt struggling to contain him. Everything about him square—shoulders, head, jaw. A Lego man, jeans and brogues his only nod to humanity. He looked familiar but not so much Rick could place why. The big guy looked from Rick to Moe and Curly.

'This isn't Harris.'

Dumbfounded expressions on their faces. The high-voiced one said, 'He come out of the apartment. Had a key.'

Lego man said, 'This is Rick Boski. He did time with my brother. You get the right apartment?'

'Course, same one we've been checking all day.' The driver this time.

The big guy didn't even glance at them.

'Fuck-off, fuckwits.'

They hung for a second, then scurried out. Then the big man turned to Rick.

'Harris a mate of yours?'

'No.'

'What were you doing in his apartment?'

'None of your business.'

'That's true, Boski. But it *is* Mr Pendle's business. Where's Harris?'

'No idea.'

'How did you wind up with his key if you're not his friend?'

Leave Zeen out of it, don't give them anything.

'He left it under his mat.'

'No, that was checked.'

Rick nodding to indicate the two stooges outside, 'By those two?'

'By me.'

'He must have come back.'

The big guy stirred, came closer. Austin, his name coming finally. But everybody used to refer to him by a nickname ... what was it? *Misery*. His brother was Mick Austin, an unsuccessful small-time crook who'd been done for boosting caravans. The rumour had been that big brother was heavy, hence the moniker.

'What were you doing there?'

Rick snatching an idea. 'He owes me money too.'

Austin stared him over like the T-Rex in that movie with Sam Neill where the guy hides in the dunny. Doug, that was his name, Doug Austin.

'I have no beef with you, Boski, but if you know where Harris is, you better tell.'

'I don't.'

'Then you need to find him quick. Otherwise, I'll be paying you a visit.'

'This is nothing to do with me.'

'His ex is your chick. Don't try and blow smoke, Boski.'

So, Austin had known that all along.

'We need our money, and if we can't get it from Harris, we will get it from those close to him.'

'I told you, I'm not—'

Austin held up a finger. Rick shut up.

'Any reasonable person would conclude that you were visiting his flat to help him out in some way.' He held out his palm. 'The key, please. I'm guessing those two never got it off you?'

Rick handed over the key. That was one good thing to come out of all this, sayonara to that fucking key.

He said, 'My car is back at Harris's place, Misery. Maybe you could—'

'What did you call me?'

Rick was tempted to say *Lego man*.

'Misery,' he said.

'Mis-*sou*-ri.' Pronouncing it long and slow. 'As in the state. And the battleship.'

Oops.

'I'm not giving you a lift. Fuck off.'

Rick didn't know where he was. Although, as he walked out into the cool night, he realised that was wrong. He knew exactly where he was—back in deep shit, courtesy of Joe arsehole Harris.

The good thing about illegal drugs, Liz Atwood reflected, was the leverage it gave you when foolish young men like Drew Waldron were sitting opposite you in a suburban Pizza Hut they would never otherwise visit, their legs jiggling with anxiety. Nine months back, Waldron had been picked up by the drug squad in a raid on a beachside coke-dealer. He was a customer, not a dealer; a typical Western suburbs type, would have gone to Christ Church or Scotch—one of those schools where they had ovals looked like billiard tables. A clear-skinned twenty-one-year-old of fuck-all use to the drug squad.

Still, when Liz was flicking through the nightly arrests and caught the name, she jumped in the lift, rode a floor and beetled over to the drug squad faster than she could down a Tim Tam on a cold night. She asked them to hold off charging Waldron, explained he might be of use to Liquor and Gaming.

'He's Dominic Pendle's penciller,' she explained.

'His what?' In unison, pizza spatter on their teeth.

'The guy who records the bets in the betting ledger, gives the bookie the correct odds, lets them know where their book stands at any given minute.'

Many pencillers were older guys who worked some boring government job and enjoyed the sideline and the extra cash. Some, like Waldron here, were students doing complicated maths majors. Waldron was extra useful because he also worked Pendle's advance-race bets. Often the advance bets would give Atwood a pointer as to which horses weren't going to be trying in an upcoming race, which might be running drug-assisted, what punters might be in trouble and about to do something foolish to resolve their debt. So had begun the relationship between the cop and the maths major, a relationship that was consummated weekly at this pizzeria.

Waldron, who had a foppish Hugh Grant fringe going on and looked offended to be seen in a place like this, said, 'Harris owes Dom north of forty grand.'

What she figured. She wasn't too proud to eat pizza right from the cardboard box. She gestured Waldron was welcome to join. He nearly recoiled.

'Why would he let Harris get that far into him?'

'I don't think he wanted to. Harris practically begged Pendle to let him bet.'

'And Harris hasn't paid, and he's going to lose appendages.' A logical deduction to draw but Waldron threw his hands out.

'I just help with the books.'

'You hear anything, you let me know.'

He assured her he would. He looked relieved, thinking he could go. Not yet.

'Anything special happen today at the track?'

Today's races had been out at Northam. Liz had already checked in with the stewards, who hadn't reported anything suspicious.

'Nope. Dominic took a few big bets, won about twenty grand all up.'

'Anything interesting in the pre-race for this weekend?'

'Not especially. John Prescott, the car-dealer, put twenty on his horse to win the two-year-old race Saturday. Odds were five-to-two. A FIFO guy put eight down to win a hundred on an outsider Saturday.'

'You know this guy?'

Liz thinking this was a big bet for a FIFO. Maybe he was dealing drugs, and she could pass the intel onto the drug squad—a little quid-pro-quo for helping her out with this show-pony.

'He's a semi-regular, but usually only bets a couple of hundred max.'

'What's his name?'

'Goose Gordon.'

She made a note to check him out.

'What horse did he bet on?'

'Hysterical in the last.'

Hysterical. Liz flicked through her mental filing cabinet. She pictured an unimpressive brown mare.

'Enzo Rapanaro owns and trains her, doesn't he?'

Waldron saying he believed she was right.

'But you know, I'm—'

'... just the penciller, I know. Anything else?'

He couldn't think of anything.

'Okay, you can go. Don't forget to tell me if Harris appears, or if Pendle lets something slip about the punishment he has in store.'

He promised he wouldn't forget and scooted out of there. Liz couldn't face the last two slices of pizza. She dumped the box in the bin and split for the office.

Half an hour later she was punching the name Goose Gordon into the criminal database.

Bingo.

'Surprise, surprise,' she said, feeling good now. Definitely a lead the drug squad could follow up. Guy had done time five years back, illegal explosives. When she got down to the Known Associates she felt like she'd just been detonated.

Under Gordon's KAs was Rick Boski!

The same Rick Boski who ran a prison-themed café and was shacked up with Zeen, former associate of the much-in-demand Joe Harris. Liz tingling all over, close to something screwy, she knew it. She sat back in her chair, mentally untangling threads. Joe Harris is more than forty grand in the hole with Pendle. Pendle wants blood. Harris wants out, but he has bugger-all friends and almost certainly no cash. What does a loser like Harris do when his back is against the wall like that? What he's always done: doubles down, borrows more money to make another bet. Except nobody is going to lend him money.

Well, maybe somebody, like an ex who still had a soft spot for him. But Zeen knew Harris, she was smart. She wouldn't be lending him money to piss up against the wall on some Hail-Mary bet. She'd want security. She'd want to be certain she would win. She'd want to know the race was fixed somehow and as good as already in her pocket.

Harris was cooking something up, and whatever that was, it would need financing. The kind of money that might come from a successful enterprise like a hip café run by an ex-con. The 'ex' being debatable—Rick Boski would prove to be just as criminal as he'd been before becoming a barista, nothing was more certain. Zeen and Harris must have stayed close. Eight grand is a fair bit, but not that much to risk winning a hundred. Harris gets half, that pays off his debt to Pendle, and sweet revenge for him that he's the bookie they're going to hit. Harris can't place the bet, and Zeen is too well known as his former grifter partner. They need a third party. Boski says, 'Use Goose Gordon, he already has an account with Pendle, and it won't raise suspicion'.

Zeen or Harris must have some connection with Enzo Rapanaro. Coke and coffee both come from South America, right? Unscrupulous trainers use coke on horses, or ketamine, depending on whether they want them fast or slow. Perhaps Zeen had access to coke, and they were going to give Hysterical a highball before the race. Or maybe Boski was a mean sonofabitch who could stand over the jockeys and demand they make sure Hysterical wins?

Liz picked up the phone and dialled. It rang several times before Candy Harper answered.

'Candy, it's Detective Inspector Liz Atwood here. Is Bryce about?'

'Sure. I'll get him.'

TV sounds filtered into the phone. Candy knew that her husband sometimes liaised with Liz. Liz wasn't stupid, she was aware that Bryce Harper, one of the state's best jockeys, never told her everything that might be going down. But she also knew he wouldn't dare lie if she asked him direct.

'What's up, Liz?' Like all hoops, Harper's voice somewhere just south of Kylie's.

'You heard anything about a fix Saturday?'

'Nope.'

'Don't lie to me.'

'I'm not. What horse?'

She debated whether to reveal that. Decided against it.

'Not important—just a big bet on an outsider.'

'Well, I know stuff-all.'

If the fix was in, the riders would have to know by now. And if Harper hadn't been included, the prospects of success weren't high.

'All right. Thanks, mate. You let me know if you hear anything.'

'Will do.'

Harper rang off.

Liz sat there and thought long and hard. Tomorrow morning she'd pay Enzo Rapanaro a little visit. One he wouldn't even be aware of.

10

'You broke into his apartment?'

Zeen loved the high ground, and Rick was pissed off with himself he'd ceded it to her. There had been no way to lie about what had gone down, seeing as it involved her, and he'd come back hours late.

'I didn't break in. I let myself in with the key.'

'What key?'

'The key you've been keeping in the biscuit tin for five years.'

'I didn't even know it was there.'

'Well, it was.'

She pointed a finger at him.

'You can't be serious. You've been sweating over that key, seeing if I used it.'

'No!'

She shook her head at him, raised an eyebrow.

'Fuck, Boski.'

He went on the attack.

'It's irrelevant, anyway. The salient point here is your mate Joe has got us in the shit again.'

'His debt, not ours.'

'Pendle's enforcer doesn't see it that way.'

The fact she didn't instantly bite back told Rick that she wasn't dismissing the threat out of hand.

Rick said, 'We have to find him.'

'I'll find him.'

'If he hasn't already gone.'

'He's onto a ring-in scam, so he's not going anywhere. He needs money. He's going to try to find that.'

'Nobody who knows Harris will give him money.'

'Fair point,' she said. 'He'll need to find someone who doesn't know him. Meantime, he'll need to stay somewhere. I'll make some calls.'

Somehow the distribution of responsibility for this latest shitstorm didn't seem equitable to Rick, so he tried to make a last point: that if anybody was the injured party, he was.

'Hey, it was bad enough last time when I had people trying to kill me over my debt. And that wasn't even my fault.'

'Marietta could never have got to your money if you'd divorced her, or just taken her off the account.'

He should have known Zeen wouldn't blink, that she'd go on the attack instead, forcing him into a defensive action.

'We're going to rake over old coals, are we?'

'You're the one started the raking. You should have just thrown that stupid key away.'

'It's not ...' he started, then stopped. It was pointless arguing with Zeen, she would never concede. 'Fine. Find Harris and then we turn him in to Pendle.'

'Sure. You're the boss.'

It irked Rick when Zeen agreed with him in that sarky tone. But then she stripped off and climbed into bed and the slate was wiped.

Dominic Pendle was not a man you wanted to cross, but even so, Zeen resented him bullying them. Harris's debt was his problem—he was a bookie for Chrissake. It was highly doubtful Pendle would resort to physical violence against her or Rick, but he didn't need to. Pendle had connections everywhere: government ministers, cops, newspapers. Easy to get a food inspector to give them a big red cross, or an article in a newspaper about unsavoury types running Northbridge establishments with a hint that Café Inside was a meeting place for crims. If Pendle wanted to give them a hard time, he could deliver.

Harris was an arsehole, that went without saying. But Zeen didn't fancy handing him over to Pendle. That bridge could be crossed when she actually found him—maybe give him some warning before shopping him, so he had time to split.

Boski was a good guy, and she loved him, full stop. If either Joe or Pendle gave him grief, Zeen would make it her life's work to destroy them. Meantime, she would try to think how Harris thought, where he could hide, where he might go to pick up a willing investor.

11

Vivid and disturbing were two words that came to mind when Paul tried to describe the dream he'd just had. He'd been in some colosseum-like structure, it might even have been *the* actual Colosseum, his body in the dirt, each of his arms and legs tied to a separate horse. He'd tried to scream but could make no words, only grunts, as if his tongue might have been cut out. The people in the stands jeered, contemptuously tossing money down at him.

As he lay there on his back, a human X, a face peered down at him, backdropped by the blue sky and white cloud—a countenance of immense sadness. It was Father John Feeney, his spiritual counsellor at the seminary. Although Paul had not seen him in over thirty years, he looked not a day older. In other circumstances, say sunbathing down the beach, the intrusion of his old mentor might have been a moment of joy. Many of his cohort found Feeney to be irascible, but not Paul, aware he was something of a favourite with the elderly Jesuit.

'You fool. You want to be the big man, the saviour. Well, newsflash, Paul Monaghan, there's only one of those. Born of a virgin, died on the cross. Ring any bells?'

Before Paul could utter a feeble protest, ask if Feeney might untie his bonds, the old priest had slapped the rump of the nearest horse.

As its huge haunches lurched forward, Paul screaming in terror, his body stretching with the tethers, he had snapped awake, breathing fast and shallow, terrified.

A glance at the clock had told him it was 4.11 AM.

He hadn't slept a wink since. Decoding the dream had been simple. He had used parish funds in an immoral and likely illegal enterprise. Perhaps his motive wasn't as pure as he'd presumed? Even though he planned to donate all his own winnings to the parish council, his subconscious motive might have been self-aggrandisement—wanting to be the one who set things right, wanting to play the hero, the saviour.

He could hear Feeney's voice as if he were in the room with him.

'You've perverted Christ's teaching, Monaghan. It's good old-fashioned pride, nothing less.'

He lay in bed stewing. There were so many separate rivers feeding into this wide ocean of anxiety. Was the horse even going to win? What if God punished him by making Hysterical lose? The parish coffers would be bare. Should he try to call off the bet? Could he even do that?

Nobody but Paul had access to the monies, and it would take all of thirty seconds for the parish council and then the bishop to determine who was responsible. His sins would be on public display. Not just in his parish, but across the whole state, maybe even the country. These days the only people who loved parish priests were compensation lawyers. Now, even though he might want to abandon the project, he couldn't repay the parish, having invested almost every penny of his own on Hysterical.

While he couldn't rid himself of the suspicion that he had fallen prey to the other fella, the one with the cloven hooves who smelled of sulphur, there was still a chance that his first instinct had been correct, that God had been the one directing him.

If the horse won, the monies went to the parish as he'd intended, and one might infer that the plan had indeed been a divine one. Should the horse lose, however, the parish would be cleaned out. Criminal charges would undoubtedly follow, and he would find himself back in the prison system, but this time in the role of prisoner. And what about all those other prisoners he had counselled over the years? How would they feel to find their moral guide was a fellow crook?

What to do? His brain was too weak a torch to find a path through this dense fog. He was groping, acting on instinct rather than carefully sifted reason, when he decided that he should head over to Enzo's to try to discover exactly what Enzo was part of.

Especially whether it might be successful.

Paul dressed quickly, jeans and shirt, a clerical collar as a prop more than anything. Old school Italian Enzo, who clearly still valued the role of the church, might be more likely to talk if he perceived Paul to be there in an official capacity.

A cool morning of dull skies and damp atmosphere didn't so much greet Paul as ignore him as he left the rectory and climbed into his Corolla. Enzo's property was about fifteen minutes east. The tardy engine coughed a few times before catching—a service was well overdue. It might be even more overdue if Hysterical didn't win.

Paul powered through the stirring streets, up to the T-junction, where he swung quickly out onto the highway for six or seven minutes before turning right down the narrow feeder road that led to Rapanaro's property.

Despite the freshness of the morning, the negative ions bombarding him, his brain hadn't yet fully engaged with the real world. As if it was hedging its bets, dwelling on the provocative dream of the arena as it calculated the cost of his vehicle repairs, money that the archdiocese would pay that might be better diverted to the school or church necessities.

No surprise, then, he literally didn't see the other vehicle emerging from his right off the little backroad until a collision was unavoidable. He hit the brakes. Luckily, he was only doing about forty-five, and the other car must have seen him at about the same time and tried to swing away as it, too, braked.

But it was all too late. The skid of the Corolla's tyres ended with the inevitable thump of metal on metal. The impact finally roused Paul to full consciousness and focused him on the here and now. He switched off his engine, sat for a few seconds taking in the unpleasant reality: he'd hit the front passenger side of a Ford sedan that looked far newer than his ageing car. It could have been worse—only a driver in the Ford, no passenger to be injured, and the damage, from what he could discern, minimal.

Paul slid out of his car. The woman of the other car was already out, calmly assessing the situation. She looked about forty, was wearing jeans and a windcheater.

'Are you okay?' Paul asked, studying her for any sign of injury. Nothing obvious, no blood. 'I just never saw you,' he said, then recalled you weren't supposed to admit fault, although there could be no question he was the negligent party here.

'I'm fine, Father,' she said, studying the damage to her car. 'Doesn't look too bad.'

The Corolla's front was crumpled a bit, the right headlight, he now saw, broken.

'No, not too serious,' he agreed. 'I'll just get a pen, get your details.'

In the console he found a biro and some parish newsletters with space to write. 'Probably just wasn't expecting anyone this time of day,' he babbled. 'You local?'

'I'm not.'

He ripped a chunk of paper from the bulletin.

'Here are my details.' He started writing his name and address. 'It's insured through the church policy, so there's no problem.'

She had pulled a camera from the car and was taking shots, getting the damage and number plates. When he'd finished writing his details, he handed over the paper. She reached into her pocket, pulled out a small business card. He nearly fainted when he read it. *Detective Inspector Elizabeth Atwood.* The next words screamed out at him. *Liquor and Gaming.* Maybe he groaned audibly.

She said, 'Yeah, you hit a cop.'

Paul feeling a weak smile trickling over his face.

'Sorry, didn't mean to ...'

'Don't worry, you're not going to prison. I'll get this in the works.' She wagged the ripped piece of paper he'd given her. 'We can both drive, right?'

Some words of assent stumbled off his lips.

'Okay, well, till next time,' she laughed and climbed back into her car, then drove off and turned back towards the highway.

For a long moment, Paul couldn't move.

Liquor and Gaming, coming from the direction of Enzo's property but dressed in civvies. His head was beginning to pound. This was bad. This was very, very bad.

Any other day, Liz might have been pissed off: the priest day-dreaming, all the bureaucratic shit she'd have to attend to. Today, though, she was seeing the lighter side of the planet: it wasn't her car, just one from the motor pool. Yes, the report she'd need to file was annoying, but that was small beer after what she'd just discovered.

Parking off the road beside a deserted part of Rapanaro's property, she'd snuck through the fence into one of the pad-docks, checked out some horses but had not laid eyes on Hys-terical. She'd circled around, edged closer to the house. There was a young lad tending the stables, but no horses. Which was when she'd caught the faint sound of galloping hooves and worked her way around behind the buildings to a rear paddock. One horse quietly grazing there. She pulled up the binocs, headed towards it. Looked like Hysterical all right. The sound of galloping was a little louder here, the source most likely over the back of the hill. She'd jogged across the paddock, past Hys-terical, hugged a line of trees to near top of the hill. By now she could tell it was a single horse, though it was still hidden by the hill's crest.

As the treeline ended, she threw herself flat on her belly, crawled through wild oat grass. Down below was a circular track of compacted dirt. She figured this must be where Rapanaro worked the horses into something like a track gallop. Nothing fancy, but the track was graded and smooth except for where the horse's hooves puffed dirt. Somebody was giving it a solid workout. Even with the naked eye she could see the rider was too large for a jockey.

Picking up her long-lens camera, she fine-tuned, recognised Rapanaro. But that wasn't what caused her to nearly drop them.

The galloping horse was a dead ringer for Hysterical. If she hadn't just passed Hysterical in the other paddock, she would swear this was her. Or maybe it was the other way around, though she gave that idea less credence because her brain had been rapidly calculating what all this could mean and had already selected an explanation. One that made everything clear to Liz Atwood, both metaphorically and in terms of the images she began to snap.

That was why, now, heading back towards the city, she wasn't worried about the ding in the vehicle, and any pain-in-the-arse paperwork. Instead, she was doing something she would never have believed herself capable of, listening to breakfast radio and singing along with Bobby McFerrin's *Don't Worry, Be Happy*.

Rick studied the small cardboard rectangle up close: *Detective Inspector Elizabeth Atwood, Liquor and Gaming.* He felt his balls contract.

Of course, it might be nothing but coincidence. He'd been surprised to see Paul back at the café so soon. Saw straight away, too, he was jumpy. Assuming, when the priest told him he'd had an accident, that was why. Even when Paul told him it had been a cop driving the other car, Rick still blasé. The card changing that.

'Did you speak to the trainer guy?'

Rick hoping there might be some logical explanation, the cop there checking on a licence or something. Paul explained he had driven straight over there, but Rapanaro wasn't around, only some stable hand, so the priest had made up some excuse like he was just passing and thought he would drop in, see how Enzo was doing while Marie was off in Italy visiting family.

Zeen had been at the back of the café, clearing tables and stacking the dishwasher as the morning rush dwindled, and she hadn't been privy to all this.

'Hey, Hun—you got a sec?' Rick signalling with a crooked finger.

She came over, carrying cups.

'You know this cop?' Rick passing her the little white rectangle like it might be a phial of avian flu. Zeen studied the card.

'Hardwood. Shit yeah.'

Zeen looking from him to Paul like she was catching the smell of burnt embers from an encroaching bushfire.

'What's going on?' asking the way someone does when they're afraid of the answer. Rick gestured for privacy, Zeen put down the dirty cups, and the three of them moved to a deserted table as far away from the scatter of customers as they could.

Rick ran her through the story so far. Zeen sitting back, a look on her face that Rick had seen lots of times before that meant she was way ahead of him.

'Wait up. You came here yesterday?' Zeen looking at the priest. 'Wanting help to put on a bet, because you got a tip that a horse was a certainty to win?'

Paul agreed that summed it up adequately.

'When you two spoke, where did this conversation take place?'

Rick felt Zeen's gaze like a dentist's probe.

'Out the back.' Rick couldn't see what the big deal was.

Zeen made a noise that might've been a doomed penguin falling to its death.

'You had this conversation out the back, right where Joe Harris then ambushed me.'

Rick seeing it now. 'He was hiding out there.'

'I'd say so. He probably came earlier while I was at the bank, heard you guys talking. Then sprang me when I got back.'

'Can I cancel my bet?' Paul clearly wasn't too interested in what must have seemed to him like minor details.

Rick said, 'Even if I could reach Goose, there's no way they'd let him cancel without taking at least half what you put down.'

'Half might be better than nothing.'

Rick could see that Paul was reeling. Reminded him of how he felt in court that fateful day when the magistrate got ready to sentence him, painting Rick as some cannabis kingpin.

A kind of wavering moan had started creeping out of the priest's throat.

Getting twitchy, Rick said, 'Maybe getting half back wouldn't be such a terrible result.'

Zeen put up her hands. 'Just cool it, guys, we need to think. Joe mentioned Fine Cotton to me. That was a famous ring-in—where you replace a bad horse with a good one that looks just like it.'

Zeen nodding to herself, as if one piece of the puzzle had just slotted into place.

'Yep, that's the scam. I'm sure of it. And your problem is, Paul, that somehow or other, Hardwood has found out about it. That is really bad news. Hardwood is tenacious and she's tough. She'll trace the bet back to Goose.' Fixing Rick with a sorrowful all-knowing look. 'That's not good for us. Goose leads to you, you lead to me, I lead to Harris, which is likely how she has got wind of the scam. He probably went to a dozen people begging for funds and couldn't keep his trap shut. With Pendle on his arse, he'll be desperate. The bet Goose made with Paul's money—that's with Pendle too, right? And he already suspects you of something.'

Rick, the shipwrecked sailor, grasped at a floating spar.

'Maybe she doesn't know the nature of the scam?'

'Any other L&G cop, perhaps, but Atwood is smart. You notice if she had a camera?'

Paul gave a slow nod.

'I'm gone.' He'd turned white. 'They'll put me in prison.'

Rick felt the need to reassure him.

'Hey, we'll cover the eight-grand bet.' Meeting Zeen's glance with a plea. 'We'll have to postpone the import, but he can't go to jail for trying to do the right thing.'

'The first payment has already gone. Soon as the bank doubled our overdraft, I upped our order to the max. Right now, we're tapped out.'

'When can we get money in?'

'Twenty-eight days my end. We'll have to rely on the café.'

'I'm so sorry to drag you into this,' Paul said.

Rick guessing Goose likely had few thousand spare. But how could he contact him?

Rick said he knew a few ex-cons who might chip in for their old chaplain.

The priest shook his head. 'I couldn't do that to Goose or to any of them. I don't want them to lose faith in me.'

Rick certain that would happen anyway if Paul wound up in jail.

'I've let everyone down.' He put his face in his hands. Zeen and Rick swapped looks. They were in this together, and unfortunately it was a deep well of sewage.

Zeen said, 'We can't worry about what's done. We need a plan to minimise damage.'

Rick was thinking that if they cancelled the bet, even if they lost half, Paul could pay back most of the funds to the parish. But they might not be able to reach Goose in time.

'Should I try calling Enzo?' Panic etched over Paul's face.

Zeen shook her head.

'No. Right now, you do nothing. At the moment, there's nothing linking you to the scam. I need to think.'

She picked up the empty coffee cups, handed them to Rick and pulled out her car keys.

'Where are you going?'

'A facial. That's where I do my best thinking.'

Paul kept trying to apologise. Rick felt bad: the priest was shaking.

He said, 'Go home and think about something else. Let us figure out the best move here.'

The priest nodded, shuffled off in a daze. Rick hoped he didn't have another accident on the way home.

After he'd settled Harris into the guest room, Oscar Cornelius tried to calm down by shooting pool. Couldn't concentrate though and had a little K to chill. What had him on edge was that arsehole bookie Dom Pendle, ripping him off way back when. It would give him great satisfaction to return the favour.

One thing troubled Oscar, though. Whoever had organised this ring-in was going to put a great deal of money on

Hysterical—or the fake Hysterical, to be more accurate. Okay, so maybe it was all SP they were going to bet, and the price would stay at better than double-figure odds. But it only took one crack in the dam to let those odds out. One loose-tongued nephew or flunky and the odds would plummet. Say the horse started at two to one, he'd have to put on six times as much money to win the same amount he could if he bet right now. On the other hand, let's say he had a little dabble right now at the pre-market odds, maybe put on five large. That's sixty in his fist, and no share to Harris, even better. What's more, he could let Pendle see who was putting the money on. And later, if Pendle tried to come back at him, tough. Oscar was confident he could match any muscle Pendle had at his disposal.

He was warming to this idea the more he thought about it. Harris was a worrywart. Oscar figuring what he could do, without involving Harris, was go up to Pendle, put on three bets, all outsiders, bury Hysterical in there. Yes, this was a very cool idea. He picks a couple of longshots and pops a grand or two on them, then adds five on Hysterical. Harris had been adamant there was no money on it yet, or it wouldn't still be the odds it was. So, the bookie would just assume that Oscar's three bets were entirely amateur.

All Oscar needed was to find out where Pendle liked to lunch and engineer an introduction. His old man would know the bookmaker's haunts. Calling his father had always seemed like an admission of defeat, but it had been years since he'd hit him up for funding. Nowadays, Oscar was a success and was totally secure in who he was. He picked up the phone.

As a potential buyer, Oscar had run his thumb over the Salisbury Hotel a few times, but decided it was too small for his needs: virtually no car park and hemmed in by offices and a botanical garden. It was primarily a lunch and after-work drinking hole for the nearby office crowd: car dealers, real-estate agents and turf types. Most of the Salisbury's patrons lunched in a small beer-garden with lush plants and bamboo furniture, but the serious old guys who still wore suit jackets and ties and spoke in hushed voices preferred the dim, dark jarrah saloon bar.

It sometimes happened that Oscar would get this drug-free organic high just from knowing he was on the right side of some deal that was about to go down. Right that minute he felt the familiar buzz, spying the bookie at a table of five sitting under framed black and white photos of various sports legends.

Even before the old man suggested the Salisbury, Oscar had it marked down in his head as a likely Dominic Pendle habitat. It was steak and chips, lamb shanks, oysters and barramundi served by waitresses in skirts with hems below their knees. It was the last place you would have found Oscar and his pals.

Larry Hacket, the pub's septuagenarian owner, was a driving force on the board of the local hotel and club owners' association, and he was always calling for help in planning the annual fundraiser for their nominated charity, the Royal Flying Doctor. Ostensibly, Oscar had called over to offer any of his venues for the annual lunch.

'I'll pick up all the staff costs and donate the bar take.'

Hacket, a diminutive man with leathery brown skin who fitted neatly into slacks and a dark shirt, was very grateful.

'That's terrific. We need more of you younger publicans and club-owners involved.'

They celebrated with a lemon squash, during which Oscar made out like he'd just clocked Pendle.

'Is that Dom Pendle over there?'

'That's him.' Hacket rattled off the names of the others at the table. One was an ex-footy coach, but sport wasn't Oscar's thing.

'I wanted to get some bets on. Would he do that for me?'

'If I ask for you he will. Come on, I'll introduce you.'

As they drew close to the table, Oscar could see the guys were on their main meal.

'Pardon the interruption, gentlemen. Is everything to your liking?'

Hacket the professional 'mine host'.

'Except the prices, you tightarse.' The footy coach, laughing as he said it. They all chuckled.

Hacket returned jovial fire.

'Mate, the way you coached my boys, I should charge you triple.'

More guffaws. This matey-mate stuff bored Oscar shitless, but old guys loved it.

Hacket said, 'Gentlemen, I want to introduce you to my fellow publican Oscar Cornelius. If you think my prices are high, try his.'

Genial nods. Oscar enjoyed being welcomed.

Hacket adding, 'Oscar is Tiny's boy.'

Of course, they all knew that, though a couple made an effort to act like it was news.

'Oscar has generously offered one of his venues for our Flying Doctor fundraiser. September third, mark it down.' All of them making out like they were interested.

'My daughter is always at the Globe,' said a fit-looking guy with glasses and a striped business shirt. Oscar, good with names, thinking it might have been Brendan.

'Tell her to introduce herself. I'll look after her.' Oscar spreading the largesse. Hacket dropped a palm on Pendle's shoulder.

'Oscar wanted to ask you something.'

Oscar acted coy. 'Sorry, I don't want to interrupt your lunch, but I've been doing this thing lately, it sounds dumb I know, where I close my eyes and literally stab the racing guide with a biro, and back that horse.'

'I might try that,' the footy coach buttering another roll. 'Can't be worse than following those mugs in the paper.'

'Actually, I've been doing it for three weeks, no betting, just for a lark. And two out of three I've won. Anyway, I have three bets I want to get on Saturday, but I have a ton of stuff on. Then I saw you ...' gesturing bashfully to Pendle. 'I wondered if you'd accept the bets. Not big, less than ten grand all up, just to try this thing in the real world.'

Pendle looked at him calmly, reached into his pocket, pulled out a business card that had nothing but a phone number written on it.

'Call this number, ask to speak to Drew. He's my main guy. Tell him you spoke to me, and I said you're good.'

'Thanks. I really appreciate it, Dominic. Leave you to it, gentlemen.' Playing up the deference, letting them know he wouldn't intrude. A hint of magnanimity to exit on: 'Hope to see you at the fundraiser, but please, if any of you find your way over to one of my venues, say hi and I'll look after you.'

A chorus of farewells, Hacket seizing his hand, one last back-slap, choosing to stay yakking to the guys while Oscar was a hovercraft across the floor all the way back to the car. Walking on air. Bets would go on, and it all seemed perfectly natural. No suspicions raised.

You could get newer cars that cost a lot less to repair, but Dominic Pendle wasn't replacing his old Jag. When he'd first started out in the racing game as the bagman for Hugh White, 1965, Light Fingers winning the Cup, he'd park his old FJ in the bookies' carpark and drool over the Jags, Mercedes and Statesmen lined up like thoroughbreds. Back then, to own one of those cars had been Dominic's main goal in life. After a lot of hard work, he'd managed it.

Over the years, the cars in the car park had got smaller, in synch with the bookies' ring.

Everyone had told him online gambling was going to replace bookmakers. And though he'd been sceptical at first, he accepted that was likely a reality sometime in the future. There would always be cash bets—money that nobody wanted funnelled into a system that authorities had access to—but once they let the online bookies out of Darwin, it was going to prove tough for every on-course bookmaker in the country, no matter where you might be based. Keeping his Jag was him saying *fuck the future*. If he was going to become extinct like the dinosaurs, then he was going to die a T-Rex.

Normally after a lunch he'd slide across the smooth leather seat of the Jag feeling bolstered by the conviviality of his peers, ready to take on the weekend, but today frustration clung to him like lint to a freshly pressed jacket. By now, Joe Harris should have been picked up and dealt with, but thus far, all efforts to locate him had failed.

Austin reported that his new muscle, a couple of dumb gym-junkies, had picked up a small-time ex-con café owner at Harris's place by mistake. The guy might have been trying to help Harris, or he might be telling the truth, saying he was trying to get Harris too. Austin had made it clear that, regardless, Harris's debt had just become his responsibility, but of course there was no point actually trying to extract that unless this guy had the readies.

Pendle pulled out his mobile phone. He still couldn't get used to these things. He'd write a phone number down on a scrap of paper and look at it while he tried to hit the tiny keys with his fat fingers. But he'd recently discovered there was a little button you could press that redialled the last number you called, and he hit that now.

Austin answered, 'Sorry, Dom. Nothing.'

'No one will loan Harris cash. He's a bad risk. He's hiding somewhere.'

'I'm outside his apartment. I've got guys at the Apostrophe, even Fremantle.'

'What am I paying you for?'

'If he's here, we'll find him.'

Pendle killed the call. He'd drop into the office, see if there was anything on the pre-race he should be concerned about.

His office was about as low-key as you could get: one of six single-level shops in a strip block in East Perth, brick, aluminium sliding windows. At one time he'd owned the complex, but a few years back he'd sold up, retaining just the one unit that bore no signage. On one side was a print works, on the other a place that supplied water coolers. He aimed the Jag at a rusting metal cross that announced 'MD' and slid into the bay beside Waldron's old Mazda.

In summer the concrete burned the soles off your shoes, but today was okay. He pressed the intercom, waited while the CCTV was checked. The trouble with gamblers was a great many of them were desperate arseholes whose grand plan was to rob the man they'd lost to. Nobody had ever successfully robbed Dominic Pendle.

'A bookie needs security, aspirin and big balls', Pendle had once quoted to the local press when asked what it took to be top-line bookmaker. The balls had never been a problem. The buzzer went, and he pushed in.

There were benches on three side of the office: two fax machines, two computers, three monitors, four phones. A nook held a bar-fridge and sink. Waldron was sitting reading a magazine on the cane sofa Pendle had got from the auctioneer across the road.

'How's it been?' Needing a slash, Pendle wishing now he'd put a toilet in the office here.

'Quiet.'

Not surprising, the Spring carnival was still a few weeks off. Waldron put down his magazine, got up and walked over to the exercise book where he'd handwritten the bets.

'Brian Caligaro wanted four grand on Immense Beauty.'

'You give him an extra point?'

'Five to one instead of four. It can't beat Patronise at those weights.'

Pendle approved, what he reckoned, too. Waldron scanned the book.

'Nothing much else except for that guy you got to ring me, Cornelius. One grand Motorpede twenty to one, two grand Sapphire Cult sixteen to one, five grand Hysterical, twelve to one.'

Hysterical? His urgent need to piss was relegated.

'The same horse the miner bloke backed.' Hearing himself say it the way Sherlock Holmes might ponder over evidence.

'It should be fifteens but seeing as we already had the—'

Pendle not waiting for him to finish. 'Doesn't it strike you as odd?'

'Not that odd. It's only two bets.'

True. But now he thought about it, right in the middle of his lunch: here's the Cornelius kid turning up at the Salisbury. Never been in there before, spins a yarn about dropping a pin on the form guide. Two other bets on random horses, smoke-screen. At least that's how Pendle would have done it.

Something was rotten in the state of Belmont race seven.

Pendle reached over and picked up the receiver of the closest phone, real buttons, not those pissy things on the little mobile. He punched in a number. The call was answered on the third ring.

'Hello?' Bobby Baker was the crookedest hoop to ever sit in a jockey's dressing room.

'Bobby, Dominic Pendle.'

'Hello, Mr Pendle. How can I help?'

'Tomorrow at Belmont. Anything I should know about?' Not giving away too much, keeping the exact cause of his interest close to his chest.

'There better not be, because nobody's cutting me in.'

'You hear anything, give me a call. I'll look after you.'

'Will do, Mr Pendle.'

Baker would know if the jockeys were in on it. The bookie looking at another angle now.

'Enzo Rapanaro trains Hysterical, right?'

'That's correct.'

Waldron was watching him closely. Pendle had an inner chuckle, imagining himself in a deerstalker with his offsider here—Waldron/Watson, it kind of fitted. He liked the idea, a sidekick who was always three steps behind the principal, in awe of his logic.

Enzo Rapanaro was a battling trainer, though not given—so far as Pendle's extensive inside knowledge went—to doping horses. But then every man has his breaking point. Most likely the trainer was going to dope the horse up and then use a masking agent, so a positive result didn't show.

'You think Hysterical could win if it was doped?' Pendle mulling, ceiling gazing.

Waldron shrugged. 'It'd be borderline unless the other favoured horses were being doped to slow down, or the jockeys weren't trying.'

Pendle didn't give much credence to that second possibility. Baker wouldn't dare lie to him, and you couldn't fix a race unless you had Baker. So, the more likely scenario was dope. Pendle wondering if it could be coincidence, these two unrelated bets. Maybe he was too suspicious in his old age? But then, being too suspicious was what had allowed him to thrive this long.

Waldron must have been reading his expression.

'You think there's something—?'

'Afoot? Yes, I do Watson.'

What the scam was, he wasn't sure, but there was something going on.

'I want everything you can find out about that miner bloke, see if there's some connection to Cornelius.'

It was time to pee.

Zeen was right about the facial. Her Croatian beauty therapist was cruel but effective. As Sylvia worked down deep into some troublesome whiteheads, Zeen's brain freed up and she started to consider what her next move should be. Inevitably, she came back with one answer: call Harris, tell him this had gone far enough.

She didn't have his number—if he had a mobile it had probably been hocked—but she knew somebody who might. When Sylvia had finished, Zeen's face feeling like fresh snow, she dialled Ronny Weitz, another old punter pal.

'Zeen, long time no see.'

'Hi Ronny. You by any chance have Joe calling, asking you to loan him money?'

Of course he had. Ronny had told him to get lost.

'Does he have a mobile phone?'

He sure did. Ronny was happy to give Zeen the number.

'Say Zeen—you're not getting back with him?'

'Not in a million years, Ronny.'

Ronny said he was glad to hear it and signed off with an emphysemic wheeze.

She dialled the number Ronny had given. Harris wouldn't recognise her number, so he might not pick up. But he did.

'*Ello*?' A bad Mexican accent.

'Cut the shit, Joe. It's me.'

'Sorry, Zeen you're too late. The position I offered you has been filled.'

'Where the fuck are you?'

'I'm in a sweet spot, eating the best cannoli, waiting for my ship to dock. Oh, there it is on the horizon.'

No time for this shit.

'Pendle threatened Rick, believes we know where you might be. Where are you?'

'You really think I'd tell you, so you can save little Ricky's arse and serve mine up to Pendle. No siree.'

'I know you have not a single shred of human decency, but I'm appealing to your self-interest. Tell me where you are, then skip. I tell Pendle, but you're smoke. Or don't tell me, and I'll contact every single person I know and get them looking. And then I'll tell Pendle.'

'No can do, Zeeny.'

She could imagine his smug weasel face, wanted to smash it.

'Listen to me. You're not going to pull this off. Hardwood is onto you.'

'Yeah, sure. Bye, Zeen.'

He hung up. Zeen cursed, held off throwing her phone against the wall.

He'd found a backer. That was the only explanation. Zeen had been hoping he was petrified, looking over his shoulder, sleeping rough. But their conversation showed he was confident, swaggering. What an idiot!

I4

THE DAY BEFORE THE RACE

The first thing you noticed about Perth was how clean it was. That won Lionel's approval right off. Like the Gold Coast, the concrete was smooth and new. The sunlight bounced off the glossy surfaces, making everything brighter, and Lionel always felt better when it was light, especially in winter. The expensive prossie he'd been gifted last night by one of his Gold Coast brothel tenants, who'd expanded operations here to the west coast, also met with his approval. Long legs, pert breasts. He'd dropped an extra couple of hundred on her, told her to let him know if she was ever visiting the Gold Coast. Lionel a single man these days.

Few years back thought he'd try the marriage thing: Daniela, a Brazilian, twenty-five and firm as a front-row's handshake. They'd met in a Gold Coast bar, had a couple of good years; then things buckled, and he'd repatriated her to Brazil with enough money to start her own swimwear shop. Trouble with young women, they expected too much, but women his age expected even more: conversation and walks along the beach at sunset. No, he was better off single.

Telling himself now he should have come west sooner, sussed out opportunities. Truckloads of money coming out of the ground. Western Australia and Queensland keeping the other lazy fuckers afloat, but those Melbourne and Sydney suits still looked down on the resource states. Thought they were sophisticated. My arse.

A light knock on his door. Lionel approached from the side, a long-held habit just in case some hostile fired through it.

'Just me, Mr Howard.'

Davis. He'd been working in KL for some kind of sultan when Lionel had lured to him to Australia. The guy had been a bodyguard for the Brit royals before that, and they'd never lost anyone, right? Davis was purely a driver and bodyguard. For the other stuff there was Tongan George, who was probably snoring his fat arse off down the hall, and Kieran, who likely had his skinny psycho arse in front of some Nintendo shit. Lionel had brought the two of them just in case. No matter how well you planned, history had taught Lionel that it was always wise to have a just-in-case option.

Lionel opened the door. As always, the six-foot-three Davis was wrapped in suit and tie with polished shoes. Lionel liked that he had class. It was important, when you went to charity dinners and gala events, to set the right tone with your driver.

'The car is ready.'

'Let's go,' said Lionel, closing the door behind him. For now, he'd let Tongan George and Kieran relax. Apparently Rapanaro's place was only around half an hour's drive. Langer, Lionel's horse guy, had flown in that morning and was in a cheap motel by the airport, no point wasting money on him. Langer's job was simple. Come out to Rapanaro's, check Double Volley was in peak shape for the race, then get his arse back east.

Lionel didn't like being around stables. Too many flies coming after the horseshit. But he'd be a liar if he said he wasn't enjoying this. Langer giving him the thumbs up, having inspected Double Volley and watched Rapanaro take her on a training gallop.

'Rapo's done a good job, she's looking great.'

Langer already bosom buddies with his new trainer mate. Lionel called Rapanaro over. The guy was about sixty, squat, brown-grey skin, the sort given to skin tags from the looks.

'Has anyone else been here since Double Volley arrived?'

'Just me and my odd jobs boy, my nephew. He couldn't tell a mare from a stallion.'

Lionel gave him his granite stare. The old boy stared back, unblinking.

'And you have told nobody else?' Offering one last out.

'Nobody.'

Good. The fact the odds were still about fourteen to one in the pre-market backed that up. If word had got out, those odds would have tumbled, and Lionel would be sending Tongan George on an errand.

'We'll be at the course tomorrow, but don't acknowledge us. We're just holidaymakers checking out the west.'

Lionel jerked his head, and Langer followed him back to the hire car, where Davis waited. So far, everything had gone perfectly. Another thirty hours and one of the most satisfying coups of his career would be under his belt.

'Davis, some Burning Red Ivanhoe if you don't mind.'

He'd made a shitload on them back in the day, a few thousand albums in Scandi and double that in the UK. Lionel never grew tired of reliving his triumphs.

He was positively yearning for tomorrow.

15

Pendle was sitting out by his pool, which overlooked the Swan River near the old Hotel Majestic site. Like everything stately in this town, the Majestic had been bulldozed. In the city, the replacement buildings were office blocks with all the personality of a Weeties box. In this suburban grotto the houses were too big for the small families who could afford them.

Daylight was lowering itself into bed, a cool wind flowing off the river guttering its candle, challenging Pendle's heavy Jenny Kee knit, a gift from his wife Shirl that he was too embarrassed to wear in public. The white cordless was in Pendle's fleshy hand, Waldron on the other end.

Seemed his Watson had been busy.

'The miner, this Goose Gordon, has a prison record for explosives.'

That could be bad news. 'Bikies?'

'Doesn't appear to be connected to any, although get this: Gordon's address is care of Café Inside in Northbridge, run by another ex-con, Rick Boski. He did time for cultivating a dope crop.'

And there it was. A clear picture forming in Pendle's sharp and inquisitive brain: dope crop, explosives, an Italian horse-trainer ... and Joe Harris. This Boski was the same fellow that Austin's knuckleheads had picked up coming out of Harris's flat. The plot thickened.

'Either of these guys got connections to Rapanaro?'

'Not that I could find.'

Pendle had a proper detective he could get to chase that up if he needed, but there wasn't really time for that.

'How about the Cornelius kid?'

'All I could find was the mining thing. Maybe Gordon works for old man Cornelius?'

Pendle said, 'It doesn't matter. It is obvious there is a fix on. This Boski is connected to Joe Harris.'

Waldron said, 'So, I should halve the odds on the pre-race, or not take any bets?'

Pendle's reaction would usually have been to keep himself safe and halve the odds he was offering, but no, this was an opportunity.

'We keep the odds twelve to one, maximum payout per bet five hundred dollars. Forty-five minutes before the race I want fifty K on Hysterical. Spread it over Melbourne, Sydney and Brizzie, small bets, various SPs.'

'That's six hundred thousand if it wins?'

'Less the one-fifty-odd we'll owe Cornelius and the miner.'

Of which, he was thinking, fifty grand would be deducted from Harris's cronies to pay off Harris's debt. If they didn't like it, he would send Austin and his boys to convince them it was actually generous.

'Good work, Watson,' he said. It was time to go inside and warm the box for Friday Night football.

For the last ten minutes, Atwood had been in his face. Now he was trying to calm himself by looking at the purple bug zapper fixed to the wall.

'He told you that Boski was connected to Joe Harris?'

Drew Waldron just wanted to get home and watch the footy. This place was the pits. Lately he found himself stressing the moment he turned into the car park here. He wondered if Atwood lived out this way. Some dude was ordering like nine pizzas for his family. Natural selection in action: none of them would make forty, eating this crap. Atwood was still staring at him, waiting for the same answer he'd given her not a minute before.

'Yes, he said they were connected, wanted to know if I'd found any relationship between Rapanaro and these guys. I haven't. Pendle has private guys for that stuff, but the race is tomorrow, there's not a lot of time.'

'So, Pendle knows there's a fix in, but doesn't know what that fix is?'

'Right, he's just following the money.'

'But he is intending on profiting from this fix?'

'You bet. He stands to make half a mill.'

'And he has no idea what the scam is?'

'Not from what he's told me. He doesn't think jockeys are involved. Most likely dope. Apparently, this Boski guy is some drug-dealer. Pendle was wondering where Cornelius fits. I'm thinking, the guy has all these nightclubs, maybe there's a drug connection.'

Wanting to show how helpful he was trying to be. Atwood said nothing, like she had her own ideas about that.

'All right. Good. Pendle has no intention of reporting this to the authorities?'

'Not from what he's said. I mean, it's the smart move. Everyone else does the work and he cashes in.'

The cop sat back thinking for a long minute, finally said, 'Okay, you can go. But if anything changes or you learn anything new, call me.'

Waldron couldn't get his arse out of there quick enough. He thought it was strange that she hadn't mentioned arresting anybody. Maybe she wanted a cut too?

Liz watched the bookie's clerk all the way to his car. She didn't take drugs but guessed this was what it would be like to be high. Not only was she going to nail Harris, his mate Boski, and Boski's mate Goose Gordon, but Oscar Cornelius might be involved somehow. Maybe he was the one financing the scam?

Could all come back to drugs, like she'd thought initially.

Pendle thought so, and Boski's CV fitted. Best of all, she had the start of a case against Pendle. But only a start. Waldron's testimony on Pendle and the illegal SP bookmakers might be shaky. A smart brief would paint Waldron as a doper looking for a deal. But the fact Pendle hadn't shared any suspicions with the stewards, or with Gaming, would raise questions about his fitness to hold a licence. And if they got evidence of him placing bets with SP bookmakers, that would sink him.

All the same, Liz had no intention of calling attention to the ring-in just yet.

Pendle was waiting until tomorrow to put on his bets, and she wanted him to suffer at least some financial loss. She would hang on until the last minute, wait till all the scammers had their money on the ring-in, then she would step in and have the horse checked—and down they would all go, losing money and freedom.

That was what got her high!

When Zeen was miserable it caused Rick physical pain. It was going on for ten, and they had finally shut the café doors for the night and were relaxing in their bedroom. Or trying to. Rick had drawn a bath for Zeen, and when she had bathed and thrown on a bathrobe, he massaged her with some kind of peppermint body lotion. To no avail: the gloom hadn't lifted from her sculpted shoulders.

'We'll be okay,' trying to reassure her as his thumbs pushed into her shoulder blades. 'Even today I made a grand. The most important thing is we keep Paul out of it.'

'The most important thing is we find Harris. And he's not playing ball. You don't know Pendle. When he finds out this place is successful, he'll come for us.'

'We could tell the cops.'

She groaned like she was trying to explain physics to the village idiot.

'For an ex-con you are very fucking Pollyanna.'

Way Rick saw it, he wasn't really a con. He might've done time in prison, but most of his sentence had been unjustified. In Rick's opinion there were cons—guys whose way of life was to move ahead at somebody else's expense—and then there were idiots like the younger Rick Boski who had only ever done anything criminal out of desperation or self-preservation, much like the original convicts sent to Australia for stealing a loaf of bread.

Rick didn't really think he was smart enough to be a successful criminal, but he was way too smart to be an unsuccessful one. He'd spent most of the day trying to work out what their next move should be. And still had nothing.

'Atwood is going to nail our arses on this,' Zeen settling on the bottom of the ocean with the heavy metals.

'She doesn't have anything on us.'

Rick had examined their position with the thoroughness of a gambler checking the floor for a mistakenly discarded ticket and still couldn't find any direct link to Zeen and him. 'All she has is Goose's bet.'

'*All*? Atwood is sharp. She's going to gut Rapanaro, and eventually he's going to say he told his parish priest about the scam. And then she's going to work out that the parish priest she had the accident with near Rapanaro's property was your prison chaplain. Are you getting the picture?'

When Zeen put it that way, he could see Atwood might infer some connection, but—

'She still has no evidence we did anything, because we didn't.'

'How long do you think Paul will last once she drags him in for questioning?'

Okay, she had a point, Father Paul Monaghan wasn't equipped to be on the wrong side of the inquisition. He would break and quickly. Something occurred to Rick.

'Why hasn't she busted Rapanaro already?'

'Maybe she has, we just haven't heard.'

'No, she hasn't.'

Zeen looked at him sharply. 'How do you know?'

'I've had Sandy up there watching the property since this afternoon. Everything is normal.'

Zeen sat up. Rick tried to pretend he wasn't looking through the gap in her robe.

'You thought of that?'

He was pleased to say he had.

'That's a waste of a good man.'

Rick was affronted. 'It's important we know when she's moving on Rapanaro.'

'Atwood's not going to do anything up there yet. Rapanaro would just say he had two similar horses, and he was going to run Hysterical tomorrow. She won't act until Rapanaro brings the horse to the course tomorrow and submits the papers with the wrong one.'

Rick had to admit it made sense. 'I wish you'd told me that earlier,' he said.

Now he knew exactly what they needed to do.

16

Rick hesitated over telling Zeen his idea. She'd likely shoot him down with her trademark ridicule. But sometimes a man had to gird his loins. Here went nothing.

'We have to swap the horses. Let Rapanaro think he's bringing the fake Hysterical to the races, but we make sure it really *is* Hysterical.'

Zeen looked at him with an expression the correct word for which he believed was *quizzical*.

'Is this like a play on words? Like hysterical as in funny? Or are you serious?'

Should he pretend he actually had been joking, retain some dignity? He was torn, like in blackjack when you're sitting on seventeen.

'Wouldn't it solve the problem of Atwood nailing our arses to the wall? And she won't be able to bring Paul in if there's no substitution.'

There was a silence. Then Zeen said, 'Even if we could pull that off—and that's a big "if"—it makes us personally involved, which right now we're not. And the good father can kiss the eight grand goodbye.'

Way Rick saw it, they didn't have a choice.

He said, 'Why don't we drive up there tonight, swap the horses around. That way, when Rapanaro leaves tomorrow, he'll just take the horse he thinks is the ring-in, but it'll be the real Hysterical.'

She shook her head. 'Too risky. The horses might have identical markings, be the same size, all that. But someone who's been with them every day will still know. Soon as he sees the mistake, he'll swap them back.' But he could tell Zeen was starting to groove to his thinking now, mulling it over and saying, 'It's not such a bad idea, and it might present some opportunity to get our money back.'

'What opportunity?'

'I don't know yet, and if I did, you wouldn't want to know.'

Which was probably true.

She said, 'The swap will have to be done tomorrow, at the course.'

That worried Rick. 'What if Atwood checks as soon as the horse arrives?'

'She's going to want to cause maximum grief. She won't act until all the bets are on.'

Rick said, 'But maybe you don't know Atwood as well as you think. Why don't we just warn Rapanaro? Tell him Atwood is onto him, and he should walk away.'

'We have no idea who's behind Rapanaro. If it's somebody big and nasty—and it most likely is—we're drawing a target on our backs. Right now, nobody knows who we are. I'd like to keep it that way. Let's have a look at tomorrow's program.'

She pulled her laptop over.

'This is good,' she said, pointing at the screen. 'Rapanaro has one other horse running tomorrow, race six, Green Wizard. He'll probably take it up with the fake Hysterical, in the same float.'

Rick asked why that was good.

'They'll take Green Wizard to the mounting yard in the lead up to its race. That's our opportunity.'

'What if Atwood acts before that?'

'Sometimes you have to punt, baby.'

Rick did not like the sound of that. Zeen though was charging ahead.

'We'll bring the real Hysterical up prior to race six.'

'Can we get into the right area?'

'Won't be a problem. Somebody leads the fake Hysterical out from the box and swaps it with the real one.'

Rick could imagine a million holes in this plan, but Zeen just swept him up when she was like this.

Rick mentioned they'd need a horse float.

Zeen had an idea where she could lay her hands on one.

Rick said, 'We also need to get you into one of your sexy dresses ...'

'I have sexy dresses?'

'With you in them, they're all sexy. And if it's men we have to get by, it'll help.'

She leaned in so close that he could smell her sweet breath when she spoke. 'One thing I like about you, Boski, you're an optimist.'

But even as she kissed him, he was thinking of all the things that could go wrong; and chief amongst those was Liz Atwood.

Liz sat at her small wooden table in a kitchen that had seen its heyday in the mid-seventies, when Abba were huge and young single women cooked apricot chicken for prospective boyfriends. These days, some guys even cooked and invited the woman to their place. Mind you, none Liz knew. She never had time to cook. Luckily, you could just go to Coles and grab pre-cooked pasta. This week she'd managed to make one packet last three nights, a boon for her mortgage. Her apartment mightn't be much—it was on the first floor of a small block in suburban Como, too close to the noise of the highway to leave the window open—but it was the only worthwhile reminder left of six wasted years with Darren. Two years back, the would-be tennis coach had walked away from her and the two-bedder, of which she'd paid all the mortgage apart from a flutter on his part in year one. So far, he'd been replaced only with a collection of brightly coloured bottles of spirits and liqueurs that Liz never drank, on a wobbly bamboo stand that she never dusted.

What Liz was thinking, as she forked the very last portion of rav-ioli, was that something was missing from her plan. She couldn't shake the thought that there was more to be wrung from this opportunity. Okay, she'd trap Rapanaro in her net—that was a given—but he was a very small fish. Maybe she could lean on him to implicate others, but who exactly? This petty crim Gordon wasn't going to be the brains behind the thing, that would be Harris, Boski and Zeen, or possibly Cornelius. But right now, she couldn't connect Cornelius and the others. Maybe there was another party lurking behind them who was the common link, a Mr Big. It would be a travesty to let him go free.

Now she was twirling her fork, running the probabilities. Probability that Harris knew, or was, Mr Big? Say fifty-fifty? Reasonable odds. He had decamped suddenly because Pend-le was after him. He hadn't been back to his flat. And as she savoured that last pillow of ravioli, she was wondering whether this might present an opportunity? Could there be something incriminating at his flat that he hadn't been able to destroy or take with him? Something that remained there because he was too terrified to return?

Every chance.

She turned her attention to Zeen and the ex-con Boski. The problem with them was they hadn't gone anywhere, still at the café large as life. No way would she be able to glean any in-telligence from their place. And Rapanaro was too risky. She already had him lined up and didn't want to blow that lurking around his property. But Harris ... his flat was vacant, and it might hold treasure.

Of course, breaking into his apartment without a warrant could get her drummed out of the service. If she got caught. On the other hand, if she found a trail that led to Cornelius or some other Mr Big, advancement would undoubtably follow. The old risk/reward paradigm.

She carried her bowl to the sink. Not only did she know how to pick locks, she practised regularly. She wouldn't just waltz on up to his apartment; she'd take her time, watch carefully. Growing excited now. Imagining some little black book, or some hand jotted notes about the split-up between the scammers just waiting to be discovered by her.

Liz scooped her keys and was at the door in one motion. The wind was up, the highway traffic a rasp. She kept a Velcro pack of blank keys and a set of picks in her glovebox. This would be the perfect way to end what had so far been a very excellent day.

17

When Missouri had offered him and Scooter a job that would keep them fit and maybe give them a chance to flex their muscles without the consequences of legal action, Colby had been right into it. The pay was low, but it was cash, and that meant he didn't have to lug boxes of vegetables every morning at the warehouse if he didn't feel like it. Instead, he could sleep in, on a good day be lying in the sun, down Scarborough beach, chatting up girls from the eastern states staying at the hotels there.

However, things hadn't turned out as Colby had anticipated. Their immediate boss Missouri was forever fucking riding them about something. The Boski guy a case in point.

How could they be blamed for bagging Boski's arse instead of Harris's when he'd come walking out the flat with a key in his hand? The two men were practically the same age. It's not like they'd been shown a photo of Harris. And then Missouri tells them he's docking the entire day's pay.

'I have to answer to Mr Pendle. Consider yourselves lucky I'm not docking you the whole week.'

Well, that just stank. And now here they were back again in Harris's flat. In the dark. A total waste of time because Harris wasn't going to be turning up here, was he? Nobody would be that stupid. But Missouri overriding any protest with that endlessly repeated saying of his: 'We have to cover all bases.'

'We could do something more constructive,' Colby had said. To which Missouri had replied, 'You *are* doing something constructive. You're keeping out of the fucking way of professionals.'

Now that was disrespectful. Not to say plain mean.

They were going on for six hours in this dump, just sitting there. They'd played cards by the light of their mini-torches for the last hour or so; and then, hungry as well as tired, had flipped to see who got to go outside for chicken burgers. Colby, of course, had lost. So Scooter was back out in civilisation, while Colby slumped on the worn sofa and stared at the dormant TV set.

'No, you can't watch fuckin TV,' Missouri had said. 'You think Harris will come in if he hears *Happy Days*?'

Happy Days? How out of touch was this guy? But Colby had said nothing, just soaked it up.

He yawned. This was soooo boring ...

Some sound pricked Colby awake. He'd slumped to a forty-five-degree angle, and his neck was cricked, but surely he couldn't have been out long, because Scooter still wasn't there. It must be him coming back. Colby was about to call out, but at the last second had the good sense to check himself. Whoever was at the door was scratching around, and Scooter had a—

That was as far as his reasoning got before the door creaked open and a thin train of light floated in.

It had to be Harris. Fuck! Where was the gun?

In the gloom he could make out a human shadow stepping into the room. He'd had the pistol on his lap. There!

Panicked, he swung and fired at the shape, just as the lights went on.

Holy shit. It wasn't Harris. It was a woman.

And he'd hit her in the chest.

'What the f—'

She started towards him. He was whimpering as he reloaded and fired again, this time striking her in the neck. Her face registered shock. Then rage. She charged.

Colby managed to throw himself sideways, and she collided with the sofa. She pivoted, snarled and reached for him, her hand seizing his shirt.

Then she gave a small cough and collapsed.

'Who the fuck is she?' Scooter looking down at the body wasn't waiting on ceremony. He was eating his chicken burger. There had been a long queue, and he was starving.

'Maybe his girlfriend? I don't know.'

Colby flapping his hands like one of them big penguins. They'd left one of the lights on because what the fuck did it matter now?

'If she was his girlfriend, wouldn't she have a key? Why would she be picking the lock?'

The roll was surprisingly tasty, although Scooter could have done with less mayo.

'How the fuck should I know?'

'Did you fall sleep?'

Colby's hair looked suspiciously matted.

'I was sitting here, thought it was you coming back, next thing I know somebody's coming into the room, so I picked up the pistol and fired.'

Okay, he'd finished the burger now he could start to think. He picked up the pistol.

'How long will she be out? Did your mate tell you?'

'He only told me about how long it takes them to go down. It depends on the size of the dog: a St Bernard takes longer than a Jack Russell.'

'Who would shoot a St Bernard?'

Scooter was thinking the world was fucked if there were people out there who would shoot a St Bernard. A Jack Russell he could understand. There was one of the noisy little fuckers two doors up from him and it never shut the fuck up. He would have loved to shoot one of these darts up the noisy little shit's arse.

'You put two darts in her?'

'The first one didn't slow her down much,' Colby said. 'What the fuck do we do with her?'

'Did you check if she has a wallet or something, find out who she is?'

Colby shook his head.

'I didn't want to leave DNA.'

'You watch too much TV. Check her.'

Colby got down and checked the woman's jacket, pulled out a small wallet.

'Oh, fuck no.'

What was it now?

Colby handed him the wallet, her ID card clearly visible: *Detective Inspector* Elizabeth Atwood. Scooter nearly choked on the last of the roll. 'She's a cop! Jesus, Colby.'

'Not my fault.'

'You're the one that shot her.'

'Because it was dark. If I could have had the TV on this wouldn't have happened.'

'What the fuck are we going to do?'

'Did she get a look at you?'

'It was dark.'

Scooter decided what they were going to do was tie her and gag her and leave her in the bedroom, comfortable on the bed.

'We lock the flat up, and we get the fuck out of here and as far away from Perth as we can—and hope she doesn't come around for twelve hours.'

'What do we tell Missouri?'

'We don't tell Missouri fuck all. We get out of here and hopefully never see that prick again.'

It was just going on midnight. Scooter was thinking Broome, Darwin and a flight to Indonesia. Somewhere far enough away they wouldn't get splashed by the bucket of shit about to drop.

18

RACE DAY

Zeen had been awake since just after five. She'd gone to bed around one, after calling everyone who might have any idea where Harris was holing up. She'd grilled the ones he'd called looking to stake him, pulled their recollections apart searching for a clue, even asking about the background noise because you knew in any of those thriller films there was always some bell or PA announcement in the background that meant you could pinpoint where the call came from. Not this time, though: anybody got a call from Joe Harris it was only ever going to be about loaning him money, so the conversation was terminated as soon as possible.

Boski was in a worse state than she was, which only made her more anxious. But the idea of swapping over the horse was better than anything she'd come up with.

It was going on eight and Zeen felt no less desperate than she had at seven. Harris wasn't far, she could be certain of that. If Harris had a potential score he was going to stay where he could get to the track easy. Any sensible man wouldn't risk running into Pendle's heavies at the track, but everything she knew about Joe Harris told her he would risk it just so he could make sure the bets were down how he wanted and then gloat when he won big.

He was in for a surprise.

Her brain was getting tired, going round in circles and coming back to the same question: who would be insane enough to stake him?

This was the busiest time of the week for the café, a load of breakfasts to make and deliver, a thousand coffees to pour.

Thankfully the staff was handling that. Zeen looked up to see Rick coming through the back door, could see straight away he was in a state. She'd sent him off to pick up a horse float she'd organised with a couple of old pals.

'That float is a bitch to tow. I don't know how I'm going to manage with a horse inside it.'

'If you're worried, get Sandy to drive. He was a getaway driver, wasn't he?'

'Thirty years ago. And they didn't get away.' Rick with a big baby woe-is-me sigh.

A potential hiccup occurred to Zeen.

'Sandy know anything about horses?'

'I don't know. Why?'

'You have to load the horse into the float.'

'We'll be fine.'

Cocky for someone who'd never done it before.

'It can be tricky, getting a horse into a float.'

'I got you into bed, didn't I? That was all kinds of difficult.'

'That's true,' she said, 'but only after you wooed me.'

'How did I woo you?' Getting in close, a smile on his face, anxiety gone all of a sudden. Men and sex, truly.

'The kiss helped,' she said.

'I'm not sure I want to kiss Hysterical.' Almost nuzzling her as he said it.

'Like that,' she said, pulling away, 'that's how you get the horse to cooperate: sweet talk. But first you need to get a halter over its head and attach a lead rope. And don't get yourselves kicked in the head trying to load it up the ramp.'

Rick gave thumbs up. 'We better get going, make sure we grab Hysterical soon as Rapanaro leaves for Belmont.'

The plan was, they would wait off the road up the street, watching for Rapanaro's vehicle.

Rick kissed her. 'Wish me luck.'

'Good luck.' The marks where his fingertips had squeezed her shoulder while they kissed had already faded. Soon as he was out the door, the anxiety flooded in again. It was a shit idea. The whole enterprise was amateur, with a hundred things that might go wrong.

Rick came back in, fast, like something already had.

'What's up?'

He swept her into his arms and kissed her again.

'It's going to be okay.' He turned to go, stopped. 'Oh, and we need croissants.'

He ducked out again, leaving her wondering if the kiss was just a pretext to the croissant chore.

Zeen pulled into the bakery car park, unable to shake her unease, like a parent listening to the cough of their sick child. Then, at least momentarily, all concerns disappeared. There was an empty space inviting her in. And right beside it was CORN 001. The car was unprotected, vulnerable. She was reaching for her glovebox and the screwdriver she'd left there when a bell dinged in her brain.

'I'm in a sweet spot, eating the best cannoli, waiting for my ship to dock.'

That's what Harris had said when she called him. It had been staring her in the face, and she had been too dumb to recognise it. She slammed the glovebox back up and jumped out of the car.

Oscar Cornelius was a big-boned, fat-arsed, curly-headed blond. And he was standing right in front of her at the counter, dressed Malibu cool: sports shirt with pineapples print, loafers no socks.

'I'll have three vanilla and three with the ricotta.'

Zeen watched his fleshy lips as he spoke, his gleaming eyes scanning the pastries. While his cannoli were being carefully packed in a little cardboard box, she retreated, climbed back into her car and reversed so she could follow him easily.

He was already eating one of the cannoli when he left the bakery. He clicked open his car and sat his fat arse down on the driver's seat. Then, still cramming the pastry into his mouth, he reversed and headed out.

Zeen followed.

'She's not budging.' The two men trying and failing to get Hysterical up the ramp and into the float. Sandy leaning back, straining with all his might, the cords on his forearms popping up, Rick shoving her from behind, careful to keep side-on to the back legs, like Zeen had told him.

'I thought you said you knew about horses.'

'Only the ones on a merry-go-round.'

Hysterical reared, her flank knocking Rick down on his backside. The second time he'd been on the ground. The first time he'd wound up in fresh horseshit—at least this time it was only grey sand and gravel. Like they'd planned, they had parked off the road some distance from the gate, Rick getting out and trudging closer to the driveway, finding a clump of trees just inside the property where he could monitor proceedings. Soon as he had seen Rapanaro leave and checked there was nobody else around, he'd called Sandy on the mobile and told him to drive the float into the property.

They caught a break when they decided to check the stables first and found Hysterical still there in its stall. Rick couldn't imagine how they would have managed it if she'd been free in a paddock.

As it was, they were going on fifteen fruitless minutes trying to get her up the ramp into the float.

'At least I got the bridle on,' said Sandy.

Rick wasn't sure if it was called a bridle, the guy with the float, like Zeen did, calling it a halter—leather headgear that had a ring to attach a lead rope. Hysterical had been well named. Trust him to find the equine equivalent of Zeen. The horse backing down the ramp now, Sandy's heels skidding as he tried to restrain her.

'Reach into my pocket,' Sandy yelled.

'What?'

'My pocket. I've got an apple.'

Sure enough, he did. Rick pulled the apple out, started wiggling it.

'Look at this, girl! Big juicy apple.'

Hysterical's evil eye zeroed in and she calmed.

'That's it, girl. Come on, now.'

She moved toward the apple. Rick had to abandon his position, get in front of Sandy, and then back up the ramp holding the apple out. Hysterical followed.

'Yes!' he hollered. 'We did it, mate.' So much for Zeen's lack of faith in him.

Rick put the apple flat on his palm, Hysterical's big mouth opened, Rick felt slobber and the apple was no more. Feeling proud of himself, even though Sandy was the one who'd had the foresight to bring horse food.

Rick and Sandy tied Hysterical in, making sure the padding was secure. Zeen had been right, the horse just needed to be wooed. An apple was all it took to tempt Eve; he should have thought of it himself.

Sandy looked him up and down. 'Unless you've got another pair of pants, you better go hose off.'

The cannoli was sweet, and so was the sight of twenty grand of cabbage in Oscar Cornelius's hands. Joe couldn't believe it had all come together so effortlessly. He'd been pacing around the room for hours, prepared for something to go wrong, but for the first time practically since Rick Boski had entered his life, nothing had.

'Last I checked, the odds were still twelve to one. So that's two hundred and forty grand worth right there,' he told Cornelius.

Cornelius handed over the money. The touch and smell of cash was, to Joe, life's most pleasurable sensation. Today that was heightened by the long drought since he'd been afforded such an opportunity.

'I'll be watching you every step of the way, Joe. Don't try and play me.'

'Hey, Oscar, please. This is a mutually beneficial arrangement, and I hope just the first of many similar enterprises. End of the day you'll have one hundred and sixty grand plus this stake back in your hands.'

'Good. I'd offer you a lift to the track, but better we're not seen together.'

Joe didn't take offence. Cornelius was being pragmatic. Joe said he'd get out there around the start of race three, didn't want to be too exposed.

'Unless I see somebody else making a move,' Joe licking his fingers to get the icing sugar off, 'I'll wait until about fifteen minutes before the race before placing the bet.'

Cornelius said, 'Don't miss out, that's all.'

'You can count on me, Oscar.'

When Cornelius left, Joe hesitated for a moment, then brought the cash up to his nose, closed his eyes, and sniffed. Nirvana.

When he opened his eyes, Zeen was standing there.

'What the—?' He couldn't find the words.

'It was the cannoli. By the way, you have some …'

She indicated his top-right lip, where a bit of ricotta must have lodged.

'Fuck off, Zeen.' He wiped it anyway. She didn't move, instead sat down on the chair opposite the bed the way she always did, like she was the one in control.

'When I saw Oscar's car at the bakery this morning, I suddenly remembered telling you about him and his Mercedes, out the back of the café. Then I remembered that time in Kalgoorlie when he went on a streak at two-up. You didn't forget that either, did you? You thought, *This could be my guy.*'

Time to get stern with her.

'The boat has sailed, Zeen. You are not climbing on.'

'I don't think you mean that, Joe.'

He was about to assure her he most certainly did when she said, 'Who's going to put the bet on? You?'

Before he could answer, she said, 'That's not going to work. Pendle is going to take that cash and tell you that you still owe him thirty grand on top. And then he's going to turn his guys loose.'

That might or might not be true—okay, it probably was, but whatever she was going to now suggest would mean cutting herself in on his deal. No way was that happening, and he told her so.

Zeen shrugged. 'That's very short-term thinking, Joe. Give me the money. I place the bet and in return I get half your cut with Cornelius.'

'Yeah, sure.'

'I could call Pendle right now and tell him where to find you. Get me and Rick off the hook.'

That, she would do.

'What's your deal with Cornelius? Fifty–fifty?'

He scoffed. 'Twenty-five.' Low-balling her.

'So, forty.'

'A third!' He realised she'd fucked him over even as he spoke the words.

'Thirty-three percent of say two hundred and forty. That's eighty grand. Tell you what, I'll let you take the first fifty, to pay off Pendle. That leaves thirty. I'll take half of that. I'm being generous, offering you fifty–fifty of your net for old times' sake. Considering the trouble you've put us through …'

Fuck, Zeen.

'All right, fifteen.'

'And you stay out of my life for good.'

That he could answer sincerely.

'With pleasure.'

19

Australians of the sixties and seventies who first ventured overseas with little more than an Instamatic and can-opener in the free Qantas bag slung over their shoulders were as foreign to the custom of tipping as Rick was to a racetrack. He had no idea what awaited him, but whatever his vague expectations might have been, it turned out he knew far less than he'd anticipated.

He cruised in the loaner Territory, Sandy beside him in front, Hysterical hooked behind in the horse float—aiming for a gate where crudely drawn letters on a white tin cross said *Trainers*. Here he got a gander at the track's clientele. White belts, desert boots, jeans and short-sleeved rayon shirts proving particularly popular among the thin scattering of patrons arriving on foot. If you were looking for glamour and spectacle, this would have been a disappointment, but in this case disappointing was good. The less fanfare the better.

He turned off the road that ran towards the main entrance into the trainers' designated car park, where the sentry was an overweight, elderly, florid gentleman in a white coat, a fold-out stool struggling to support him. Busily engaged in conversation with a skinny chap of similar age in a suit that might have seen in the Queen's inauguration—around the time beer came only in large brown bottles—the sedate attendant just waved them through.

'Didn't even check. Zeen was right,' said Sandy, who had no more racetrack experience than Rick.

'Zeen is always right,' said Rick, this time with a smile. The car park was nothing but a paddock, really, loads of horse floats parked willy-nilly, and one or two horses being led out of the trailers, a few others criss-crossing the paddock. Some of the horse handlers were snappily dressed men in trilbies with binoculars wrapped around their free arm; others he presumed strappers, men and women in worn jeans who looked a lot like the patrons he'd clocked en route.

Rick cruised over to a vacant area. His instructions were to wait for Zeen and this he was happy to do, especially as he had no idea how to get Hysterical out of the float.

'So, this is our little star, Hysterical,' said Lionel, emphasising the horse's name the same way you might wink. He was feeling chipper: the stewards had done a perfunctory check and signed off on it as bona fide.

Enzo Rapanaro played his part, just in case anybody was listening. 'She's twelve to one, and it's not a strong field, so if ever she's going to win a metropolitan race, it could be today.'

The stalls where horses waited pre- and post-race were at the back of the course, near the trainers' car park. They were open stalls, and the public could walk past and take a look. Some of the horses had strappers with them, but many were left unattended if the stable had horses running in the next race.

Though he bet frequently and fixed many a race, Lionel didn't really know a lot about horses themselves. There hadn't been many around Streatham when he was growing up. Double Volley aka Hysterical looked a little on the small side compared to some of the other horses dotted around the stalls.

'Does your wife come?' he asked the trainer.

'She's spending time with her family in Sicily,' said Rapanaro.

That was something Lionel approved of. The less people in the know, the better. What he did not approve of was Tongan George's dress sense. Polo shirt, flip-flops and black footy shorts, topped with Shane Warne white-frame sunnies. It was almost disrespectful. Davis, on the other hand, in a well-cut suit and shining black leather footwear, reeked of class.

'The jockey?' Lionel making sure his instructions to leave the rider ignorant had been followed.

'No idea. Hasn't ridden Hysterical before, so won't be any the wiser.'

Exactly how Lionel liked it. The fewer moving parts to an engine, the less could go wrong.

'Good luck,' Lionel tapping Rapanaro on the shoulder with his racing program, the way any passer-by might do after a friendly chat, wanting to keep his contact with the trainer to a minimum. If the stewards were to get wind of the ring-in, they'd be looking at whoever was behind it, and Lionel's presence would be a beacon.

A precautionary squiz had revealed that the only other occupants in the area, beside a couple of grooms, were an elderly couple and a sexy woman in an expensive outfit, her short skirt showing off her great legs. Lionel heartily approved. A man needed something to look at in between events.

When Lionel found Davis waiting by a white cast-iron table beside a furled umbrella, champagne and glasses chilling up nicely in a bucket, he asked if he'd any word from Queensland on the pre-race odds.

'Still holding at twelves.'

Davis gestured at the bottle, Lionel nodded. Davis popped expertly and poured. Lionel took the proffered champagne and swigged. Everything was going to plan.

The big guy in the suit with the Islander hanger-on had been checking Zeen out. She knew it the way women of her mother's generation could tell the ripeness of fruit at a glance. The big guy might have been one of the crims in on the deal, or just as likely a publican from somewhere up north. Either way, he wasn't of particular interest to Zeen. Detective Inspector Elizabeth Atwood, however, who *was* of particular interest, was so far nowhere to be seen.

Zeen had been quite certain that Atwood or one of her minions would have been stalking, but there had been no sign of her or anybody who looked like Liquor and Gaming squad.

She'd clocked the stewards going about their business, but everything seemed normal.

After she'd collected the cash off Harris, she'd gone back to the café and changed into a sexy frock with a big hat. If everything went to plan, that hat was going to be important.

She'd resisted calling Boski and giving him the good news about finding Harris, and the even better news about the money she'd got from Harris. Rick needed to be fully focussed on bringing Hysterical to the track. If she told him her plans, he would argue with her, or worry, or both. She'd save the reveal till the horse was at the course. Hopefully that would be some time soon.

From the speakers behind her she heard the caller announce the start of the next race. This was when the area was most deserted, and in thirty-five minutes' time, when the sixth race was being run and Rapanaro and his strapper were busy getting their runner to the mounting yard, that was when Hysterical would be unattended and they would strike.

Her Samsung buzzed with a text message. Rick.

Here.

A wave of relief swept through her. First part of her plan was progressing well. Once the horses were swapped, she would get to work on the rest of it. But she was still bugged. Where the heck was Atwood?

As she scanned about, she saw a figure emerge from behind a large tree some forty metres away. Joe Harris. He signalled: *I'm watching you.*

Good, Joe, watch all you want.

'Please, Lord, if pride was involved in my actions, forgive me. I told myself I was following your divine plan, but now I'm not sure, and I'm confused. Surely, you wouldn't weaken my resolve with doubts.'

Paul, kneeling in front of the altar, crossed himself and shakily got to his feet. It was a small, unprepossessing little church, but it had been his shop for a little while, and only now was he beginning to realise how much he would miss it if things went awry.

Rick had called him last night to say he could already chip in about nine hundred dollars from his day's trade, but there wouldn't be enough to cover the shortfall by Monday, when the finance committee met. Not unless the horse won. And, quite apart from that, Paul felt awful about taking Rick and Zeen's money. They owed him nothing.

He had already decided that he should make his own weakness the subject of his sermon. It would be a public confession, in which he might salvage some respect from God by owning up to his prideful behaviour and accepting the vitriol that would undoubtedly, and justifiably, be delivered his way by parishioners and bishop alike.

The whole episode had also given him a chance to reflect on the kindness of friends. No doubt Zeen and Rick had had plans for that money, a chance to improve their café and their place in life. But Rick hadn't hesitated and, just as impressively, Zeen, who had no prior connection to Paul, had stood by him.

He exited the church, reminding himself the confessional box still needed sanding. He crossed to the rectory, checked his watch. Already past two. Believe it or not, he still possessed a transistor radio, and come race-time he would listen in and learn whether it had been the Lord or his old adversary who had initiated the chain of events that had generated so much self-reflection.

He retrieved the transistor from the drawer in the kitchen, clicked it on and thumbed the dial until he located the nasal tones that signalled the racing channel.

The horses were moving in for the next race. He wondered whether Rick and Zeen were out at the racetrack. If they were, he prayed they would have a day to celebrate.

Ever since Rick had come up with the idea of swapping back the real horse, Zeen had felt that old familiar zing crawling up and down her spine. Pulling off a scam always had the greatest chance when everybody else thought they were the ones in the know. A bunch of greedy arseholes believed the race was rigged but, in fact, it was going to be unrigged. That offered a situation Zeen could exploit. Already she had performed the first and most important step—she would be playing with somebody else's cash. But with a little luck she reckoned she could leverage that into a real win.

Of course there were hurdles to jump, dangers lurking at every turn. That's why she'd kept Rick in the dark. He'd worry too much. For the critical stage of swapping Hysterical back in, Zeen had chosen Sandy over Rick for the role of the stand-in strapper.

'He's stooped, balding, looks like he's smoked a packet of Winny Reds a day for the last thirty years. Stick him in this smock coat, nobody will look twice,' she'd explained when making the call the night before.

Now she met Sandy on the car park side of the gate. It was ten minutes until the sixth race, when Rapanaro's other horse would be engaged.

'Rick's at the float. We haven't got the horse out yet,' he confessed.

'Why not?'

'I only had one apple.'

Typical. Zeen got him to lead her to the float. Rick was standing beside it looking useless.

'Really?' was all she needed to say.

'You think it's so easy, you do it.'

Zeen walked to the back of the float and unbolted it. It was boggy here, and her shoes were two hundred bucks. Any permanent damage, Boski was paying up big time, likely extra-long massages all week.

'Come on girl, showtime,' she said.

Zeen had been around horses plenty. She stroked Hysterical and sweet-talked her.

'Don't worry about these dumb-arse men. They're not going to hurt you.'

She hooked a lead rope onto the halter, then guided Hysterical down by gently pushing her backwards.

'That's how you do it,' she said and handed the rope to Rick. 'By the way, I found Harris. He was hiding out at Oscar Cornelius's pub. He's here at the course.'

She almost told him she had twenty grand sitting in her handbag but decided against it. It would get too complicated, and Boski was the kind of guy needed things kept simple.

'What are you going to do?' he asked.

'It's what I'm not going to do that's important. But you need to trust me.'

He gazed at her long and soulful; said, 'I do.'

Kissing would have to wait. She gestured to Sandy.

'You come with me,' turning with Sandy and the horse because she didn't want to look back at Boski and find herself getting emotional when she needed a clear head.

'I'm nervous, Zeen,' Sandy said as he followed her to the gate leading into the track.

'Don't be.'

The recording of the bugle heralded the runners in the next race onto the track. Zeen swung around, expecting to see the place clear.

No sign of Rapanaro or any strapper with the ring-in horse, but Oscar Cornelius was standing at the stall, gazing at the horse that was supposedly going to be carrying his twenty grand.

Shit.

Well, Zeen had a saying: a negative can always be turned into a positive. The second part of her plan had involved encountering Cornelius before the race, and this opportunity had now presented itself without any effort on her part.

'Sandy,' she whispered, 'While I'm talking with this guy, you need to untie the horse and lead it back out to the car park and bring Hysterical in.'

His jaw went slack, but then he nodded. Zeen swept up beside Cornelius.

'Tell me you're not thinking of putting your money on this sorry piece of horseflesh.'

Cornelius turned in surprise, maybe ready to tell her to mind her own business. One look and his fleshy lips started oiling up.

'As a matter of fact ...'

'Oh, come on. She has about as much chance of winning as you have of buying me dinner.'

Out the corner of her eye she saw Sandy moving to the horse. Cornelius cracked a grin, as she knew he would. Swung her way, leaning back against the rail like he was Gene Kelly in a sailor suit ready to swap wisecracks with Mitzi Gaynor, or whoever was the love interest in those movies she used to watch on Sunday afternoon TV.

'I'm sure dinner with you ...?'

'Sarah.'

'... Sarah, would be delightful, but the thought hadn't crossed my mind.'

With Cornelius facing her and not the horse, she could follow Sandy's progress as he fumbled with the knots on the stall ropes.

'No, I was just playing with you ...?' leaving it for him to supply—

'Oscar Cornelius.'

'Oscar, I am sure you are beating those ladies off with a stick and that offering to take me to dinner would be the last thing to cross your mind ...' Here she deliberately angled her body so her plunging neckline was seen to its best advantage 'But irrespective of that, Hysterical cannot win. And believe me, I'm a fine judge of horseflesh.'

Sandy had the horse now and was leading it off. The horse seemed happy to follow. Cornelius looked Zeen up and down—*ogled* might be too dramatic a description, but not by much.

'I'm sure you're a fine judge of horses, Sarah, but on this occasion, you will be proven wrong.'

'It's double-figure odds.'

'The odds should never discourage you, if you believe.'

He'd glanced over his shoulder at the anonymous strapper and horse but quickly refocussed fully on her. The next race started, and the commentator's animated call was blowing in on the wind. They had maybe three minutes now before the area filled up again.

'So, you're a betting man, Oscar?'

'You bet.'

They shared a laugh.

'Is that what you do for a living, or a side hobby?'

'I own pubs and clubs. You ever been to the Globe? That's one of mine.'

'I'm fairly new to town, but I'll look it up.'

'And might I ask what you do for a living?'

'I could tell you, but then I'd have to thrill you.'

Oscar laughing, enjoying the repartee.

'Unlike you, however, Oscar, I am something of a professional gambler. That's why I know Hysterical cannot win.'

'You might be surprised.'

'Nope. Tell you what. I have ten thousand dollars here,' tapping her handbag. 'I'll bet all of it Hysterical doesn't win the race. You match me, winner takes all.'

He was intrigued.

'Ten thousand?'

'Yep.' She opened her bag and gave him a glimpse of his own money. 'What do you say, Oscar? You got the *cojones*?'

Getting in real close as she said it, almost brushing his thigh with hers, like he was the sexiest man alive. He was wallowing in it, pressing closer.

'Indeed, I do have the *cojones*, but I would hate to take your money.'

'I don't need any misguided chivalry.'

'Here's the thing, though, Sarah. The odds are twelve to one, and you're only offering me even-money. That's a substantial discount in your favour.'

'But you're certain that it'll win, aren't you?'

She'd backed him into a corner, now it was time to seal the deal.

'Tell you what, Oscar; I lose, you not only get my ten thousand, but I'll take you to dinner at the venue of your choice.' She ran her tongue around her lips. 'Including my apartment— if that's what you desire.'

She knew even before he started drooling that she had him hooked. Rick had been right. Sometimes it was handy to be able to go back to the old ways: a sexy dress, a husky voice.

'Do you have ten thousand, Oscar?'

'I certainly do.'

He fiddled in his trouser pocket and brought out a couple of thick rolls. She nodded in appreciation.

'Well, we need an uninvested third party to hold the money for us.' She caught Sandy wandering back in with Hysterical. He gave the slightest of nods.

'You can't trust anyone here, we're at a racetrack.' If only Oscar understood the irony of his own words.

The race was over, and people were drifting their way. Sandy was tying the horse back into its stall.

'What about the race photographer?' she suggested. 'They can't afford to rip us off. They need to work here.'

Oscar thought that an excellent idea. They headed off to find him or her, Zeen relieved to be moving away from Hysterical. Her heart was in her mouth. There was always a chance that

Rapanaro would recognise the real Hysterical, but she reckoned his subconscious logic would tell him it couldn't be Hysterical, because he had left her back at his stables in Helena Valley.

But what was worrying her even more, was: where was Atwood?

In her student days, when she was planning to be a primary school teacher, Liz Atwood had enjoyed some big nights out. But never had she woken with such a pounding headache and dry throat. Where was she? She went to push herself up, couldn't. Her hands were numb. Her legs, too. For an instant she panicked, she'd had a stroke.

Her blurry vision tracked around an unfamiliar room, settling on a dressing-table mirror. The reflected image of herself was, if anything, even blurrier, but it told her what she needed to know: she was trussed and gagged on a strange bed. Fuckers!

She tried to yell, but because of the gag could manage no more than a grunt. The nylon cord they'd used on her wasn't so tight that they'd cut off the blood to her wrists, which were behind her back; but the rope wasn't loose and even wiggling her fingers her hands were still all pins and needles. More attempted yelling only meant more razor blades in her throat. She felt her pulse racing, was growing quickly exhausted and more anxious by the second. Calm, she told herself.

Slower breathing. Good. Relax. Think. Easier said than done. Her brain was soup.

Coming back now. Last night, she'd wanted to find a link between Harris and whoever the other conspirators were, so she had driven to his apartment. This, she was thinking, is most likely that same apartment, although she couldn't be certain. She had seen nothing of it, really; it had been in darkness when she entered, and she'd not got as far as the bedroom.

She replayed the events from the moment she'd entered the building. Coming up the stairs, kneeling in front of the door and listening. Not a sound. She'd picked the lock, walked in, a shadowy figure in the living room ... *Bam*!

A memory lurked that she'd been fired upon, but it was like the smell of a dish that has already left the room, a hint only. Had she been hit? She twisted this way and that, could see no blood or feel any obvious wound. But her head? Maybe they'd pistol-whipped her?

How long had she been out? No sign of her phone, and she couldn't feel the weight of it in her jeans pocket. Could have fallen under the bed, or whoever assaulted her, Harris maybe, had taken it with them.

Her brain was functioning now. What time was it? There was a digital clock on the dresser, but it had been shifted around at some point and was facing the mirror, so she had to decode the reverse image and that told her it was ...

2.06! In the afternoon!!

What a complete disaster. She had to get to the track. Because she had told nobody else about what was going to be her coup, nobody would be looking out for the ring-in. It occurred to her that she could be in a lot of shit for breaking in here, but she couldn't worry about that right now. She wriggled and screamed.

And got nowhere. The bed was too soft and absorbent. She had to make a noise, and to do that she would have to get to the floor. There was no easy way. She struggled to the edge of the bed and flipped herself over.

She might have got away with nothing worse than a bruised arse, except that the bottom drawer of the dresser had not been shut the whole way.

Her head hit the drawer, and she promptly knocked herself out again.

Rick knew there had been no point asking Zeen to divulge her plans. If she told him, he was going to worry; and if she didn't tell him, that would lead to some argument that she would undoubtedly win or at least act like she'd won. So, he'd taken a deep breath and concerned himself with the task at hand, getting this second horse up into the float. Once Sandy and he had swapped horses, and Sandy had started back to the track with the real Hysterical, Rick employed lateral thinking on how to get the new horse into the float.

A kid about thirteen helping load another horse out of its float seemed to know his way around horses. He was leading his horse towards the gate from the car park to the stalls, a route that took him right past Rick. The kid was a redhead and wore his hair in a rat's tail.

'Hey, Ginger. You good with horses?' Rick asked.

The kid gave him the kind of look Rick would give a pervert if he were a kid.

Rick said, 'I need help to load this horse into the float. Twenty bucks.'

'Wait there,' the kid commanded.

Rick did as he was told, and upon the kid's return, following advance payment in full, the horse was loaded into the float.

Sandy, returning to catch the last stanza, said, 'So far so good. Zeen's leading some guy around with her cleavage.'

No matter that Zeen was doing something to help him, Rick felt a pang of jealousy. He dampened it, concentrating on the greater good his sacrifice might bring.

'The trainer hasn't noticed the switch?'

'I wasn't exactly hanging around, but let's say no alarms have gone off.'

Rick told Sandy it would be up to him to get this horse back to Rapanaro's.

'You think you can handle that by yourself?'

'I'm getting the hang of it,' Sandy said.

Joe Harris had spent enough time with Zeen to know that she couldn't be trusted. He would have kept a closer eye on her, except that he had to watch out for Missouri and any of Pendle's other guys who might be looking for him. And as well he did. He was just zipping up after a nervous slash in the gents when he saw Missouri lumber in. Joe swiftly retreated into a stall and snapped on the lock, terrified he'd been made, but nobody pounded on the door. He gave it five minutes, snuck a peek to check the coast was clear, then skedaddled.

Joe was playing a dangerous game, and this forced him to the periphery of the track, finding cover where he could while trying to keep an eye on Zeen, but that trip to the gents had cost him time. He was relieved, not just in the bladder sense, when he happened to pick up on Zeen walking back from the edge of the track, past the finishing post where the race photographer had his tent.

What did not give Joe any sense of comfort, however, was that she was in the company of Oscar Cornelius, and they seemed to be very buddy-buddy. They stopped, Oscar said something, she said something, and then they went their separate ways.

She was double-crossing him!

After explaining the nature of the wager to the photographer, and entrusting the money to him, Zeen and Oscar had started back towards the grandstand area.

Oscar said, 'I have a fine table in the Members, and a chilled bottle of Veuve if you'd care to join me.'

Zeen had been expecting just such an invitation. She replied, 'Much as I enjoy your company, Oscar, I'm not sure it's a good thing to have two people betting for opposite outcomes in close quarters.'

'I can assure you that I'm not a sore loser.'

'No, but I am,' said Zeen. 'If you're quick enough, I'll see you after the race when I collect.'

Cornelius laughed. '*Au revoir*, Sarah. I'm partial to duck, by the way.' He strode off towards the Members, while Zeen angled in the opposite direction.

Already she was torn whether she should have bet the whole twenty, made a profit on the side; but she'd promised Boski she was out of those scams, and it was just one piece of a much larger puzzle. So she parted with just ten and retained ten thousand in cash in her handbag. So far everything was going well. Maybe too well. Getting worried again Rapanaro might spot the horse-swap.

Suddenly her arm was grabbed, and she was pulled behind a huge potted palm.

'You trying to cut me out?'

Harris's eyes were dancing like Lotto balls in the airstream.

'What are you talking about?' Playing it cool.

'I saw you with Cornelius. What are you cooking up?'

Zeen pulled her arm away.

'I went over to check out the horse, and he was there too. We got talking.'

He tried a sneer.

'Oh yeah, I translated. Boski not good enough for you? You going to dump him now?'

Ignoring him. 'I never told him I was the one placing his bet. Didn't want him confused.'

'That's all you *are* going to be doing. Got it?'

She'd had enough.

'I've seen Missouri walking about. One shout from me, you're history.'

'Where's the money?'

'You think I ripped you off and stayed around to have a flutter or two?'

'Show me.'

Zeen snapped open her bag, gave him a glimpse of the cash she still had, snapped it shut.

'Don't look now, but that's one of Pendle's guys over your shoulder.'

She was lying. It was just some dude in a cap and sunglasses. But he induced the requisite fear in Harris, though he tried to mask it. She pushed her advantage.

'Why don't you go wait somewhere safe? I'll bring you the money after I collect.'

Harris shook his head. 'No way you're collecting. You bring me the ticket, soon as that bet goes on.'

'It's dangerous here for you, Joe.'

'Leaving you with a quarter of a mill would be a lot more dangerous.'

With that he broke away.

She started back towards the trainers' car park. Boski was heading her way.

'I've been looking for you. All good?' he said.

'The horse is switched. Nobody's noticed.'

'Sandy said you were leading some guy around.'

'Don't get jealous.'

'I'm not.'

She didn't mind he was.

He gave it all of twelve seconds, then asked, 'Who was he?'

'Oscar Cornelius.'

Registering the confusion on his face, she said, 'You have to trust me.'

'I do.'

Whether he did or did not was immaterial. He had no choice in the matter. Right now, she had other things to worry about.

She said, 'One problem—I don't see Atwood.'

'And that's a problem?'

Gut instinct told her it might be.

Using your phone on a racecourse in Australia to make bets was forbidden. Not that this bothered Drew Waldron, because the bets he was making with SP bookies scattered around the country at the behest of his boss were illegal anywhere.

Custom at the course was light today, and Pendle was more interested in getting on those bets than in having his penciller on hand at his bookie stand. That job, as he'd told Waldron numerous times, he could do himself. As the runners for race six trotted out onto the course, Pendle had told Drew to put down his pencil and start putting bets on Hysterical.

By the time race six had been run and won, Drew had accomplished his task. So far, to his great relief, no sign of Atwood. He'd expected her to be prowling nearby, demanding updates right under the nose of his boss. Drew came back from his chore to see Pendle taking a quick slug of Somac.

Leaning in close enough Drew could smell his aftershave, Pendle asked, 'How much did you get on?'

'All of it.' Fifty K spread around a dozen different SP establishments in various states. You didn't ring up and say, 'Dom Pendle wants five thou on Hysterical', you just quoted an account number. Years of expecting phones to be tapped, Drew supposed, or maybe wanting to screen anything from the tax office if they ever got a whiff of it.

Not that Drew believed that likely. He'd only been in the racing game for three years, after answering an ad in the paper calling for somebody quick with math, but from what he'd learned already, so many powerful people were mired in the game—cops, politicians, judges, media moguls—that if any investigation was mooted, it would be stillborn.

Atwood was an exception. She was a zealot. It was the drug bust that had him on the hook. That were to become public, his next career move might be checkout chick. Atwood nailing Pendle was nothing to Drew, so long as he skated on his drug charge. He resumed his place at the book.

Pendle said, 'Word will get out soon that money has gone on Hysterical, and then we'll have them all trying to bet with us. But at five-hundred dollars payout limit, we won't lose too much.'

'And you'll keep the price out even if the punters jump on?'

Normally a bookie would shorten the odds as his liability stretched.

'We might pull it into elevens just so the stewards don't get curious.'

Pendle was a wily old dog; he had to hand that to him. Pull the odds in by a point, Pendle could be seen to be reacting to the demand from punters, but it was in Pendle's interest to keep those odds out—he stood to gain a lot more from his own bets on Hysterical than his payouts would cost him. Even with a starting price of eleven to one, there'd be five-hundred and fifty grand heading Pendle's way. Pretty good for an afternoon's work.

Supposedly Atwood was going to blow it all apart. Though exactly where was she? Drew shooting a sideways glance at his boss, an idea leaping out at him like a skeleton in the ghost train. Would Pendle ... if he found out that Atwood knew and thought she was going to do him out of half-a-mil ... would he have her eliminated? A cop! Would he dare?

Fuck. Pendle was so well connected that if Atwood was taking her ideas to a superior, that information could be looping straight back to Pendle.

And what if he found out that Drew had been her snitch? Could Pendle know they'd been meeting in secret? Could he be toying with him?

The pencil in his hand was shaking. For weeks he had been desperate to see the end of Atwood, but now he was scared that what he wished for might have come true.

There was the type of anger where people shouted and stomped and thumped fists on desks. And then there was Lionel anger.

That was the kind where all sound evaporated, and the world went into ultra-slow motion, like right now. Lionel had taken a call in the Members' dining room, the fizz in his flute of Moët bubbling, blissfully unaware, to the surface.

'Say again. Slowly.' When he'd recognised the number calling as his own office, he had not been overly concerned. Arnold would be giving him a courtesy call to say the money was on as arranged, just before race six. But that wasn't what Arnold was telling him.

'Someone's already put a heap on Hysterical. A couple of the smaller outfits just refused to take our bet. Said they were tapped out already.'

Lionel almost strangled the little phone. The plan had been to put off laying their bets until twenty minutes before the race, reducing the chances of big money being put on Hysterical here at the track, forcing the odds down.

'What about Donovan?'

'Donovan said he would take ten as a personal favour, but he was capping his payout at a hundred. Said it was too suss.'

Perhaps Lionel should have been thankful that Donovan, the largest SP in the country, was prepared to at least offer double-figure odds, but thankful Lionel was not. Normally, Donovan would have been good for twenty at twelves. Now Lionel would only get a hundred grand max off him.

'What is our precise position at the moment?'

'Apart from Donovan, I've been able to place a total of thirty-seven thousand at starting price.'

A quick calculation told Lionel that if the starting price held at twelves here on the course, that would be a total of four-hundred-and-forty-four, plus Donovan's hundred would lift it a bit over half-a-mill, less than half of what he had been expecting. And if the bookies here dropped the starting price, he wouldn't even get that. It was a fucking disaster was what it was. Somebody had double-crossed him. Somebody had cashed in.

'Did you ask who put the bets on?'

'None of them would spill, but they must know whose accounts the winnings would be going to.'

Lionel was wondering how widespread the breach was. Were there lots of people out there cashing in on his hard work and planning? He had a gut feeling this would come back to one person. Likely betting by numbered accounts to cover their tracks. That's what he would do. And for somebody to wait this long and not hit the bookies on course, which would have shortened the starting price, that felt organised, disciplined. Like they knew when he was going to put down his bets and had nipped in just before. What a shame he had brought both Kieran and Tongan George over with him; right now, they could have been usefully employed paying a visit to a couple of these SPs on the other side of the country.

'What do you want me to do?'

Lionel's first instinct was to tell Arnold to send George's baby brother Max to Wes Jackson, one of the smaller SPs. Persuade Jackson to talk. But he scratched that idea before it could leave the barrier. The only people at the Queensland end who knew of the ring-in were himself, Tongan George, Kieran, Langer and Arnold. Davis, who had not been privy to the scheme, might potentially have put things together. But instinct told him Davis was too English.

Lionel himself had told nobody. George was a loyal soldier; Langer did too well out of Lionel to bother. Kieran had a bent, violent streak, and just maybe he would dare to double-cross his boss, but if Kieran were behind it, he wouldn't have had the smarts to hold off. This was clearly the work of someone clever—sharp enough to suss out Lionel's timing and place their bets just prior to him.

Or maybe this operator was not so clever as all that. Maybe they simply knew exactly when to strike because they were in on the plan. Arnold was smart. And he knew the timing.

Your first inclination was to say to yourself, 'Arnold is just a nerd who likes seeing his long-range plans reach fruition'; but years of experience cautioned Lionel against being too trusting of his minions. Who was it who had gone behind his back and sold the Deep Purple tapes in Germany all those years ago? Inge, the girl he trusted more than anybody. She'd bootlegged his bootlegs! And hadn't she started as a photocopy girl in the Frankfurt office? It was easy to underestimate somebody's ambition. Nobody was better set up to engineer this coup than Arnold, but he wasn't the only possibility. There was another leg to the operation right here in Perth.

'Mr Howard?'

Arnold calling him 'Mr Howard' as if he respected him. But did he?

'Don't do anything for now.'

For one, Lionel thinking he didn't want to create bad blood until all his winnings had been paid. Worst thing he could do would be to initiate payback, thereby calling cops down on himself. Some of the SPs might run. Or talk. No, better he held fire until after the race. Then he could root out the traitor and deliver the kind of retribution that would discourage anybody from ever again fucking over Vinyl Lionel.

'I don't want them cracking the shits and withholding my money.'

'You got it,' said Arnold and rang off.

All pleasure had gone from the day. The Moët seemed flat. Be easy for whiz-kid Arnold to set up some fake credentials with SP bookies, put on the bets, then act surprised to Lionel.

'Bad news, sir?' Davis proffered the Moët bottle, but Lionel waved it away.

'Yes, mate. Not the best.'

It took him a while to find Max's number in the little notebook he carried with him. Apparently, some phones you could put the numbers in with the name of your contact and then just press the name, but he didn't know how to do that. He was thinking that hooker from the other night would. Might be worth flying her over to the Gold Coast, give her a chore or two to go on with between the other stuff. He dialled Max, getting up and moving away for privacy. Pretty sure he could trust Davis, but why risk it?

'What's up, boss?'

Max sounded just like his brother. Lionel couldn't tell them apart on the phone. Max wasn't supposed to know about the ring-in, but now Lionel was thinking George could have told him. That would be another potential leak.

'Job for you. I want you to keep a very close eye on Arnold for me. If he goes somewhere, follow discreetly. If he makes a call, listen in. Understand?'

'Reckon he's a cop?'

'Don't worry about what I think, just do as requested.'

'You got it, boss.'

He ended the call. Yes, it could be Arnold; but perhaps he was looking in the wrong state. Perhaps the leak was right here in Perth. The trainer. He needed to have a chat with Rapanaro.

Liz wanted to scream. The traffic was not heavy but unerringly in all the wrong places. Initially a trailer full of roped mattresses in front and a learner bus-driver beside it had slowed Liz down, but she'd broken free and was powering east along Walcott Street, reaching optimum speed when the orange light ran out of puff. Only at the last second, as the light hit red, did Liz brake and skid to a loud halt.

Shit, shit, shit. Every second counted. A Hilux pulled up next to her. The driver, a guy about thirty in an AC/DC tee-shirt though she guessed he'd seen the band once and long after Bon's final encore, staring at her like she was a road menace. She hit the automatic wind-down on her window.

'You can fuck off!' she yelled, catching a glimpse of herself in the rear vision mirror. A gauze bandage oozing blood was angled above her left eyebrow and that eye was closing fast too, fat sausage skin beneath expanding.

Her good eye checked the clock on her dash. Seventeen minutes. No time to waste.

She planted her foot and shot through the intersection while the light still glowed red. Horns blared. Like she gave a flying.

From the time she'd hit her head on the drawer in Harris's bedroom till she regained a kind of fuzzy consciousness, more than twenty minutes had passed. It took her another ten to work out that she was still roped up, only now lying on the floor not the bed. Her legs were bound at the ankles, but she lifted them and then drove her heels down onto the floor hard as she could. Boards would have been optimum, but fortunately the carpet was thin as a pensioner's wallet. She kept piledriving but had no idea if anyone was actually in the flat below.

Forty minutes later, her legs heavy and dull as concrete, and her with nothing to show except a steady trickle of blood from what she reckoned was a scalp wound, she started flipping around, kind of ugly break-dancing. She discovered that by leaning back on her shoulders and propelling herself from her arse and hips up and forward, she was able to pummel the dresser with her feet. Some strikes were good enough to make items topple onto the floor. A heavy brush, a few pens, a small bottle of cologne. She'd zeroed in on a big old crystal decanter and, by concentrating her attack on the wall side of the dresser, managed to set it teetering on the edge. One final kick and it toppled into the windowsill, bounced off and plummeted to the floor, creating an almighty din and smashing.

She'd got the hang of things by then and was creating even more havoc, sweeping her legs around like the arms of a deranged clock, knocking over anything she could reach.

Eventually, worried neighbours had come to her rescue. Using the key that her assailants must have left under the mat, they'd opened the door and discovered Liz, trussed in the bedroom. They'd already called her fellow cops, but there was no time to hang about and wait. The couple who found her, a nurse and a tradie, sorted her out: the nurse dressing her forehead, the tradie slicing the ropes that bound her. Three deep glasses of water and she was out of there. She gave the couple her card.

'Tell the uniforms I'll speak to them later. I've got urgent business,' she'd said, running down the steps and trying to remember where she'd parked her car. Took her a valuable couple of minutes to locate and hobble to it. Time she was trying to make up now, roaring under the East Perth subway twelve minutes to start time. Whether it had been Harris, Pendle or Boski who had physically attacked her, she currently didn't care. They were all going to pay.

She tuned the radio to the racing station. Race six had been run and the runners for the last were already out in the yard. She pressed her foot down far as it would go.

If something was going to go badly wrong, it would be right now, reckoned Rick. Atwood had to be lying low, watching on concealed cameras or something, because she still hadn't made her move and the race was only minutes away. Rapanaro had heaved the jockey up into Hysterical's saddle but still no whistles or alarms. Zeen was rarely wrong—in her own mind she was never wrong—but could she be wrong about this? Could the accident with Paul have been a fluke? Probably Atwood had been out there because she was suspicious about Rapanaro. But maybe she wasn't as clever as Zeen supposed. Maybe she hadn't seen the two identical horses and hadn't realised the nature of the scam. Had she, she would've come down like a ton of bricks well before this.

A moderate crowd had gathered around the mounting yard. No sign of Cornelius, or for that matter Harris, but Missouri's big head swivelled like his namesake's guns—the ones Cher had straddled singing 'Turn Back Time'—and when he clocked Rick, his eyes narrowed.

During Rick's jail stint he might sometimes look across the courtyard and see some arsehole giving him the exact same stare. A bilious feeling would rise in his stomach. Rick registering that feeling now. If they didn't pull this off, he was destined to become Doug Austin's punching bag.

Bang! Rick was nearly skittled, but not by Missouri. Some big Islander, shoving forward to get a ringside view of the mounting yard. Rick catching Rapanaro exchanging a look with the Islander, who jerked a thumb as if to say the trainer was wanted right that minute. The trainer ignored him and kept speaking quietly to the jockey.

Rick checked the Islander out more closely: a head that looked like it had been lifted straight off Mount Rushmore, shoulders wide as the poles used to hitch oxen together. First thought, he was a cop, one of Atwood's crew, but Rick quickly ditched the notion.

The guy was wearing thongs. He could be an undercover cop, but no, the longer Rick looked at him, the more he got a prison vibe. Rick couldn't pinpoint the giveaway, but when your everyday survival depended on recognising threats, you got damn good at picking up on things you weren't even conscious you had done. Yeah, this guy had done time. A worrying idea assailed Rick: this bloke might be one of the ones organising the ring-in.

The early warning biliousness gave way to crawling tendrils of fear. The Islander meant business. Had they twigged that somebody was about to neuter their scam? If so, you'd think there would have been more action. Okay, there wasn't real urgency yet, but all the same, the big fella looked pissed off about something.

A heavy hand fell on Rick's shoulder and his intestines convulsed.

'You here looking for Harris or trying to back a winner to pay off my boss?' Missouri squeezed Rick's shoulder.

'I don't bet,' said Rick.

The horses were leaving the saddling paddock now and starting to head out to the course.

'So, I'll take it you're hoping Harris might show his face here. You'd be better off backing a longshot. Listen, Boski, personally, I have nothing against you. I asked my brother about you, and he told me you're a decent guy. I'm sorry you're caught in the cross-fire, but what I think doesn't matter. For some reason, Pendle is sure you're into something with Harris. I'm not privy to what. If Harris isn't found soon, the debt will be extracted from you.'

'I don't have that kind of money.'

'You have a business that is doing well. If you want it to keep doing well, you'll find the money and then get the money back off Harris.'

'What if I can't?'

'Do I need to spell it out? A fire could break out, a customer could claim you sexually abused them in the toilets, the health department could find rat poo in your kitchen.'

'Thanks for enlightening me.'

The big hand patted Rick on the shoulder in what might have been meant to offer sympathy, or at least comfort, but only made him think about bruises and pain. Austin moved off. Of the Islander and Rapanaro there was no sign.

'I didn't tell a soul.'

Rapanaro had his hands apart, gesturing wildly. He was hemmed in between Tongan George and a vat of boiling chip fat. For a modest endowment to the staff, Lionel, who stood just behind George, had secured exclusive use of the ground floor kitchen for five minutes. Kieran was guarding the door.

George took a threatening step closer, his big chest almost up against the trainer's.

'Think hard, Enzo.' Despite his vast repertoire of 'inducements', Lionel had never yet chip-fried the hand of an interviewee. He had a sneaking suspicion it would work a treat.

'Your wife perhaps? Innocent chat while she was having her hair done. Or buttering sandwiches at the school canteen.'

'She never has her hair done. I tell her nothing. I sent her away three weeks ago to see her family in Italy, so she hears nothing. I tell nobody.'

He was very convincing.

'Trip to Italy must have been expensive.'

'First time in four years. We saved up.'

'That can be checked.'

'Then check it. I tell nobody. If I tell anybody the prices out there would be way shorter.'

Enzo pointing out towards the bookies' ring.

'That's not where they put the money on.' Then, with what almost sounded like empathy, Lionel said, 'You may not have meant to divulge our secret. It could have slipped out without you realising. What about the stable boy?'

'I tell him nothing. He's as thick as three planks. I tell him Hysterical has a twin that can't race.'

'Perhaps he mentioned it to someone.'

'He's not into horses. He's a farmhand, that's all.'

What was impressive was Rapanaro wasn't trying to shift blame onto the stable boy. Maybe it was Arnold, the whiz-kid, after all? One last-ditch effort, because the race was about to start and Lionel really did not want to miss it, even if it would pain him to know how much he had been denied in winnings.

'Perhaps you had to see a shrink, or were chatting with your doctor ...?'

He saw a flicker of something in the trainer's eyes.

'What? Who did you speak to?'

Enzo was shaking his head.

'No, he wouldn't ... He's a priest.'

George looked at Lionel, Lionel looked at George. Kieran cracked that psychopathic grin that appeared whenever the prospect of inflicting pain raised its head.

Lionel said, 'Tell the boys where they can find him, Enzo.' Then he swept out. The horses would be in the barriers.

There was no doubt in Zeen's mind Harris would be watching her to make sure she placed the bet with Pendle. But not up close, because Pendle would see him and that would not end well for Joe Harris. So, he'd be watching from a safe distance, using binoculars. And he'd be looking for and expecting a reaction from Pendle when she put twenty K on. The only place he could be watching from was from behind her, straight on to Pendle. There were too many people to the side.

The big hat she was wearing would help, but Pendle would be up on his bookie stand; his face would still be visible to Harris. The horses were heading to the barriers as she zeroed in on the bookie. Pendle didn't know her, but she knew Pendle. He smiled as she approached. She noted Hysterical's price was still twelve to one. She motioned for him to bend down towards her, or more specifically her inviting decolletage.

He did. 'I'm told you are the biggest bookmaker,' she whispered, emphasising 'biggest'. These older guys loved a dash of double entendre.

'I'm certainly the *best*.' Pendle's eyes twinkling.

'Twenty on Hysterical, Dominic,' Zeen winked. She opened her bag and slid across a twenty-dollar bill. Harris wouldn't be able to see their hands and would have no idea of how much she had handed over.

'Two hundred and forty to twenty for the lady,' Pendle called to Waldron.

'Do you know what all the police are doing in the car park?'

As she'd hoped, this generated a worried frown. If Harris was looking, perfect. He'd think Pendle's reaction was because of the huge bet.

'There are police in the car park?'

'Yes, quite a bunch of them.'

Pendle scrawled on the ticket and handed it across, clearly fazed. She made her escape as a swarm of punters descended. They all wanted Hysterical. She took herself around the other side of Pendle's stand where she'd be obscured, opened her bag, pulled out a black marker pen and added a *K* after where Pendle had scrawled *240*.

Harris had told her he'd see her at the back of the stand. He was waiting. She could hear the race-caller's muffled description of horses moving into the stalls.

'He take it all?'

'You were watching, weren't you?'

He put out his hand.

'Give me the ticket.'

Yes, he'd been watching. She handed it over. He glanced to confirm it was Pendle's and she hadn't swapped it out—an old trick they'd often used as a team. Zeen wasn't concerned about him scrutinizing the ticket beyond that. Bookmakers' writing was never legible. You got an idea of the horse's name and a suggestion of the payout, but it was a hurried scrawl, no more than graffiti. If she breathed easier when he slipped the ticket into his pocket, she tried not to show it.

'When do I get my money?' she asked.

'After the race. I'll see you back here.'

'You'd better,' she said.

The PA announced one or two runners were still to go in. Harris was smoke.

Liz Atwood hit the stewards' room like a cannonball. The chief steward nearly fell off his chair at the sight of her.

'We need to pull out Hysterical. It's a ring-in.'

As she said it, the loudspeakers carried the familiar line that starts every race.

'And they're off!'

She turned towards the large TV screen as the barriers flew open and the horses jumped.

Then she screamed.

When the phone rang that morning Thaiphoon Tony had been midway through a set of one-handed push-ups, having already brought Marietta her usual Saturday breakfast in bed: a light mushroom omelette, fresh orange juice and coffee. Ninety-nine percent of calls were for Marietta, and she picked up the brand-new cordless phone she'd bought two days ago from Harvey Norman as a spur of the moment purchase, having just shelled out for their brand-new dishwasher.

'Tony, it's Oscar.' Holding the phone out for him with one hand while the other forked omelette.

Brought up by a Thai mother who had taught her six children to observe the rules of social intercourse with the same scrupulous attention to detail she expected from them in personal hygiene, Tony wiped his sweaty wrists and palms with a towel before taking the phone and addressing his employer respectfully.

'Yes, Mr Cornelius.'

'Tony, I know it's your day off, but I have a job for you today.'

'That's fine, sir. Nothing I can't change.'

Cornelius assured him he would be well compensated. He instructed Tony to come to his office as soon as possible but to take the back stairs.

'I want you to be discreet,' he said, 'Oh, and dress well: slacks, collared shirt, good shoes, sunnies. And a hat.'

'I don't have a hat, Mr Cornelius.'

'A cap will be okay.'

'What do you think it is?' asked Marietta, munching her toast. Tony had showered and was dressing as instructed.

'I have no idea.'

Which was the truth. He really hadn't a clue.

'Well, it's good, right? "Well compensated"—that sounds promising.'

Tony hoped so. Prior to him, Marietta had been married to a convicted dope dealer, Rick Boski. For a time, Tony had been consumed with jealousy and rage, wrongly believing Boski to be threatening Marietta. That got settled and they were all on good terms now, but more than a few times Tony had found himself empathising with Boski, who had wound up doing prison time after falling asleep while minding a dope crop—one of three jobs he'd been working to keep Marietta in the manner to which she was accustomed.

She'd cut the omelette into dainty slices and was taking her time over the last.

'Because, Darling, we need the money, right?'

Marietta was the kind of woman with whom you were always going to need the money.

'I wonder why he wants you to dress like that. Sunglasses and hat. Sounds like you're going to a funeral.'

I hope not, thought Tony. Especially not my own.

'No,' laughed Cornelius when Tony asked if he was going to a funeral. 'It's a disguise.'

Tony wondered who he needed to be disguised from. Cornelius wasted no time telling him.

'I got a business associate staying up here in the spare room. I'm going to give him a large amount of cash, and I want to make sure he goes where he is supposed to with it.'

'Where is that?'

'The races.'

He told Tony that for reasons Tony didn't need to know, Cornelius and his associate were not to be seen together until the end of the race meet.

'Essentially, I just need you to make sure he doesn't do a runner. And if he does try—'

'I'm to make sure he doesn't succeed.'

'Correct, Tony. He should be taking a cab direct to the races. You make sure he does. And then when he gets there, you keep an eye on him. Here, you might need some cash.'

Cornelius peeled off four fifties.

'That should cover transport and lunch. That's not your wages; that's just petty cash. Don't worry about a receipt. Whatever you don't spend, you can keep.'

'Thank you, Mr Cornelius.' Tony getting even more excited now about the job.

Tony was told to make himself comfortable in the office, from which vantage he could spy on the room down the hall. Cornelius was heading home to get changed. Soon as Cornelius left, Tony pulled up a chair, opened the door a crack and spent fifty minutes with one eye glued on the guest room.

Piece of cake. Until the guest room door finally opened and he caught sight of the 'business associate' he'd be tailing.

Joe fucking Harris.

Tony and Harris had history, not the least of which was Tony mistaking Harris for Boski and giving him a fractured skull in an act of self-defence.

Harris, he knew to be a slimy double-crossing snake. Tony found himself in an invidious position. Perhaps he should tell Cornelius what he knew? Or—and here he channelled Marietta—perhaps not. What would happen if he warned Cornelius that Harris was not to be trusted?

Cornelius might want to know how Tony could be so sure, and Tony would be forced to reveal their shared history. And even if he didn't ask, or if Tony made up some story, Cornelius might break off his relationship with Harris, leaving Tony without whatever generous compensation might be on the cards.

Right now, Marietta was likely on the brand-new phone ordering top of the range cushions, blinds or towels. They would have to be paid for somehow.

No, best he said nothing. After all, he was wearing a disguise, so even if Harris caught a peek, he wasn't going to recognise him.

Harris took the stairs and Tony followed. Cornelius had said nothing about locking his office, so Tony just left it.

Harris reached the bar and walked out the front door of the hotel, down a block to a taxi rank where he took the first cab in line. Tony took the next one and told his driver to follow. Harris went straight to the racetrack, exiting the cab and following the punters through the main gates.

Tony paid off his driver and followed him in.

At this point his quarry's behaviour had become weird. He'd avoided crowds and taken himself to deserted parts of the course where he'd used binoculars to look around. With no binoculars himself, Tony had conspired to drift past Harris to see what he was spying on. It wasn't the racetrack, that was for sure: that was in the opposite direction. It appeared to be the part of the course where the horses were kept while waiting for their race. Drawing closer Tony got a pretty good idea what Harris had been spying on.

Oscar Cornelius and ... Zeen?

Zeen was Rick Boski's woman. Tony liked Zeen. She hated Harris. They used to run racecourse scams together, and he'd sold her out to a bad guy. What was she doing flirting with Cornelius? Zeen and Rick were strong. Something was going down, but what?

Tony tried calling Marietta for advice, but the call went unanswered. Oh, Saturday, her pedicure, right. Okay, so what would she tell him if he managed to get through to her?

'What are you being paid to do?' she'd ask.

'Watch Harris; make sure he doesn't skip.'

'Are you watching Harris or your boss?'

'Well, I'm trying to see what Harris—'

'None of your business. Keep it simple. Watch Harris.'

Right. Good advice. Tony turned on his heel and picked up Harris, who was heading for the toilets. Tony gave him a moment before he followed, but a real big guy cut in front of him. There was no sign of Harris at the urinals. He must have taken a stall. There was only one exit, so Tony left and set himself up in a position to watch his quarry exit too. When Harris still hadn't appeared after several minutes, Tony began to worry. It was possible that Harris was constipated, but his anxiety continued to build.

And then just when he was ready to go back in to check the stalls, Harris's head poked out like a chick's from an egg. Seemingly having assured himself the coast was clear, he'd then broken cover in a dash, making for a huge palm tree. Tony clocked Zeen heading that way, saw Harris briefly emerge and drag her in with him. Tony couldn't risk getting close enough to hear what was being said. In fact, at one point Zeen looked his way and he thought she might have recognised him. That forced him to retreat.

When Zeen reappeared, she didn't look like she needed anybody's help, striding out of there like she owned the place. Harris, on the other hand, seemed jumpy. Tony kept his distance from Harris, who wound up in the back of the stand looking through his binoculars again.

That's where Tony had been when his phone rang. Oscar.

'How's our friend?'

'He's at the course. Got a cab, came straight here.'

'So long as he stays there, all should be good.'

Cornelius rang off, leaving Tony feeling guilty. Should he warn him? How could he, though? Zeen was his friend. If she was involved with Harris again, she must have a good reason.

And then, right before the last race, he'd watched Harris slide down the stairs to the rear of the stand and meet up with Zeen again. Tony was a lot closer this time. He couldn't hear what they were saying, but it looked like she handed him a betting ticket. By now the horses in the last were taking to the track. Tony followed Harris to the members stand but couldn't go any further, as he was not a member. However, he witnessed Harris meet up with Cornelius at the top of the escalator. A moment later Cornelius rang again.

'Everything is good, Tony. I'll meet you at the bottom of the escalator after the race. You can drive me back.'

For the first time since he'd spied Zeen at the course, the pressure and anxiety Tony had felt, lowered. Everything was good.

Officially, Tongan George had fought fourteen heavyweight bouts, winning ten and losing four. But this was only a fraction of the paid fights he'd been in. Illegal fights in various pop-up locations were triple that. Then of course there were the ones that were not in a ring at all but came as part of the job. There had been quite a few of these over the last five years, since he'd started enforcing for Lionel, a job that from time-to-time required weapons other than his fists. In all his thirty-four years, however, he had never knocked a priest around. He didn't like hitting women either, knew what his mum would say if she ever found out. If a woman tried to attack him, he might give her a slap, not a hard one, more a tap, clear her head. Women usually attacked because they were defending their arsehole boyfriends or sons. Sometimes, a drug-fucked junkie might try it on. In George's opinion, that was okay to defend yourself with adequate force. But a priest?

'I don't like this,' telling Kieran as they'd lit up the highway in the hire car. The trainer had coughed up directions to the priest's house.

'Don't like what?' Kieran was driving. Like all these young blokes, couldn't wait to get behind the wheel of the Lexus.

'You know, bashing a priest.'

Kieran laughed. The guy was a psycho.

'I'd do it for free. They're all pedos.'

George didn't believe that for a second. Father Kevin who'd

taught him to play rugby back on the island, if you called him a pedo, he'd knock you flat.

'He doesn't even know if the priest was in on it,' said George by way of being rational.

'We'll soon find out,' laughed Kieran.

'Don't like it, man. You mess with a priest, bad things happen.'

'You think God's going to punish you?'

'I dunno about Him, but my mum will.'

She still expected him to go to mass whenever he went back home to the island.

'Mate, what we've done over the years, God's taking his time smacking our bums.' Kieran laughing, disrespecting God. George wasn't sure exactly where he sat on the whole God thing, but if you couldn't be sure whether God was or wasn't, why poke the bear?

'Click on the radio,' said Kieran. 'Find the racing station.'

The need for caution had evaporated: the race would be over before Missouri or any of his goons spotted him, and by then Pendle would be the one owing him money. Joe Harris was more than happy to rendezvous with his new bestie, Oscar. As he was approaching the glass doors, where an escalator would deliver him to the eyrie with a sweeping view of the track, a big Islander barrelled past, knocking him into a pirouette.

'Sorry, Bro,' boomed the bloke as he charged away, followed by a young white guy in a dark shirt with a narrow white tie.

He presumed they were hustling for a last-second bet. Probably on Hysterical. Good luck with that. By now Pendle would have it below double-figures. The other bookies, pure sheep, would follow.

Cornelius met him at the top of the stairs. He was on a phone call but ended it to guide Joe to a table by the window offering an eagle-eye view along with a handy TV screen just to make sure they missed nothing.

'We got twelves,' said Joe.

'What was the look on Pendle's face?'

'Terrified. I was watching through the glasses. I had an associate place the bet. Just to be on the safe side. Don't worry, I'm paying them out of my end.'

Naturally, he wouldn't be paying Zeen anything, but Cornelius didn't know that. Joe handed the ticket over. Cornelius glanced at it and slipped it into the handkerchief pocket of his coat. On the TV screen, the prices of the runners flashed up. Joe's neck jerked.

Hysterical was still eleven to one in the ring. Pendle had seemed shocked when Zeen laid that bet on him, but he hadn't shortened his odds by much. You had to hand it to him, the guy had steel balls. Or maybe the TV feed was a few minutes late.

'I haven't had a chance to tell you the best part yet,' said Corny. Joe was playing with that as a nickname for Oscar. He wasn't prepared to bring it out in the open just yet, Oscar might take it the wrong way, but for now that's how he was going to think of him.

'What's that?' Joe found himself grinning the way you do in anticipation when your mate is going to lay some intel on you. You want the best for them, you really do.

'Well, I was looking at the horse and got chatting to this babe.'

'Hot?'

'Scorching. Heaven on a stick. I'm glad Lucy was busy today with a baby-shower. Anyway, this vision—her opening line is she won't let me buy her dinner ...'

Corny looking his way grinning, Harris matching it. Yeah, a pretty good opening.

'... says she knows horses, tells me Hysterical can't win.' Oscar leaning in, winking, whispering, 'Which is probably true. 'Course she doesn't know it's not Hysterical.'

Sitting back cocksure, sipping his champers.

'I told her she was wrong. And she said, get this, she had ten grand to say she was right. And if I won, she'd make me dinner ... at her flat if I wanted.' Big white teeth grin. 'So, I'm looking at another ten thou, *plus* a hot date.'

There were only a couple of horses out of the barrier, but Joe had stopped registering any of that. A faint discomfort, first declaring itself in his upper digestive tract seemed to be expanding, growing into a hard knot.

'This woman, she have a name?'

'Sarah.'

'How old?'

'Early to mid-thirties.'

The last runner went into the barrier.

'What was she wearing?'

'Very sexy, silky, chiffon dress. A big hat.'

As the barrier light began to flicker, so did Joe's brain. Pendle might have big balls, but surely, when he stood to lose nearly a quarter of a mill, he would cut the price by more than one point. And Zeen had been wearing a big hat. A big hat that could block Joe's vision of exactly how much cash she'd handed over.

Harris's eyes travelled to the ticket sitting in the top pocket of Oscar's jacket. He zoomed in hard. Was the 'K' on the *240 K* the same scrawl as the rest?

'This bet you had with her was cash?'

'Yeah, ten grand each.'

What woman in a sexy dress carries ten grand in cash with her to the races? Joe's experience: none. They let their boyfriends or husbands put the money on for them. Except for Zeen, of course.

'Who's holding the money?' asked Joe, as nonchalantly as he could, though his skin was practically flaking off at the effort of holding in his scream.

'The course photographer.'

'And they're away,' yelled the race caller.

In a fourteen-hundred-metre race like this one, you didn't want to get too far back. Lionel had seen videos of Double Volley winning in Singapore from midfield, but with only a thousand metres left to run she was in the last third of the field. By the turn, a sick feeling was swelling in Lionel's stomach. She had not advanced despite the jockey's urging. Momentary hope sprang in his bosom when she ranged past a couple of plodders, but the leading pair had broken away, and she quickly died on her run to finish well back.

For a long moment it was plaster-of-Paris Lionel, seemingly stone but hollowed out. It had not occurred to him till then that the setback of not getting his odds was but an entrée to a complete rout. And there was no succour in having lost less than he might have but for some parasite getting in first on his scam. Months of prep, the logistics, all down the drain. These horses were hacks. Double Volley was two classes above them and had been trialling the house down. What the fuck had gone wrong?

The locus of all failings in his enterprise was Enzo Rapanaro, who was about to discover what happened when you fucked over Vinyl Lionel Howard. George and Kieran had been sent to deal with the priest, but this didn't discourage Lionel, nor that his pistol had gone with them. No, this was something Lionel could handle himself.

He was still waiting on a call from Arnold to tell him who'd knocked off his odds. Whoever that turned out to be was going to pay double.

Over Lionel's extensive career he had developed an animal instinct when it came to near and present threat. Right then, as he strode towards the dismount area, ready to throttle

Rapanaro, that sixth sense kicked in. He stopped in his tracks, then cautiously circled the area without drawing too close. He homed in on a woman in the dismount ring, going apeshit. Her head was bandaged in just the same way as the flute player in that famous picture of the three American War of Independence soldiers where the other two are playing drums. Now, to Lionel that was an omen not to be ignored, because that picture had been on a plate that he and Sharon, the real estate woman he'd dated, had purchased together in a souvenir shop in Boston. One of those trips you do when you think things are pointing to a long-term relationship. The relationship had been very short-term, ending with that overpriced plate smashing against his Broadbeach wall after Sharon aimed for him and missed.

The stewards were gathered around a petrified Rapanaro, checking papers and taking photos of Double Volley. Fighting the urge to flee, Lionel edged closer.

The bandaged woman was shouting, 'This horse is not Hysterical!'

'No, but *you* are, love,' called some wag from the crowd.

Despite looking like he was teetering on the edge of a tall building, Rapanaro managed to stammer, 'I don't know what you mean.'

'What I *mean*,' said bandage woman—who was obviously some kind of cop—'is that this horse is a ring-in.'

Lionel had heard enough. One moment he was there, the next there was simply foul air.

It had been a long and painful day for Liz, but now she was drawing solace from the promise of inflicting such discomfort on others. Starting with Rapanaro here.

'The game is up, Enzo. I drove out to your place. I saw the second horse, this one. What is it, a twin? Or have you painted it?'

She wet her thumb with spit, rubbed the horse's blaze. The horse pulled back. Okay, maybe it was a good paint job, or maybe it was real, didn't matter.

'That the scam didn't work is irrelevant, Enzo. You're still looking at jail time and a life ban. Unless you talk to me right now.'

Rapanaro was throwing glances at the stewards, who muttered among themselves, apparently mystified. Liz didn't know why those clowns couldn't just announce right now that this was not Hysterical.

'I'm not saying anything without a lawyer,' Rapanaro said.

She wagged a finger in his face.

'I've been assaulted, drugged and beaten up to prevent me revealing the truth about this. You need to start talking.'

'Er, Inspector?'

It was the chief steward beckoning her. She threw daggers at Rapanaro and joined the steward, who continued to back away from the crowd that was being swelled by arriving Media. A racing journo was yelling at the cameraman, there to cover the weigh-in, to get in closer.

Fighting frustration that had been exacerbated by the steward's untimely interruption, Liz said calmly, 'Yes, Walter?'

'I'm sorry, but this is Hysterical.'

God save her from these fools.

'No, it is not.'

'Every mark is identical. It's not painted.' Then, in maybe what was supposed to demonstrate some kind of sympathy, he continued, 'Perhaps with the blow you took ...?'

Walter's attempt to appear empathetic only irritated her more.

'I only took a blow because some arsehole drugged me and tied me up and I hit my head on a drawer. They wanted to stop me getting here. I saw both horses out at Rapanaro's property Thursday morning.'

Uh-oh. Maybe she shouldn't have revealed that just yet. Walter stroked his chin.

'You had evidence there was a ring-in but didn't tell anyone?'

'I couldn't.'

Now Walter was offended.

'You didn't trust us?'

'Sorry, no. In my judgement the fewer people who knew, the better.'

Walter was shaking his head. If there had been a handy stake with a bundle of faggots at its base, he might have tied her to it and set her on fire.

'Did you notify anybody else in Liquor and Gaming?'

That was a good one.

'I trust them less than I trust you guys.'

The cameras were getting close.

'I think we need to take this indoors.' Walter's eyes painting the shark pack of journos.

Rapanaro called over. 'Can I go get my horse settled now?'

This time Liz Atwood withheld the scream she so desperately desired to unleash. The DNA would nail him.

25

Rick and Zeen had watched the race together. He should have been jumping up and down with joy when he saw Hysterical beaten, but instead he stood there like a robot who'd run out of juice. He felt Zeen's breath in his ear.

'It's okay, Boski. We won.'

And when he looked into her eyes, he did get a little jolt but it wasn't enough to kick-start him.

'I know,' he said. 'So long as Rapanaro doesn't blab, Atwood won't have a case, but ...'

'But what?'

He felt awful admitting this. 'Part of me wishes Hysterical had won. That money could have been put to good use, and Paul's in the hole now with the parish funds.'

'Not any more he's not.'

Zeen shoved a wad of cash into his hand.

'That's ten grand. Enough for Paul to repay the parish with a little extra on top.'

Rick's mind was spinning.

'You backed the winner?'

'Too hard. Anything might have won. Oscar Cornelius gave Harris twenty grand to put on Hysterical. I convinced Harris I should place the bet with Pendle in return for a commission if Hysterical won. But of course, it was never likely to win, seeing as it was the real Hysterical, and Harris was never going to pay me if it did. So, I made alternative plans.'

Rick could tell she was having fun, holding something back. He asked what happened to the other ten grand.

'That I used as my stake to bet with Oscar Cornelius that Hysterical wouldn't win.'

'You used his own money in a bet with him?'

Rick felt a smile settling on his face like a sunbather at a beach.

'Yes, I did. And we just won, so I'm about to collect another twenty grand.'

He shook his head. 'You never cease to amaze me.'

'I told you to trust me.'

He always would. He asked what they were going to do with the additional twenty she was about to pick up.

'We could keep it, reduce our overdraft, but you won't want to do that.'

That was true.

'Or ...' she said, '... we could donate it to Paul for his parish. Let me get the money first, then we'll worry about what we do with it.'

'I'll come with you.'

'No, you won't. I don't want you causing a scene if Cornelius is there.'

Rick was about to dispute he would ever do that, but then his phone rang. It was Sandy. By the time he looked up, Zeen had gone.

Sandy sounded excited. 'I just listened to the race on the radio. We did it.'

For the first time in days, Rick felt he wasn't holding his breath.

'Yes,' he said, 'We fucking did!' Embarrassing himself he'd said that loud enough for passersby to look over. 'No problems with the horse?'

'Under control. I'll be back at Rapanaro's soon. I'll drop the horse off and see you back at the café.'

Rick almost couldn't believe everything had gone so well to plan. Zeen—what a woman. They were all safe from Atwood and thanks to Zeen, Paul would be able to repay the parish. Plus, twenty grand on top that. It would be fun working out the best use for that little windfall.

It had been a wonderful day.

'Lionel's not going to be happy.' Kieran shaking his head. George and he had just listened to the race on the car radio.

'Thing was never in it,' said George. 'Maybe he'll tell us not to bother roughing up the priest? I mean it didn't win anyway.' Hoping at least.

'You know the boss. That won't mean shit. If somebody tried to fuck him over, even if they didn't succeed, he'll want his pound of flesh.'

The phone rang. Lionel's number.

'Fuck me! You think he's got this car bugged?' George wasn't joking. He'd seen plenty of TV shows where that happened. Perhaps because Kieran considered it a credible possibility, he kept his mouth shut. George picked up.

'Yes, boss?'

Lionel's voice crackled over the phone.

'Listen, the cops are all over this. Somebody talked, obviously. They've still got Rapanaro, so we need to shift the horse.'

'What do you mean?'

'I mean, George, that we don't want the cops finding the real Hysterical, do we?'

George could see the problem.

'So, we forget the priest and go for the horse?' George was relieved.

'Who said anything about forgetting the priest? He's probably the one who talked. There's two of you. One for the priest, one for the horse.'

George was disappointed but not surprised. Like Kieran said, the boss hated being screwed over.

'I don't know anything about horses.'

'Then you do the priest. Kieran takes the horse.'

George looked across at Kieran.

'You know anything about horses?'

Kieran shook his head. Shit. More complications by the second.

'How we gonna move the horse? It's not gonna fit in here.'

'Find a horse float, steal one. Rapanaro's likely got a spare one. How far out are you?'

'Ten minutes from the priest.'

'Whoever's going for the horse, drop the other one, then get to Rapanaro's quick.' He rattled off the trainer's address and George tried punching it into the GPS. With his oversize thumb and fingers, it took forever.

Lionel said, 'I have to go.' And rang off.

George relayed their instructions.

'Bags the priest,' said Kieran.

That was fine by George. Except he had no idea about how to wrangle a horse. He supposed it couldn't be that hard. They gave you any shit you socked them on the jaw.

Now he knew. It was the cloven-hoofed one who had lured him to destruction, playing on the sin of pride. Paul slumped further into his armchair. He was ashamed to admit that, to the last, he'd been willing Hysterical to win. Not a chance. The best laid plans of mice and men ... hadn't that been exactly what he had warned Enzo about on that fateful day? Should have listened to his own advice.

A half-hour had passed since the race. He'd risen only to turn off the radio, grab the whisky bottle—a Liquorland bottom-shelf variety—before resuming his position. It mattered not that his ultimate intention had been good. The process by which he had attempted to achieve it was corrupt, he saw that now. A man who robbed a bank to give to the poor could confuse you, make you think he was a good person. But 'Thou

Shalt Not Steal' was a fundamental moral instruction.

Instead of robbing a bank, the fella could have worked a second job, donated all his wages. Paul had wanted the glamour and wanted to get it the easy way.

His doorbell rang.

Not now, please. He remained seated, willing the visitor to go away, just as he'd sat there listening to the race willing Hysterical to win. The bell rang again. He hoped this wasn't going to be a callout to a dying parishioner in need of last rites. He'd feel like an imposter, a fake priest, an empty vessel. He took a big slug of the cheap whisky and rose, not as steadily as he might have done half-an-hour earlier.

On opening the door, he was greeted by the sight of a youngish man, quite tall, slim, dark shirt, white tie, slacks. The outfit appeared out of place on him. Paul scotched the idea of last rites, surmised the fellow was a tradie who was looking to set a wedding date and had been told by his bride and mother to dress up before visiting the priest.

'Father Monaghan?'

'Yes.'

He opened the fly screen to be polite. It was growing dark quickly now; light had faded in step with hope

'There's no one else here, is there?'

And odd request, but perhaps not if the young man needed to confess.

'No, just me.'

The young man took a step towards him.

Paul's stomach roared in pain, and he staggered back, struggling for breath. The young man quietly followed him, closed the door and then punched him again. This time a left to the ribs. Paul went down on one knee, the just-consumed whisky rising back up in his throat, making it even harder to breathe.

'We need to talk about a horse.'

Paul heard air scrape into his lungs. Light-headed as he was, he understood. Shame was not to be his only punishment.

There was no horse float sitting in any of the paddocks, nor up the driveway of the trainer's house where Tongan George parked. And then he thought to himself, 'Wait on, does this car even have a towbar?'

He got out and checked. No towbar.

'Stuff this shit,' he muttered. There was an old station wagon along the gravel driveway by the side of the house. George hoped that meant somebody was home. They might know where there was a float, and something about loading horses.

'Hello?' he called out. Nobody appeared. He started having a look around. Fifty or so metres from the house was a big rectangular structure, a barn or maybe a stable. It looked big enough to have a horse float or truck in it. He walked to the door.

'Hello?'

Gloomy, but down the far end, beyond a row of empty stalls, he could see a horse. As he got closer, he saw it must be the horse he was supposed to take, because it looked just like the one at the races.

'Okay, horsey, you need to come with me.'

The horse was quiet, watching him warily through huge eyes as George unlatched the gate.

'Come on, we have to get you out of here.'

What George was thinking was he should at least get the horse to a paddock, maybe then he could get it out to a neighbouring property, so if the cops came looking, they wouldn't find it.

But first he had to get the horse out, and she didn't want to move.

'Hey, come on, you don't want to be stuck in here.'

Apparently, though, she did.

'We can do this the easy way or the hard way.'

The horse clearly preferred the hard way. Okay. She'd asked

for it. George had seen cowboy movies. You gave a horse a slap on the arse, and it ran off. He pushed his giant frame into the stall. He was wondering how Kieran was going with the priest. He hoped the priest had choir or something so Kieran couldn't get to him.

George brought his big hand back and slapped the horse on its shiny rump. Trouble was, nobody had told George you shouldn't be behind the horse when you did it.

Tongan George had dished out a lot of punches in the ring and had taken more than a few too. But he had never been on the wrong end of the kick of an angry horse.

The horse drove its hind leg backward with enormous power, catching George flush on the temple—right where Sammy 'The Stingray' Mahoud had landed a big blow six years earlier. George's brain pinballed around his head, leaving him brain-dead in an instant. His body hit the floor of the stall with a thud, and blood began trickling out of his ears and nose a moment later. And then the horse decided she would move after all.

26

Twenty thousand in cash, when it's in rolls of hundred-dollar bills, is lighter than a can of deodorant, Zeen was thinking as she dropped the money into her handbag. She had been relieved to see there was no sign of Cornelius when she'd arrived to collect from the photographer, who was mystified at his normally vacant turf beyond the winning post being besieged with media types. Not that Zeen couldn't have handled Cornelius, just that it would have been tedious.

Presuming that, if Cornelius were to pursue a rendezvous, he would be coming from the direction of the grandstand, she took the other direction, leaving the throng of journos, stewards and stickybeaks in her wake. She headed around the corner of the building, where an outdoor bar had now closed, leaving nothing but a padlocked rollerblind. Feeling good with herself, disaster averted, a priest saved. Maybe takeaway Thai for dinner. From the track, Atwood's voice carried shrill as a drill. All and sundry were being threatened with something. Well, not Zeen's problem.

An arm seemed to emerge from the brick wall, seizing Zeen in a tight grip while ripping her handbag from her shoulder.

'I'll take that, thank you, Zeen.'

She wriggled, stamped her heel into Harris's foot; yet though he grunted in pain, his hold did not slacken. Retaining his grip on her, he popped open her bag and confirmed the rolls of notes.

'A snake doesn't change her spots,' he hissed, which was the kind of irony Zeen couldn't fully appreciate right then. She managed to bite his hand.

'Shit!'

This time he let go, but it did her no good, as he kept the money well out of reach of her snatching hand.

'I knew you couldn't be trusted.' Harris was wringing the hand she had bitten.

'I knew *you* couldn't be trusted.' Angry with herself for not having Boski on her arse as backup. She'd dropped her guard prematurely. Joe Harris was always a mine waiting to detonate. 'You were never going to pay me my share.'

'That's moot, Zeen, because you made sure the horse was never going to win. You pay off the jockey?'

'For twenty grand? I was going to offer that money to you anyway, you arsehole.'

'Sure you were.'

This was not a lie. She'd considered the alternatives and made up her mind while en route to collect the winnings.

'Pendle's after you. You need Cornelius in your corner. And thanks to you, so do Rick and me. You can hand Cornelius back his stake, play the hero—tell him how with our help you learned the cops were onto the scam and it had been called off.'

'Oscar's going to think I ripped him off. This gets me out of the country.'

'You'll never be able to set foot back here, which I admit is something your plan has going for it. Or, you could make Oscar's day, give him back his stake. Buy us both a useful friend in times of trouble.'

'He'll ask why I didn't tell him before the race.'

'And you'll say you were protecting him: what he didn't know couldn't be used against him. Tell him there'll be other scores.'

'Nice try, but I think I'll take my chances in Bangkok.'

Harris swung around the corner of the building, out of sight, and then almost immediately marched backwards into view again—a pistol pointed at his heart by a big nasty-looking guy.

'We've been looking everywhere for you, Joe.'

'I was just on my way to see your boss.'

Harris with a full-denture smile as genuine as market-stall Versace.

Pendle's enforcer obviously, the one they called Misery she

was thinking. Zeen started to edge away. The lump noticed, seemed uncertain whether to allow it.

Probably would've too, except Harris intervened.

'That's Boski's bit. I was going to pay you guys back every cent. But she double-crossed me.'

Zeen said, 'He's full of shit. I'm outta here.'

'Not yet you're not,' the big guy said.

It wasn't like Pendle had lost big, but Drew could tell he was pissed-off. Like they always did when the race meeting was over, they'd gone to the soft-drink dispenser machine at the bottom of the stand. Pendle liked Coke but refused to pay the racetrack markup, so he would bring two cans in a little cooler bag to consume during the meeting and then they would stop here for a beverage before heading to the car park.

Drew popped his can, heard the fizz that signifies freshness.

Trying to sound upbeat he said, 'We won on the book. All those small bets on Hysterical.'

Pendle offered goanna eyes.

'Please. We lost fifty with the SPs.'

Before Pendle had capped the payout on Hysterical, they'd taken thirteen grand off Cornelius and the miner alone. They doubled that on the race from other losing punters. So Pendle was looking at a twenty-five-grand deficit between what he'd outlaid with the SPs and what he'd won off other losers. To many people that was a lot of money, but Pendle lost twice that amount regularly. Then won it all back plus some.

'I hate being played.' Pendle finished his can and crushed it.

'You reckon we were played?'

'I do. I wouldn't be surprised if Harris and these ex-con mates of his were in cahoots with the SPs. They drop the lure that the race is fixed, but it's smoke and mirrors. I load up on a horse that's never going to win. They probably split with the SPs, pick up twenty, twenty-five of my fifty for the trouble.'

'I heard Atwood yelling it was a ring-in.'

'So they fooled her, too. You saw that horse running, that had to be Hysterical.'

Pendle's phone buzzed. He answered right away.

'Yes.'

Drew could make out the unmistakable boom of Missouri's voice but couldn't hear what he was saying. Whatever it was, though, seemed to cheer Pendle.

'Good. Take them to the warehouse and we'll deal with them there.'

He ended the call more buoyant.

'We have Harris, finally.' He handed Drew the bag containing the day's take. 'Put this in the safe and I'll see you in the office Monday.'

Bloody George wasn't answering his phone. Lionel's b.p. was through the roof. He tried Kieran but he wasn't answering either. Rapanaro had been allowed to load his horses, but with Lionel needing to keep his distance from the trainer, he didn't know what had gone down between the trainer, the cops and the stewards. Lionel gave Rapanaro time to get into the car park, then called him.

'What the fuck is going on?'

'Wait a second.' Rapanaro's voice was low. 'Let me get in my truck.'

The sound of a door opening and closing was followed by rustling. Rapanaro's husky voice came back on the line.

'You tell me. The cop knew.'

'The crazy one with her head bandaged?'

'Yeah, Atwood. She was certain it was a swap. And she kept

going on about how somebody drugged her and tried to stop her getting to the track.'

This was crazy shit.

'Are you serious?'

'It wasn't you?'

'Of course it fucking wasn't me.' Lionel wondered how he'd stumbled on this moron. 'What have you told them?'

'Nothing.'

'If you've mentioned me—'

'I haven't. But listen—'

'Have they charged you?'

'No. They've headed out to my property to check for Hysterical, but—'

'We're one step ahead. I already sent my guys to remove the evidence.'

'This is what I'm trying to tell you. Here's the really weird thing ...'

Big Lionel teetered, curiosity drawing him to the edge.

'... I'm certain that was Hysterical that ran, not Double Volley. They rechecked the papers right in front of me and they couldn't find even the smallest discrepancy. And the DNA will show there was no swap.'

Rapanaro was digging his own grave with every word.

'What bullshit are you trying on?'

'Not bullshit. I'm telling you the horses are pretty much identical, but there're the tiniest differences. Hysterical has narrower fetlocks, but it's more the personality. Hysterical is laid back. Double Volley is on a trigger. The way she walked up into the float just now, it's Hysterical, I'm sure.'

Lionel's fists clenched and unclenched, willing a victim to stray within their reach.

'Are you saying you loaded the wrong fucking horse? Are you that fucking incompetent, or were you in on this?'

'I'm as surprised as you are.'

He'd be more surprised when Lionel stuck a gun in his face.

Which reminded Lionel, he needed to get hold of one.

'Are you saying somebody swapped the horses? Your stable guy?'

'I loaded Double Volley myself, this morning. She hates the float. But Hysterical ran that race. All I can think of, and this sounds crazy I know, is somebody swapped the horses here at the track.'

This guy was lying through teeth that would not be in place much longer.

'Somebody went to your property, grabbed Hysterical, brought it here, and without anybody noticing, including you, swapped the horses over before the race. That's what you're saying.'

'Yeah. Half the time the stalls are deserted. It's possible someone could do it.'

'And you didn't notice the dainty fetlocks?'

'I wasn't looking at them. I had another runner the race before.'

If you're going to tell a lie, tell a big one. Obviously, a theory this guy subscribed to.

'The good thing is,' the trainer was saying, 'that there's no crime, no malpractice. Atwood is wasting her time.'

'You think me dropping two hundred grand to set this up is a good thing?'

'Of course not.' The trainer sensibly cautious. 'But they can't pin anything on us.'

'And you swear you weren't responsible?'

'What do I get out of it?'

Which was the question, wasn't it? The horse that ran being Hysterical would explain a lot. Logically, if the trainer was involved, he had to have an angle to score big on the race. If Rapanaro wasn't involved, who had been?

'The cop kept asking me if I was involved with a Joe Harris, or Rick Boski.'

'Who the fuck are they?'

'No idea. I don't know either of them, but the cop seemed to think they were involved.'

Lionel cooling his rage enough to process. The cop figured this Harris and Boski had something to do with the plan. *His* fucking plan! If, and it was a very decrepit, dubious 'if', the trainer was right about Hysterical being swapped back in right before the race, then these two were the logical suspects.

By the time George and Kieran had finished with Rapanaro, Lionel would know whether the trainer had any part in it. Maybe it was the priest? Maybe the do-gooder priest was the one had fucked him over? Kieran or George would soon establish the extent of the priest's involvement. Then they would be free to move on to the trainer if required.

'Okay, listen. Go back to your property and act normal. I don't know where Double Volley might be, I left that up to my guy. We'll have a further chat on this.'

'I swear I didn't do anything to mess this up ... except go to confession.'

'The priest is the only one you talked to?'

'That's right.'

Lionel ended the call. He was still wondering about Arnold. Could he have engineered some coup with the help of these Harris and Boski guys?

His phone buzzed. Speak of the devil.

'Mr Howard.'

'Yes, Arnold.'

'I know you said to leave the SPs for now, but I have a contact with Bocaire.'

A middling SP bookie on the Gold Coast.

'He traced one of the accounts that the bet on Hysterical came from. Dominic Pendle. He's the biggest bookie in Perth.'

Having dropped off the horse at Rapanaro's, Sandy was musing on how at such a late stage of his life a man could suddenly see how it might have turned out so different with just a simple twist of fate. Loading Hysterical up the first time, Rick and he hadn't a clue about what to do. It was just instinct led Sandy to offer that apple.

This new horse, when Sandy tried to get him up into the float, didn't want a bar of it. Sandy had been in prison: he understood. The horse float was small and probably uncomfortable, like a cell. That could make you scared even if you never wanted to admit it.

Rather than get angry with the animal, Sandy had recalled the way Father Paul was always able to calm him, never raised his voice, never threatened. The priest hadn't been locked up at night, but he was no less a prisoner than the rest of them. He wasn't allowed a woman, had to go where his bishop told him. And these days a lot of people treated priests like crims. Yeah. Father Paul's dog collar was just a different kind of jumpsuit.

Now he thought about it, Sandy had probably spent more time with the priest over the years than anybody else. They'd played cards, talked about all kinds of things, deep and trivial. Even laughed about how they were prisoners of different systems. They were friends, was the thing. That's the approach he'd taken with the horse too.

'Hey, listen, Missy,' Sandy had said, back in the car park at the track, 'I'm your friend. You want to get home, right? Me too.'

He'd sweet-talked her for a good while, and then he'd risked stroking her and she'd let him. She'd liked it and so had he, and then when he said, 'Come on, let's get out of here,' she had trotted up the ramp no problems.

Same when he let her out and led her to her stall in the barn back there at Rapanaro's. He hadn't wanted to leave her, had walked back for one last rub of her long snout, feeling that living animal under his rough old palm, lingering, not running away.

How different life might have been for him, he'd thought sadly, if he'd discovered horses all those years ago, instead of cars and drugs.

It would be wrong to say he had been melancholy driving off, but there was a definite regret, a sense of opportunity squandered. The doctors had told him he had a year, maybe two, left, but how much of that would be standing on his feet? There was no point getting sad now—this was as good as it was going to get—but that didn't mean you couldn't reflect on what might have been. The good thing was, he had his best mate just ten minutes down the road.

He would call in on Paul.

Paul's stomach hurt like hell. He was in his loungeroom on his knees, his attacker standing over him, fists clenched.

'Rapanaro told you about a certain horse running today. Did you tell anybody?'

Given the circumstances, Paul felt a lie permissible.

'My oath prevents me from revealing what is told in the confessional.'

Strictly speaking, Rapanaro's talk about the horse could be seen as outside the actual confession, which was why he'd felt able to converse with Rick.

Satan's hound squatted in front of Paul, a sly smile spreading.

'Bet you've had a few young lads kneeling in front of your open fly, haven't you?'

Paul said nothing. Waves of pain continued to crash over him.

'You don't bet on the ponies, then?'

Paul shook his head, managed a hoarse, 'No.'

His tormentor stood, clicked on the kettle. Paul struggled to get to his feet. The thug strode around his servery.

'Radio, huh? I wonder what you were listening to, Barnesy?'

He clicked on the transistor. The racing station announcer was giving odds on a harness event. The lout feigned surprise.

'Isn't that weird? You don't follow the ponies. And looky here ...'

Oh shit. He had found the morning paper.

'If it isn't the racing pages. With a big red star alongside race seven.'

With the aid of furniture, Paul had regained his feet.

His assailant said, 'I reckon you're one big bullshit artist.'

The water was noisily approaching boiling point, the kettle rocking a bit, full.

Then the lout said, 'You know a fella named Joe Harris?'

To this he could honestly reply, 'No.'

'What about a bloke called Boski?'

His eyes probably gave him away.

'No.'

This time, the fist smashed into his nose. Blood poured.

'Total bullshit artist. Where is Boski?'

Paul had dragged Rick into this. Others must not pay for his error.

'Told you, I don't know—'

Another fist to the stomach, doubling him as ... *whack*! He was hit in the side of the head. Found himself on his back on the floor, where, despite his swirling vision, he clocked a large spider web above his bookcase.

'Talk, Father. Or I'm going to give you a special treat.'

The voice was moving away, towards the kitchen bench. Paul fought to stay conscious, then wished he hadn't. The thug stood directly above him now, holding the steaming kettle.

'We call this—hot waterboarding. Boski?'

As he spoke the man tilted the kettle. Boiling water splashed onto Paul's crotch. The trousers he was wearing offered no protection. Paul yelped.

'The rest of it will go on your pretty face. One. Two...'

Sorry, Rick.

Sandy parked the car and horse float beside the rectory. From the car park it was quicker to go through the side gate into the backyard. He was thinking that he should have stopped at a bottle shop, bought a couple of beers for Monaghan, but he reconsidered. Father Paul was battling the drink and didn't need Sandy making things harder. But maybe he could have bought a packet of Twisties or some biscuits or something.

He walked across the flat patch of lawn at the back of the house. He could see the priest's car in the driveway on the other side, so he was almost certainly home. The door that led into the laundry was open, and when Sandy stepped in, he could hear voices. He was on the verge of turning back, not wanting to interrupt a private meeting, when he heard a voice say, 'Talk, Father. Or I'm going to give you a special treat.'

And the way it was said, the tone, took him instantly back to prison. Sandy reacted immediately and was almost out of the laundry when he held up and looked back for anything that might be a useful weapon. Cup of Omo sitting on top of the washing machine ...

Sandy walked down the hall and turned into the loungeroom. A guy, twenty-five at a guess, holding an electric kettle, steam curling from the spout like he was planning to pour it down an ants' nest. Only there was no ants' nest, just Paul lying on the ground, his face cut like he'd taken a hard fist.

Sandy put the cup of powder down quietly on the kitchen servery. 'Am I interrupting something?' Not asking it for an answer.

The other guy turned, surprised, then angry, readying to swing the kettle. Sandy was ahead of him, moving around so there was nothing between him and this punk.

'You Boski?'

So, this was to do with the horse.

'Me? No.' Sandy drawing a little closer. 'This man's a priest, you know that?'

'Shut the fuck up.' Still ready with that kettle. 'Who are you?'

'I'm the gardener. Who are you?'

The guy transferring the kettle to his left hand, reaching into his coat pocket and pulling out a pistol.

'None of your fucking business is who I am.'

For some reason Sandy wasn't as shocked at finding a gun pointing at him as he assumed he would be. Even when he'd been a bad bastard, that hadn't happened. He'd been on the other end a couple of times, the one holding the weapon. Maybe it was knowing you had not much longer to live anyway? Maybe that sucked the impact of it all. Whatever, he felt calm.

'Hey, take it easy man. You want money?' slowly easing his wallet from his back pocket, opening it. Tucked in with his other cards, his blank plastic card, its bottom edge honed sharp enough to slice ham. Sandy getting his fingers around it.

'I have nearly two hundred dollars in here. It's yours.'

The intruder, greedy fuck, salivating at his unexpected score.

'Here.' With the card between his index finger and thumb, Sandy reached towards the guy, the wallet the bait. Soon as the guy's weight shifted and the muzzle of the pistol wavered, Sandy dropped the wallet.

The guy's eyes flicked to the falling leather rectangle. Sandy in one motion, like a shortstop, scooping the cup of soap powder with his left hand, pitching it into the intruder's face. The guy swinging blindly with the kettle, squeezing off a shot at the same time.

The bullet going wide. With his right hand, Sandy like he was scything wheat, arcing the card across the man's neck, the guy dropping the kettle, trying to reacquire Sandy with the gun even as a red line bloomed across his throat, a cowboy's neckerchief.

Sandy feeling a bullet hit somewhere under his arm, his feet losing traction. He was falling, his ears ringing, but his eyes didn't leave the face of his foe. Not the first time Sandy had seen fear of imminent death in a man's eyes. What had been a thin line of blood around the shooter's throat already a red scarf. The guy only now realising that was his life spilling out of him, dropping the gun, grabbing his throat with both hands, strangling himself, blood gushing between his fingers like beetroot juice from a fat burger. There was nothing Sandy could do for him. His own world was turning grey fast.

28

Zeen should have been back by now. Rick hadn't been too worried at first. The photographer was likely busy on course, maybe taking shots of the ruckus down there. Or Cornelius might have turned up, trying to crack onto Zeen. Rick had thought Zeen capable of handling that, but it had been well over fifteen minutes now, the crowd was thinning, and there was still no sign of her. After Rick tried her phone twice and received no answer, he decided he would head down to the track regardless of any potential bollocking from her.

He arrived to find the horses, cops and stewards all gone. Only a few media types remained packing up. Rick caught sight of a small marquee with a sign that read *Photographs*, a tall guy with glasses and a beard about to go.

'You the photographer by any chance?'

He was. Rick asked if a woman had come to collect a bet.

'Yeah, right after the race. Quarter of an hour ago, maybe.'

'Was she by herself?'

As far as he saw she was. Rick asked about the guy who lost the bet.

'He came by about five minutes after.'

'Was he pissed-off?'

'More distracted. He just asked if the woman had been by yet.'

Rick had no idea what to make of that, but he didn't like it. Not one little bit.

Oscar had kept watching the race through binoculars right to the end. He'd provided a running commentary on the race's progress to Harris all through, or at least he thought he had. 'Where is Hysterical?', 'She's back a bit', 'Too late'. That kind of thing.

When he lowered the binoculars at the end of that miserable run and turned to where Harris had been, the guy was nowhere to be seen.

There was not a skerrick of doubt in Oscar's brain that he'd been played. Harris was almost certainly in league with Pendle. Oh, he'd been clever, warning Oscar not to bet extra money pre-race with the bookmaker, knowing that would spur Oscar on. The twenty-grand bet with Pendle had barely changed the odds, like the bookie already knew he was risking nothing.

Then Oscar dropping another ten to the delectable Sarah.

He pulled himself up right there.

Was she even legit? Maybe she was in on it too?

Oscar started moving then, fast. He shoved past a couple of oldies, forcing his way down the escalator like a bowling ball scattering pins. His new driver, Tony, was faithfully waiting at the foot of the escalator as he had been instructed.

'I've been set up,' he muttered. 'That guy's name is Joe Harris. Call me if you find him. Try the exits!'

Maybe Harris had slipped out as soon as the race had started, got a decent head start. On the other hand, if Harris was in it with Sarah, all Oscar had to do was find her, and he knew where she would be—collecting cash from the photographer.

Even from a distance, Oscar could see there was a hubbub just beyond the finishing post. As he passed wizened punters in battered hats, cigarettes hanging from their mouths, and smartly suited young brokers in earnest conversation with old private-school friends, the words 'ring-in' jangled like shopkeepers' bells. He caught sight of the photographer hanging at the back of a media scrum, called him over.

'The girl ...?'

'Already collected.'

'Was she with anyone?'

'By herself.'

'You see where she went?'

He hadn't. Oscar headed in the opposite direction to what Tony had taken, figuring between them to cover as wide an area as possible. He spent a futile five to ten minutes wandering the near-deserted track, then called Tony.

'Seen him?'

'No, and there's hardly anyone left.'

Shit. There was an exit out into the bookmakers' car park. If Harris was in it with Pendle, maybe they had gone that way? Oscar told Tony where he'd parked his car.

'You grab it and pick me up at the front gate. The handicapped zone will be good this time of night.'

By now the bookies' car park was near empty. A few vehicles remained a good hundred metres off. Oscar swept the paddock with his binoculars.

Bingo! Sarah and Harris, just like he'd thought, being ushered into a big old Jag by a huge guy.

And there, waiting at the wheel: Pendle.

He reached for his phone.

'Found them. Change of plan. Bring my car to the bookmakers' car park and be quick.'

'Listen to me,' Harris was whining as he was shoved into the rear of the Jag, 'I did not scam you. She did it.' Pointing at Zeen like something out of the Salem witch trials. 'She's poison.'

Talk about history repeating. Zeen knew any time spent with Joe Harris would likely see you wind up with bitumen scrapes from where he'd thrown you under the bus. She wondered what Rick was doing: was he just standing there where she left him or was he already looking for her? Her handbag was now firmly in the grip of the huge guy who had already assured himself it was full of cash.

She tried to delay getting into the car, said to him, 'You're the one they call Misery.'

'It's Mis-*sou*-ri.'

Sounding pissed off as he bundled Zeen into the Jag and dropped the handbag on the front passenger seat while Pendle got behind the wheel. They hadn't tied her hands. She figured it would be difficult to explain if they had an accident or somebody reported it. Pendle set the car rolling out of the car park, down the feeder road. Harris agitated, jumping up in his seat.

'Hello? Are you fucking deaf? I'm telling you she's the problem here.'

Zeen was pleased Pendle did not dignify Harris with a response. Time she went proactive.

'This is kidnapping,' she said. 'You drop me up the road, we'll forget about it. You've got Harris, extract your debt from him.'

'Or?' said Pendle, politely slowing to allow traffic to enter from his right.

'Or I will inform the police.'

The rear-vision mirror showed amusement on Pendle's face.

'You know how much the Commissioner of Police owes me?' he asked.

'Impress me,' said Zeen.

'Half as much as the Minister. You see where that would be headed? A complaint that angered their major creditor.'

Harris shot her an angry look, like she should shut it. The car resumed its unhurried journey. Traffic thinned out. They seemed to be heading into the city.

'Besides, Zeen,' said Pendle, bringing the car to a gentle halt for a kid waiting at a crosswalk. 'I doubt you want to go to the police. I have a feeling they might look at you and Joe here a lot more closely than at me, especially when it comes to a certain ring-in.'

'There was no ring-in.'

The words hissed out of Harris like air from a deflating tyre.

'Detective Atwood seems to think differently.'

They had turned into a wasteland of largely abandoned factories in East Perth. Zeen guessing this was where they had brought Rick. Harris was back with his trowel trying to dig her a grave.

'She fooled Atwood too. Don't you get it? That was Hysterical that ran today.'

This time it was Harris that Pendle found via the mirror.

'You're saying they never switched the horses?'

'That's what I'm saying.'

'And you're certain of this because …? You were involved?'

'I wasn't involved. I know *her*.'

Trying to point across Missouri to her. He swatted Harris's hand away.

'So, you're *not* certain.'

Pendle sounded like a barrister cross-examining Harris.

'I'd lay my left nut on it,' said Harris.

Pendle smirked, 'That one's already spoken for. It will have to be the right.'

Zeen enjoyed Harris's discomfort. She could see sweat bubbling on his top lip.

'Come on, Dom. I admit I was out of line doing a runner instead of accepting my punishment.'

'You're out of line for using my first name without permission.'

'I apologise. But the way it went down, she lured me into thinking there was a switch on. And I admit I wished to profit from that. But I didn't organise anything.'

Pendle showed interest for the first time.

'So that was the plan? A ring-in?'

'That's what I took to be the plan.' Harris trying to act like Pendle's pal. Zeen wanted to puke. 'See, they're friends with the priest, who's pals with Rapanaro …'

Proceeding to tell Pendle then the guts of what he had heard while hiding out at the back of the café.

'So, I go out to Rapanaro's property to see for myself what this might be about, and what do I see? Another horse, the dead spit of Hysterical. What would you construe from that evidence?'

'A ring-in. Fair enough. And then?'

'And then ...'

A phone buzzed. They'd removed Zeen's and Harris's. It was Missouri's.

'Yes, mate?' he answered.

Zeen couldn't hear what was being said, but the guy on the other end sounded animated.

'Okay, thanks mate. I'll tell the boss.'

Whatever it was, it wasn't good news.

29

It was lineball, but Drew reckoned the parking lot of the Belmont McDonald's, where Atwood had demanded they meet, was a step down from the pizza place. As he was buckling up in his car, about to leave the course, he'd received her text.

He parked and waited, figured she knew his car well enough by now. It had grown dark the last few minutes, criss-crossing headlights marking anonymous cars' entries and exits. He'd tuned into the footy, a Melbourne game. His rear door opened, and Atwood slid in.

'What the fuck is going on, Drew?'

Though he had a fair idea what she meant, he played ignorant.

'What do you mean?'

'Pendle. He kept his price high on Hysterical. Like he knew it wouldn't win.'

'He only did that because he'd backed it with SPs and wanted to keep the odds high.'

'So, he thought it was going to win?'

'He was really pissed off. He put like fifty grand on it, stood to win more than half a million. And he capped payouts at five hundred, apart from those first two bets he took from the miner and Cornelius.'

'You're saying he was caught by surprise?'

That was what he'd just said, wasn't it? He rephrased. 'He absolutely expected it to win.'

'Did he have any explanation for why it hadn't?'

'It's racing, detective, there are no certainties, only probabilities.'

She left without another word.

Drew fired up his car. He couldn't wait to get out of there.

If anything, Liz was comforted by what she'd heard. She'd been worried somebody might have caught a whiff that she had been onto the ring-in and consequently nixed the scam. The logical suspect in that case would be Pendle, but she believed Waldron. Pendle had thought he was going to clean up. Cornelius had also expected it to win. Maybe somebody on the inside double-crossed their partners, maybe doped the ring-in so it wouldn't win? But the momentary fear she'd had that the horse running might have actually been Hysterical—that she could pretty much lay to rest.

Major Crime was still waiting to interview her about the assault at Harris's, but she was avoiding any contact for now. To admit she had broken into the apartment would go badly for her. But she had an idea for how she might get out of it. When the neighbours had opened the door to free her, they'd found the key under the mat. She could say she'd done the same after knocking on the door and getting no answer but hearing movement inside. Say she'd found the key, opened the door, poked her head in and called out, and had been shot right then with what must have been a tranquilliser dart of some kind. Truth was she remembered stepping inside and not much more, so not admitting to actually entering was only a small fudge. Her spare keys and set of picks had still been in her pocket when she'd struggled out of there, so nobody knew she'd had those on her. They could remain a secret. Unless it was Harris, whoever attacked her had no business being there. If they said she broke in, she would deny it. Anyway, for now all that was unimportant.

She'd sent her sergeant, Van Lentides, on ahead to Rapanaro's while she detained the trainer after the race. She'd given Rapanaro no opportunity to make a call. There was a good chance he'd moved Hysterical away from his property in the last twenty-four hours, but if he hadn't the evidence would be even more telling. Mind you, the DNA they had taken from the ring-in would prove it wasn't the right horse that had run. They'd also swabbed the horse, which would reveal if it had been drugged.

Her phone rang. It was Lentides.

'You there yet, Van?'

'I'm here at Rapanaro's. And you're not going to believe this.'

What now?

'Surprise me.'

'There's a dead guy in the barn.'

The dead man was big, lying on his back, wearing shorts and thongs that hadn't budged off his feet. Van Lentides was just on forty, had a little silver showing through a bottlebrush comb-back otherwise black. Could have done with some more height. His wife made fabulous shortbread almond biscuits. Liz didn't think he was a brilliant detective, but she believed he was honest and that's what she preferred. It had taken Liz on the fat side of twenty minutes to get here.

'The ambos were on their way,' Lentides said. 'I called them right away. Soon as I was certain he was dead I let them know, which was good because they were able to divert to some other emergency. Sirens have been going off. I told base this guy needs an undertaker and a tailor more than an ambo. The medical examiner is supposed to be here any minute.'

If the death had occurred in other circumstances, Liz would have simply called for the body to be removed. Soon as Lentides said it looked like a suspicious head injury, she'd told him to call the medical examiner.

She squatted down to check the corpse more closely. Lentides ran commentary.

'Blow to the head. There's a shovel over there could be the murder weapon.'

Atwood stood. 'He wasn't murdered.'

'He didn't do that to himself.'

'He was kicked in the head by a horse,' said Atwood.

'What horse?' Lentides looked around the barn.

'The horse that was in here. I'm guessing Hysterical.'

She didn't hold it against Lentides that he'd missed this. His background was illegal dogfights and gambling dens. Not a lot of either in Perth. Atwood had read somewhere that Perth had the highest percentage of migrants of any city in Australia: pretty much all Poms. You might arrest them for excessive sunbathing, their red skin a crime against humanity, but they were loath to frequent any casino that didn't offer an Asian buffet.

As she swung open the stall gate, surgical gloves donned out of habit, Liz heard a car arriving. She walked out to find Rapanaro at the wheel of an old Landcruiser with a big horse float on the back.

'What's going on?' The trainer climbing out to see what the fuss was about.

'Follow me. Don't touch anything. Van, you checked the vehicle?'

Nodding at the fancy Lexus just outside the barn.

'Waiting for you, boss.'

'Do it.'

She asked Rapanaro if the car was his.

'I wish,' he said.

'Know who it belongs to?'

He shook his head. Lentides opened the driver door and began to poke around. Liz led the trainer inside the stable to where the body was sprawled.

'Something to tell me, Enzo?' Pointing at the body like it was proof against him, hoping to shake him up.

'Don't know him,' said Rapanaro. Atwood studied his face, didn't believe him.

'He's part of your attempted scam, right? I'm guessing he got asked to move Hysterical but had no idea what he was doing.'

'I've got Hysterical right there in the back of the float, and I'd like to unload her.'

More confident than he should have been. Liz had a feeling she was missing a piece of this puzzle. Not going to give Rapanaro any inkling of that. Keep him on the back foot.

'Nice try. We took DNA, but that'll take time. You could save the taxpayer a lot of money and get yourself a lighter sentence by just admitting what you did and telling me who else is involved.'

'There's nothing to be involved in.'

'I think the dead body here in your stable begs to differ. After we've checked the property for other horses ...'

Talk about timing. Wherever Hysterical had been, she must have heard the car and come back to be fed. There she was, standing about twenty metres off from the stable.

'Speak of the devil. Hello, Hysterical.'

'That's not Hysterical,' said the trainer. 'That's a mare I've been agisting.'

'What's its name?'

'Double Volley.'

'Who's the client?'

'A syndicate based in Queensland.'

At last, she was getting somewhere.

'You have the papers?'

He said he did.

Lentides advanced.

'Car's a rental. Corporate hire. Waiting on a name.'

Another siren burned away in the distance. Not a good day for someone.

30

His loungeroom crackled with radio static. He was observing the physical world but not somehow part of it. Paul Monaghan's whole being had been reduced to a single question. Had he caused all of this?

His hands still dripping blood, he hovered at the periphery watching two ambos work furiously on the man who had attacked him, while another pair lifted Sandy, attached to an IV but conscious, onto a gurney and wheeled him out. From what Paul glimpsed between the crouched bodies of the remaining ambos, his attacker had an oxygen mask clamped on his face like one of those parasites in the Sigourney Weaver movie. One of the ambos, a young woman, lifted a blood bag from her stockpile, its plastic tube descending out of sight.

'Could you hold this for us, Father?' His legs somehow managed the short trip, and he stood holding it—like a tree branch with a big red fruit dangling from it. He was wondering if the guy was going to make it, supposed this wasn't the time to ask. The male ambo jumped up and dragged over the gurney they'd left in the doorway.

The girl, who had mousy blonde hair, seized the thug's legs, the other ambo the shoulders. He said something like, 'Ready and ...'

And the two of them lifted their patient onto the gurney, Paul still holding the bag, feeling useless. The girl swiped the bag off him.

'You might have saved his life,' she said. The gunman seemed white and brittle as a stick of chalk.

'I didn't know what I was doing.'

Paul finding himself speaking without initiating the thought to do so.

'Wrapping the towel tight around his neck, calling triple zero ...'

Was that really him? Jumbled images slid in and out of his mind. At the time it had been happening in slow motion, yet trying to look back now it was like he had cut and pasted somebody else's experience. From outside came the sound of another siren heralding yet another vehicle to his personal war zone.

'Let's go,' called the male ambo and they rolled out urgently, Paul pulled behind them in their wake.

A police car had arrived. Paul watched the body loaded into the ambulance, the light flashed, and they were away with the siren blaring. Sandy's ambulance had already disappeared. Two uniforms, also one male and one female, climbed out of the police car. Paul had no idea yet what he was going to tell them.

A couple of junior detectives from Major Crime had interviewed Liz soon as she got back to HQ, the senior guys with hands full over some attempted homicide and assault that had been the reason the ambos never made it to the dead guy at Rapanaro's.

Liz stuck with her cock-and-bull story of the key under the mat. The detectives had no idea yet who the culprit was but had made Harris a priority. Liz had offered up a blood sample so they could try and trace what she'd been injected with. There were marks where her skin had been punctured. They'd taken photos and were hoping a doctor or a vet could tell them whether it was a hypodermic needle or a dart, but Liz had a distinct memory now of being shot. The super had tried to get her to go to hospital but she'd refused, saying she felt fine. He hadn't been impressed by her keeping things to herself, but she'd covered her arse there, saying she had nothing concrete to go on until she'd spoken to her informant, and that before she could then assemble the troops, she'd been bushwacked at Harris's flat.

Meanwhile, Lentides had just called. He'd traced the hire car found at Rapanaro's to a Mr Crispin Davis who was staying at the casino hotel.

Figured. That's exactly where crooked gamblers would stay. Liz was all alone in the office, her feet up on a chair, river views just gloom this time of night, a bucket of soggy crinkle-cut chips her dinner. She'd worked her way down near the bottom of the bucket now, where the salt gathered.

She had to lick a finger before dialling. The phone only got to ring once.

'Davis speaking.'

English accent. Almost posh but not quite. Atwood had a good ear for English accents. Back in her student days she'd worked as nanny for a Pimlico couple slumming it in Perth, the husband forced to command this distant outpost of a multi-national insurance firm if he wished to one day head the London office. Now, *they* were posh. Mr Crispin Davis wasn't, but you could tell he had spent time with those who were.

'Mr Davis, this is Detective Inspector Atwood of the West Australian Police, Liquor and Gaming Squad.'

'Indeed? How may I help you, Inspector?'

'You hired a Lexus from Galaxy Luxury Vehicles. Is that correct?'

Only dark-brown fingernail scraps of chips remaining. She crumpled the cup, aimed for the wastepaper basket, missed.

'Yes. Has it been involved in some accident?'

She took her feet off the chair, sat up to give her spine a rest and make sure her BS detector was fully charged. Davis was the only driver listed on the form but odds on was going to deny he'd been at Rapanaro's. She'd be listening to his every breath to try and detect a lie.

'Are you not in control of the vehicle at the moment?'

Watch, he was going to say it had been stolen.

'No. I loaned it to an associate.'

That was a surprise.

'Could you tell me the name of this associate?'

'I'm afraid not.'

'Are you refusing to help the police?'

'Not at all. I meant I can't tell you his name other than it is George.'

'You don't know his surname?'

'I do not know it accurately enough to report.'

Atwood's bullshit detector was in overdrive.

'Yet you loaned him a vehicle? Of which he was not a listed driver? What is your relationship to George?'

'We met yesterday for the first time at Gold Coast airport. We are … were … part of a potential racing syndicate put together by Gordon Langer, the trainer. He suggested we take a look at some potential gallopers here because the prices are lower than in the east. We're only small investors.'

A good cover story, but she wasn't buying it.

'What does George look like?'

'Big fella. Tongan, I think he said. One of those four syllable surnames which I couldn't tell you with any exactitude.'

'I'm sorry to inform you we found a gentleman an hour or so ago, deceased. He was carrying no identification. We believe it is your friend.'

Silence, then a gasp.

'God, no.'

Atwood was thinking he already knew. Probably via Rapana-ro on the blower. Her guess, these guys part of the ring-in syndicate and dead George had been asked to remove the evidence.

'What was he doing out at Helena Valley?'

'He asked me to borrow my hire car, wanted to pay a friend a visit.'

'He mention the name of this friend or where they lived?'

'I thought he said Scarborough. Is that a place?'

'He wasn't found anywhere near Scarborough.'

'I can't help you.'

'He didn't mention a name?'

'No. I had the impression it may have been family. I barely knew the fellow, but we are both staying at the casino hotel and I didn't need the car to get back.'

Liz told Davis she'd like him to come to police headquarters to identify a photo of George.

'We might need to take your fingerprints too.'

'Happy to be of service.'

'As soon as you can, please.'

He said he would grab a taxi. She told him she would meet him in the foyer, ended the call, put the phone back in its cradle, apologising mentally to the next user for the greasy film she'd left all over it. Her head was hurting, and possibly it was her ribs too, somewhere around that torso area.

Something was going down, yet Liz still had no idea exactly what.

31

Soon as Atwood had left his property, Enzo Rapanaro had phoned Lionel to tell him Tongan George was dead.

'Who killed him?' Lionel already planning a vendetta.

'Pretty sure it was Double Volley.'

This was an unfortunate turn of events, but at least it rendered revenge unnecessary and let Lionel consider how he was going to spin the situation. The cops would find the hire car. Fortunately, his precaution in hiring the car in Davis's name would offer a smokescreen. If George had been dealing with the horse, Lionel had to assume Kieran would be dealing with the priest and would have the gun. Which was untraceable, of course, but you didn't want complications. Claiming the car to have been stolen would only foment suspicion; better to acknowledge the men were known to one another, but say they were not close associates. Well, George being kicked to death by a horse certainly suggested a man with equine interests. Why not a horse-owner syndicate? Syndicate members often didn't know one another but were introduced by a trainer.

Lionel could also drop Langer into the mix, make out he was the common connection. Sooner or later the cops would uncover Lionel had been in Perth, but that could be explained. Davis worked for him and wanted to get into horse ownership. Lionel was there to hold his hand and enjoy some racing himself. They'd know it was bullshit but couldn't prove otherwise.

Okay, with the basis of a defensive strategy, Lionel had prepped Davis for the inevitable police call, and as expected, Davis had acquitted himself well.

Since then, Lionel had packed Davis off to the police in a taxi, called Langer and warned him to expect a call from the station, briefed him on what to say. But where was Kieran? He'd heard nothing from him, but that wasn't surprising as George and Kieran were only allowed one phone between them, and they constantly used up their prepaid plan. Kieran, though, could have called him from the priest's landline, surely?

Now, Lionel was without transport himself. That wouldn't do while revenge against a certain bookmaker remained outstanding. A quick phone call to his brothel connections had secured a car for Lionel. It would be brought to him at the track.

'Don't worry about anything fancy. An old clunker will be fine,' he'd told them.

And here it was now, pulling up where he'd told them, on the corner, away from any potential cameras. It was an old Pajero. The young guy driving leaned his head out.

'Mr Howard?'

'That's me. You can leave it running.'

The driver put the car in neutral, pulled up the handbrake and got out. He was skinny, about twenty, Australian. That was another thing about Perth reminded him of the Gold Coast: the criminals all seemed to be white guys.

'I've loaded the destination you needed into the GPS,' said the driver.

'And the other thing?'

'Under the back seat.'

Lionel thanked him and offered him a fifty for a cab.

'No need Mr Howard, it's all taken care of.'

A second car swung by and the young guy climbed into that. It pulled away and Lionel settled behind the wheel of the Pajero. He liked the feel of it.

The day so far had been a disaster, but Lionel wasn't one to dwell on the past. His phone rang. He had an inkling it might be the phone Kieran and George shared.

'Hello?'

'This is Detective Sergeant McGlashen of WA police. To whom am I speaking please?'

Lionel had to check the back of the phone to find the name it had been registered in. He had several aliases for this kind of thing.

'Graeme Kolzac. I'm in Brisbane.'

'Mr Kolzac, we found this phone on a young man who has suffered a serious injury. Do you know who the phone belongs to?'

The police hadn't mentioned a phone when they'd spoken to Davis about George.

'I'm not certain of the number. Can you describe the man?'

'Mid-twenties, slim, light brown hair, slightly above average height. He was wearing a jacket, leather shoes.'

Sounded like Kieran. What the fuck now?

'That sounds like Kieran. Kieran Nettle.'

The cop asked him to spell the surname, so he did.

'What kind of serious injury?'

'We can't go into that.'

Send a guy to do over a priest and he winds up with serious injuries? What the hell was happening? The cop, McGlashen, asking now how they knew one another. Lionel said they worked together in the storeroom at Aqua Sports in Brisbane.

Lionel had set up the company for the express purpose of providing fake employment to his various enforcers. Lionel told McGlashen that Kieran had been heading to Perth for a holiday.

'Do you know where he was staying?'

Lionel said he did not. McGlashen asked if he had any family contacts. Lionel said he didn't know.

'Mr Kolzac, does Kieran have any psychological issues?'

'Yes, I'm afraid so. What's happened to him? Most of the time he's fine but, I don't know, sometimes ... Why? What's happened?' Setting it up like there was a history there. If something had gone wrong at the priest's, it would provide cover. There must be no link to the ring-in.

'I can't really say any more at this stage, Mr Kolzac. But thanks for your help. I may be back in touch.'

'Could you let me know what hospital he's been taken to?'

'Royal Perth.'

He thanked the cop and ended the call.

What had happened at the priest's? You send two men out on a simple job, one winds up dead, the other seriously injured. Had he been kicked by the horse too?

Lionel set the car rolling and punched in the number of his brothel connection. Whatever the cops knew, his brothel friends would know very shortly after.

Dominic Pendle's day was growing worse by the minute. Doug Austin had pulled him aside once they'd escorted Harris and the woman into the East Perth factory unit and lowered the roller-door to keep out prying eyes.

Austin kept his voice low so Harris and the girl couldn't overhear.

'Bilko called.'

These stupid nicknames. 'Bilko' was one of the men Austin used. Pendle didn't know his first name, guessed it would be Jayden or some other name a tattooed, mulleted father would pick. Bilko's surname was Sargent, hence the moniker, after Sergeant Bilko from the old TV show.

Austin continued, 'Those two dickheads I had watching Harris's rang me this morning at breakfast, whingeing about not being able to watch TV all night. Saying they'd spent the whole night in the dark at the flat and nothing had happened. I told them to shut the fuck up, stop griping and stay there till I said otherwise.'

Pendle wondering where this was going, guessing it was nowhere good.

'When I grabbed Harris at the track, I texted them they could go home. I'd arranged for Bilko to relieve them, and with all this shit going down, forgot to tell him not to bother—'

This was getting longer than *Lord of the Rings*.

'So, Bilko rocks up to Harris's flat and the place is covered in cops and crime tape.'

Pendle's head was already booming. Bilko had apparently asked one of the neighbours what had gone on.

'From what Bilko could gather, some policewoman was ambushed in the apartment last night and tied up. They'd only found her because she was trashing the place to get attention.'

Policewoman? Atwood ranting ... Fuck!

'Your two guys?'

'*Our* two guys.'

Austin having the temerity to correct him.

'*Those* two guys, that *you* hired ...'

'On behalf of you.'

'... have assaulted and tied up a cop?'

'I'll find them,' said Austin.

One thing about Pendle's brain, it calculated odds at warp speed. Any immediate action might get overly messy. There would be awful blowback if the cops connected the two morons to him. Revenge was a dish best eaten cold.

'It might be better to let them go for now. Somewhere far away. Then you can deal with them.' Right now, he needed to turn his attention to two other irritants. He considered Zeen and Harris.

'So,' he began.

Zeen cut in, 'I'm tired of this shit and I want to go home, Pendle. That twenty grand you took off Harris is mine. Right now, you've abducted me, and you are an accomplice in the theft. You agree to call this quits, I'll give you the twenty grand for his debt. The rest you sort out with Harris.'

Which was tempting, except that he already had the twenty-grand. And it was not only a matter of mere shekels. He wanted to find out who had ruined his scheme, then make them pay in an excruciating way.

Pendle said, 'I respectfully decline your offer.'

32

The uniformed cops didn't interview Paul, they just asked if he needed to be checked out at a hospital while they secured the crime scene. A delay would give him a chance to decide what he was going to tell them, so he said yes.

'Detectives McGlashen and Martinez from Major Crime will interview you at the hospital,' they told him as they called for yet another ambulance.

Paul should have known that the case would go to Major Crime. All the same, it shook him. He was worried the assailant had died. He asked the uniforms, but they said they had no idea.

The new ambulance arrived. Two females. They checked his blood pressure and did some other tests, like they do for footy players with concussion, asked him where he hurt and he told them most places. They made him lie down on the ambulance gurney and took him to Royal Perth Hospital. By the time he'd been checked out yet again by the Emergency doctor, he'd decided what he would tell the detectives.

This wasn't a clever film script with comic casting surprises. The white guy with wavy hair and the build of a rugby player was McGlashen. The slimmer, brown-skinned detective Martinez. They asked him to tell them what happened.

'It was about a quarter to six. I was sitting in my chair, having a whisky, when my doorbell went. I got up and opened the door and this young man was standing there. He asked me if I was the priest, and pretty much before I could say anything more than yes, he hit me hard in the stomach, then followed up hitting me in the face.'

McGlashen said, 'Have you ever seen this man before?'

'No. Not so far as I am aware. He's not one of my parishioners.' No lie there.

Martinez asked if his assailant had demanded money.

'No. It started off he was verbally abusive, implying that I was a paedophile priest. That seemed to be his thing. He was angry. Maybe he's been a victim, I don't know. I'm not a paedophile.' And all that was true too.

'And then what happened?' McGlashen asked.

'He was going on about horses, I think. He made no sense. I realised then he probably had mental issues. When I tried to get up off the carpet—I'd fallen after that initial assault—he kicked me.' Okay, some omissions here and there but none of it an outright lie. Paul pretty sure his assailant did have issues.

'How many times did he kick you?' asked Martinez.

'Twice, I think. Then he boiled a kettle. He scalded my crotch. He was going to tip the rest over my head. A hot water boarding, he called it. And then Sandy entered.'

'Sandy Hearne?'

'Yes.'

'He's a friend?' McGlashen.

'Yes. I suppose you could say I am his spiritual counsellor.'

'Were you expecting him?'

'No. He's only been to my house once before, I believe. Normally I catch up with him in the city, at the place where he works.'

Martinez asked where he had met Mr Hearne.

'Casuarina. He was an inmate there, and I was the Catholic chaplain. He has continued to seek my counsel since his release. And I'm very glad he did today.'

'Can you describe how the intruder received his injuries?'

He explained that being on the floor, he didn't get a clear view. This was true. At the time he didn't know what had happened, it was only after that he had pieced it.

'But pretty much as soon as Sandy arrived, the other fellow threatened him. Then he pulled a gun. Sandy offered him everything he had in his wallet.' That was true. 'Then I think he dropped his wallet to distract him and threw some washing powder in his face. The other bloke fired ... twice maybe? It was very loud. Sandy went backwards and when the intruder turned towards me, he was holding his throat and blood was pouring out, and Sandy was lying on his back. How's Sandy doing? Have you heard?'

'We haven't,' said McGlashen.

'The other bloke?'

Martinez's turn. 'ICU. Sounds like you saved his life.'

McGlashen asked if he had seen who slashed the assailant's throat.

'Wasn't it the intruder himself? I just assumed ...'

'Still looking into it,' said Martinez.

Okay, that was misdirection, but not an outright lie—as that had indeed been what Paul had thought at first.

'I saw him holding his throat and blood pouring out, then he collapsed. I checked on Sandy, who was *compos* but maybe in shock, then staunched the blood as best I could for the other bloke and called triple-o.'

What Paul didn't tell them was he'd found the sharpened card on the ground and placed it between the injured man's fingers. McGlashen mentioned a car and horse float they'd found in the car park.

'Would that be Hearne's?'

Paul had no idea. 'As far as I know, Sandy has nothing to do with horses.'

'Did you see what vehicle the intruder arrived in?'

Again, he replied truthfully, he had not. The detectives thanked him and told him he could go. He wasn't going anywhere until he'd seen Sandy, though.

The café was empty. Rick had closed up and was sitting on a stool in front of the Milano. No word from Zeen. Beyond worried, Rick was bouncing off the walls. When the landline phone rang, he dashed to answer it. Paul's voice greeted him.

'You okay, Rick?'

The priest sounding stressed and anxious. Rick was going to mention Zeen right off, but that could wait.

'What's happened?'

'Sandy's in hospital. He's been shot.'

Rick listened to the priest's report with growing horror, felt like throwing up. First Zeen missing, and now this?

'Is Sandy going to be okay?'

'He's sedated, on a drip. I spoke to the doctor. He said the bullet itself didn't do a whole heap of damage, but his system is weak from his cancer anyway, so what might be plain sailing for a healthier person is a lot more treacherous.'

'And this guy who attacked you, he say who he was? Who he was working for?'

'Nope, but he did talk about the horse. Asked about you and a fella named Harris. I didn't say anything, but Rick, I'm ashamed to say I was about to.'

Rick assured the priest he would have done the same thing.

'The cops asked about a car and horse-float left in the car park beside my place. I told them I knew nothing about it, but I'm assuming that might have been Sandy.'

'Yep.'

By themselves, the car and horse float were no damning evidence of anything. Atwood might have her suspicions, but she couldn't prove a thing.

Rick said, 'I'm worried about Zeen. She was supposed to be coming home with me from the races but never came back after she went to collect some money she won. I waited half-an-hour.'

'She hasn't contacted you?'

'Not a word.'

'Oh, Lord. I don't want to carry that on my conscience too.'

Monaghan was on the verge of crying, Rick could tell. Rick could easy join him.

33

When Tony had got that call from Cornelius saying he'd spied Harris and 'Sarah' getting into Pendle's car, he was torn. Yes, he wanted to keep working for Cornelius, but Zeen was a pal, and whatever con she might have been working would be justified, at least in her brain. If he'd been the one spied them, he would have said nothing, let things work themselves out. And sure, after the call, he could have dawdled, pretended he couldn't find Oscar's car, but that was unprofessional, and even to help a pal, Tony couldn't perform less than his professional best. Besides, Marietta was counting on him, and friends had to take a back seat to his woman.

When you were used to a beaten-up old Torana, a car like this made you pinch yourself: the purr of the engine, the way it handled easy as a toothpick, it was heaven. Gripping the wheel in his hands gave him goosebumps. All this might seduce a less principled man, but Tony was not one to place material goods above love, family and friendship.

So, Tony had been conflicted when he wheeled into the paddock, now deserted except for Cornelius, who was a lighthouse. Cornelius had run towards the car the moment it came into view. He ripped open the passenger door, jumped in.

'Like I thought. They were all in on it. Harris sets me up, Sarah cashes in, suckering me to a bet, then Pendle takes my money. Step on it. They'll be stuck at the intersection up here.'

Zeen willingly having anything to do with that lowlife Harris didn't jibe for Tony. He had fished for more information.

'You sure they're all in on it? Even the girl?'

'Large as life, the lot of them, climbing into a Jag, Pendle, Sarah, Harris and some giant. Faster ... there!'

Sure enough, there was the Jag turning the corner up ahead, just getting off the feeder road onto the highway. Tony was thinking the big guy was Pendle's muscle, and maybe this wasn't the big happy family that Cornelius supposed. The Merc zipped through traffic, closing the gap like Tony had to do no more than think what he wanted to happen, and it obliged.

They tailed the Jag to East Perth, where it turned off into some kind of industrial area. It was growing dark, the brake lights of the Jag red coals when it paused before a factory unit roller-door.

Tony switched off the headlights and parked behind another warehouse from where they could keep eyes on the Jag. The roller-door lifted, and the Jag moved inside. As the roller-door began its descent, Tony saw Zeen climb out immediately followed by the giant, who grabbed her and shoved her off to the side.

'You see that?' Tony had said, indicating the unit to Cornelius, who was fiddling with his phone.

'What?' Cornelius squinting through the windscreen too late.

'The big guy just manhandled Sarah.'

'You think she might be innocent?'

'She might be.'

'Why would Pendle scoop up Harris and her?'

'That Harris looks slimy to me. Maybe he asked her to put that bet on with you. Maybe she just wanted to meet you?'

Cornelius was dubious.

'More likely she's sucking his dick and doing what he asks.'

'Or, Harris has something over her.'

'Blackmailing her?'

'Could be. I don't see him being her type. More you.'

Cornelius was interested now.

'You think?'

'What do I know? But I'll tell you one thing, she ain't friendly with the big guy. My guess, he's Pendle's muscle. I bet she'd be very grateful to anyone who rescued her.'

Priming the trap like that, Cornelius dwelling on what he'd said.

'What are we going to do?'

Which was what Tony had hoped he might say.

'I got an idea, but you won't like it.'

Cornelius said, 'Try me.'

Zeen didn't like where this was going one bit. There would inevitably be pain. The only question was how much, and for whom? She'd tried to bluff Pendle, but he was calling her on it.

'I'll make you a counter-offer,' the bookie said. 'Tell me if you were the one behind this, as Harris suggests, or somebody else was the brains.'

Harris weighed in. 'I'm telling you; it's Rick Boski. He's got a café in—'

That was as far as he got, because right then the walls imploded.

In fact, it was just the roller-door buckling inwards, and now spearing in after it ... was that ... a Mercedes sports? It got weirder. The driver, who looked a lot like Thaiphoon Tony, jumped out and yelled at her to 'Get in the boot!'

And she was preparing to do just that until she noticed her handbag with the twenty grand in it on the concrete floor. Pendle, who had dived for safety to the other side of the unit, must have dropped it. She grabbed it and turned to head towards ... well, she could see now it *was* definitely Tony, when a giant arm seized her.

'Sorry, honey.'

Missouri's arm like a steel cable around her chest. She tried stamping down on his foot, but he was too fast, dancing away, still holding her, a smile spreading over his face.

Until his jaw was smashed by an airborne foot. Missouri's whole face seemed to wobble, then his eyes rolled up and he checked out of consciousness, his arm falling away like somebody had taken a machete to it, leaving the big man to hit the floor with a thud.

'Go!' Tony yelling as he landed like a ballet dancer and spun towards the car in one motion.

Zeen didn't hesitate this time; she ran through debris, passed Oscar Cornelius in the passenger seat, who seemed to be loving every minute, jumped into the open boot and wedged herself in as the car reversed at speed. As it swung into a one-eighty-degree turn at speed and then powered into the night, Zeen managed to catch a glimpse of Harris darting across the industrial wasteland.

Almost anywhere in this fair city was preferable to the McDonald's car park, but hunched over ledgers in Pendle's office, Drew was thinking this was lineball. It had been a nightmare day, stressing every single minute that Pendle would find out he'd been snitching to Atwood. Thankfully, Pendle was so obsessed with Harris and Boski that he hadn't considered he might have a traitor closer to home. It was going on 7.30, getting cool now, and Drew wanted out of there before the Goan curry place in Beaufort Street closed.

Him being here was literally a roll of the dice. At the end of every race meeting, Pendle—always worried that some mug would pull a hold-up to get his cash—determined randomly who would be responsible for getting the day's takings into the office safe. He would toss a die, and if the number came up one, two or three, he would bring it here himself. Four or five, it was Drew, six it would be Henry the bagman. They were the only three with keys to the office. Today, Pendle had rolled a five.

The failed betting plunge aside, Pendle's returns had been fair. Not a great day, but not a bad day. Sure, Pendle had lost his SP bets, but on Hysterical's race he'd won with every mug punter who'd been duped just as Pendle had. The other six races he had three winning and three losing, but overall, he had won ... Tallying it right now ... sixteen thousand, four hundred and eighty dollars.

Anybody else would be thrilled with that for a day's work. Of course, Pendle would say it was all in the preparation, which took a lot more than a day, but it was still nothing to be sneezed at.

The door buzzed. Nobody buzzed at this time of night. Drew checked the grainy black-and-white vision from the front-door camera. A bloke was there, neatly dressed in a jacket and trousers. Looked like one of Pendle's old mates. Probably some ex-footballer.

The buzzer sounded again. What a loser. Drew leaned down to the microphone.

'Sorry, sir. This office is not open.'

'Are you Dominic Pendle?'

Not an old friend then.

'No, sir. Mr Pendle isn't here.'

'Where can I find him?'

Drew didn't like the guy's pushy tone.

'I really don't know. Maybe his house?' Saying it smart-arse, with a bit of attitude. These old guys thought you were their secretary. If you gave them any latitude, they would have you putting the SIM card in their phone next. 'Or could be out at dinner.'

'Where does he live?'

'Sorry, sir, can't disclose that. Goodnight.' Turning back to the ledgers. The buzzer went again. And kept going. And going. And going.

And then it stopped.

Thank fucking Christ.

And then it buzzed again. Drew flicked his eyes across to the monitor. Now the guy was standing there with something in his hands. Drew used the zoom-stick.

A fucking sawn-off shotgun!

Drew reached for a phone.

'If you're trying to call out on a landline, I cut that before our first discussion.'

Drew patted his pockets. Where had he put his mobile?

'And if I were you, I wouldn't try calling anybody with your mobile.'

Found it. 'I'm calling the police.'

He was safe in here, wasn't he? His phone was suddenly a cake of wet soap. Fuck!

'I wouldn't do that. What's your name?'

'None of your business.' He had the phone in his grip now. 'I'm calling …'

'Can't you smell it in there?'

'Smell what?'

Drew started dialling 999. No. That was UK TV shows getting the better of him.

'The petrol.'

He looked at the camera image again. The old guy was brandishing a jerry-can. He turned it upside down for emphasis, patted it to show it was empty. A few drops came out.

'Old place like that will go up so quick. I bet your boss is too cheap to have sprinklers.'

Of course he was.

'Not that they would likely save you. I mean, you could risk it, the fire brigade would get here eventually. They might save your life, but you'd be burned like a fucking Pommy tourist at Bondi on New Year's Day. Skin grafts …'

'All right. Please, don't do anything stupid.'

'That's my advice to you, son. If you don't open the door, I'm dropping a lit match. And if you try to run out after …'

He wiggled the sawn-off.

'I have no beef with you, son. But your boss fucked me over today. So, let me in, and I promise you, I will not set fire to the place. Or shoot you. Unless you don't behave yourself.'

Drew had dialled one zero. He could probably keep the guy talking while he dialled the next two. But then, fuck it, why should he carry the can for Dominic? Sounded like it was this guy's scam that Dominic crashed, and Drew hadn't been in line for any of Pendle's spoils, so why should he cop the consequences?

He pressed the switch. The door clicked and the guy stepped in. Then the door snapped shut. The man must have been close to sixty. Dark jacket, collared shirt, shotgun.

'What's your name, son?'

'Drew.'

'All right, Drew. Cooperate, nothing bad will happen to you. What do you do for Pendle?'

'Penciller.'

The man nodded. 'Good. So, you would know about the bets he placed with SPs all over the country.'

Drew thinking he could plead ignorance. The shotgun persuaded him otherwise.

'I put them on. Thirty grand. But he lost.'

The man got in close now.

'How did he know?'

Drew felt his Adam's apple bob.

'About the ring-in?'

'Yes. About the ring-in.'

'He didn't really. Know it was a ring-in. We only figured that out after the race, when Atwood the cop started on about it.' Drew hearing his voice, shaky and high, like it was coming from a doll with a pull-string. 'Pendle just followed the money.'

'Explain.'

'First off, in the pre-race, last Wednesday, some nobody put eight grand on Hysterical. Nothing too unusual. Somebody knows an owner or a trainer, hears the horse is a chance ... they stick their free cash on. Then Thursday at lunch, you know Oscar Cornelius?' The unblinking eyes suggesting apparently not. 'He owns pubs. He's never bet with us before. He tracks the boss down at lunch to put five grand on Hysterical. Pendle figured the race was fixed. He didn't know how and he didn't care. He wanted to cash-in. He's pissed off.'

'*He's* pissed off? It was my fucking scam!'

Touchy. Drew put his hands up. The man's brows furrowed. Drew tempted to say, 'sorry for your loss', stymied the impulse.

'Pendle didn't interfere in the race, then? Buy off the jockeys?'

'No. He reckons it was some guys—Joe Harris, this punter who's into him for like fifty grand, and a guy named Boski.'

The man's eyes straying to the cash Drew had been counting. Studying those notes like he was a philanthropic passerby could offer street orphans a new home.

'How much is there?'

'Twenty-six thousand, four hundred and eighty dollars.'

'Put it in the bag for me.'

Nodding at the bag it came in. Drew obliged.

'Where's the safe?'

'There's no ...'

A shotgun levelled at his forehead. Drew nodded in the direction of the safe, which was behind a wood panel in the rear wall. It was about head high and looked like a cupboard for glasses or coffee mugs.

'Key or code?'

The safe had been there well before Drew's time. Drew had suggested installing an electronic lock with code. Pendle had said that if anybody managed to break into the empty office an electronic lock would be useless, the thieves would just blow it. And if he or Drew were around when somebody was asking this question, like right fucking now, it would probably be at the end of a gun. In which case, Pendle said he didn't want to misremember some combination and wind up with a hole in his head.

Drew tried handing the man the key, but he waved it away.

'You open it.'

Drew did, warned, 'I don't know how much is in here.'

This was where Pendle kept some of his undeclared winnings. Bets with regular clients on a cash basis that never went through any books. The cash was in neat bundles. Seven bundles of ten grand each: Drew discovered this when his visitor made him count the stash. He was instructed to put that money in the bag too. That made seventy plus the sixteen-four-eighty plus the ten-grand float. Almost a hundred grand.

The man zipped up the bag.

'Where do I find these guys you mentioned?'

'Joe Harris, who knows? Pendle's been looking for nearly a week. Boski apparently has a café in Northbridge not far from here, but I don't know the guy personally.'

'Name of the café?'

It was just outside the perimeter light in his brain. Shaking his head, apologising.

'Something with a prison theme. Café Jail, or Café Stretch or ... something to do with prison.'

Enough to work with, Lionel reckoned as he started to back out.

'You've done well, Drew. Adios.'

Eight at night Saturday and this part of the city was deserted. Lionel climbed into the Pajero, feeling a bit more at ease now. He knew Northbridge was a bit west of here. Figured it wouldn't take him that long to find this café. He had half a dozen cartridges, which ought to be enough. A hundred grand almost reclaimed.

That was a start, but there was a long way to go.

35

What had impressed Oscar was how well the Mercedes had stood up to the ram-raid. He guessed that's why a Merc was so often the vehicle of choice for smash-and-grabs. Right now, the front of the car looked like one of his dog Wilbur's chewed toys. But did he care all that much? That had been such a blast, driving through the roller-door like Mel Gibson, and then this new guy Tony jumping out and going Bruce Lee on the goliath. Fucked Pendle's plans right up. Whatever they might have been. They were heading south now into Northbridge. Tony a dark horse.

Oscar said, 'So you know Sarah?'

'Her name's not Sarah, it's Zeen. Yeah, I met her a few years back. I didn't want to say anything before. I'm sorry. I know she lied to you, but I'm sure there's a good reason.'

Oscar liked this guy despite the fact he hadn't been upfront. And that ram-raid had been a helluva buzz. Besides, Tony knew this Zeen, and Oscar was intrigued by her.

He said, 'You think she's straight, even though she lied?'

'Not sure why she did that. She had a past. But long as I know her, she's a good person. Her partner is a guy named Rick Boski.'

'Partner as in business partner?' Oscar was hoping. Zeen *née* Sarah was going to be awful grateful for her rescue. The idea of a woman with a past excited him.

'Yes ...'

Oscar's heart leapt—

'... but also, the other kind. They have a café.'

—and crashed.

'Boski was married to my wife Marietta. That's how I know him.'

Jesus, Perth was a small town.

'You get on with him?'

'He's okay. He did time but he's not a crim crim.'
'What'd he do time for?'
'Fell asleep minding a dope crop.'
'You ever do time?'
'Not me, no.'
'Not that it would matter, just ... curious.'
'We should go to the café now.'
'She going to be okay in the boot?'
'She's used to it.'
Whatever that meant.
Tony said, 'Sorry about the car.'
'That's okay. It's insured. I'll figure something out. How tight are she and this guy Boski?'
'Pretty tight, Oscar. You're wasting your time.'
'Okay, let's go to the café. But pal or no pal, you're working for me.'
'Yes, Mr Cornelius. Of course, sir.'

A clusterfuck of the highest order. That's what this was. Pendle had ruined his suit when he went diving into an oily patch on the concrete floor as the unit seemed to be collapsing. The so-called 'Missouri' was sunk. The big man had tried to stand but had just toppled back over, and now lay on the floor of the industrial unit, counting stars. Whether it was the karate guy's kick or Austin's head hitting concrete or a bit of both was irrelevant. He was out of the fight. Pendle, on the other hand, was working up to a frenzy.

That bastard Harris was gone. Again. And so was the girl who maybe was the brains in all this. And so was the money he had so recently reclaimed. The one positive was that, remarkably, the Jag remained without a scratch on it. The Mercedes had smashed in and stopped inches from the Jag's rear bumper.

Pendle had been lying on his side to protect himself from falling debris and had only caught a glimpse of the triad guy who'd taken out Austin. He couldn't say offhand if he had been alone or with a team.

His phone rang. It took him a moment to locate it in his left jacket pocket. It was Waldron, screeching like a cat in a fight.

'Boss, we've been robbed—' The words a tumbling waterfall, so Pendle had to concentrate to make sense of them. Certain highlights stuck, like 'robbed'.

'All the cash?'

'All of it. The safe, the float, the takings.'

'You let him in?'

'He splashed petrol all around outside. He had a shotgun.'

'His name?'

'Never gave it. Wanted to know where you lived. I wouldn't tell him.'

Making out like he was some hero. Kid would have shat his pants. As he was talking, Pendle was feeling in Austin's pocket for his gun. It wasn't there. Or on the ground. Fucking Harris or the girl must have taken it.

'Wait there. I'm coming over.'

No traffic this time of night; Pendle was at the office in seven minutes.

'That was water, not petrol.' Pendle ropeable that anyone could be so easily conned, part of him wondering if his penciller could be in on it, but the kid looked too scared. 'And it was probably a pop gun he was carrying.'

'Nnnoo,' Waldron stuttering, pointing to the picture he'd freeze-framed.

It looked like a sawn-off, all right. The CCTV quality was shit, though, the man's image grainy, unclear.

'Can you get a better photo?'

Waldron clicked and a different picture appeared on the monitor: the guy leaving the office with Pendle's bag. An older guy, pushing sixty, the face not familiar but showing the kind of hardness men acquire with constant physical labour. Or battle. A tough son-of-a-bitch.

'And he was looking for Boski?'

'Café Inside. I couldn't remember the name with the gun pointing at me, but it came to me after he went.'

'And he said we gate-crashed his scam?'

'You. He said you'd ripped him off, or words to that effect.'

'And he had no one with him?'

'Maybe outside, but just him in here.'

With any luck, Pendle might still get him. Using a small key from his keyring, Pendle opened the locked bottom drawer of his desk, not caring he was sharing this with Waldron for the first time. There was a pistol in there, a Beretta. Pendle had scored it on the nineteen-eighty-four Railway Stakes. A punter couldn't pay up and the pistol was given in lieu. Over the years Pendle had scored a few strange items: a backhoe, numerous vehicles, a guitar, a truckload of timber, more televisions than the Good Guys had on display. The pistol was the sole thing he'd kept.

He'd only ever fired it a few times in the year or so after getting it, the novelty of it entertaining him on the way to and from some country race meetings. So it had been lying there for twenty years, but no reason it shouldn't work.

'Where are you going?

Pendle thought it was pretty fucking obvious.

'Get my money back for starters.'

36

Chaos reigned in Rick's brain. Should he call the police? He was certain something bad had happened to Zeen, and there were any number of culprits lining up. The scariest was the crew who'd set up the original ring-in. They had to be behind the intruder who'd shot Sandy and beaten up Paul. Rapanaro must have told these guys he'd spoken about the scam with his priest. Maybe they'd recognised Zeen at the races, realised she'd been part of the switcheroo. Right now, she could have a gun to her head. Or worse.

He prayed it wasn't them. Could be Pendle and Missouri who had grabbed her. Or Harris. He had that kind of form and would happily trade Zeen to Pendle as the scapegoat.

Or perhaps it was Oscar Cornelius, who she'd won the money from. He could have been at the photographer's waiting for her to show up, maybe twigged he'd been scammed, wanted payback. Rick cursed himself for not going with her. What scared him was, by now he might have expected a call from Pendle or Cornelius, some kind of blackmail. But nothing.

He picked up the telephone book, found a number for the Globe Hotel. A woman answered.

'Is Oscar in, please? It's important.'

She hadn't seen him. 'I'll ask the others.' Suddenly Rick with an urgent desire to pee, forced to hold it in while he waited. The phone scooped up.

'No, nobody has seen him. Would you like to leave a message?'

'Thank you, I'll try later.'

Fuck it. He had to call the cops. It would likely mean fessing up to the whole thing sooner or later, but he would do that gladly to bring Zeen back. He was about to dial when he heard a car arriving fast out the back. Doors opened and closed, and the sound of voices wafted in.

The door was thrown open. Zeen stood there, her dress and hair askew ... and was that ... Thaiphoon Tony?

Rick raced to her, crushed her body into his.

In his ear he felt her warm breath. She whispered, 'Yeah, I'm glad to see you too.'

The four of them sat around the counter, the Milano rumbling like a locomotive, 'Arrivederci Roma' playing from its speakers, Rick delivering Tony his requested long black, a macchiato for Oscar Cornelius. Guy had a big arse splayed a little over the stool, big boned, not all that fat but soft, you could tell. Far as Rick was concerned the guy could have free coffee here the rest of his life.

'You like a cannoli, Oscar?'

Zeen playing hostess despite still wearing her scrunched dress. A lot less scrunched than the front of the Merc, mind you. Wonder the thing could be driven. Rick remembering, just a few days back, Zeen wanted to scratch that very car. She'd certainly got her wish. And then some.

'Love one.'

Rick offered the cannoli around. Tony declined. Oscar started in on one with the little pastry fork.

Zeen said, 'I'm sorry about the deception, Oscar, it was necessary,' tipping her handbag up so the twenty grand from their bet spilled out over the counter along with a lipstick, sugarless lollies and the black marker pen she'd used.

'That's your twenty grand back.'

Shooting Rick a look to stay silent about the ten large she'd laid on him earlier. 'I was about to give you this, but Harris stole it off me and then Missouri, Pendle's muscle, grabbed us.'

Cornelius took a sip of his coffee, raised his eyebrows a little like he was pleasantly surprised.

'What happened? Was it a con from the start?' The cannoli nothing now but a stain on his plate.

Not wanting to be stuck on the outer here, Rick pushed his way in.

'A cop, Detective Atwood from Liquor and Gaming, tumbled to the ring-in two days ago. She could have wrapped it up early, but we figure she was holding off.'

Zeen tag-teaming, 'Our guess: she wanted all the major players, not just Rapanaro and whoever he was prepared to spill. You would have been one of those in her net.'

'So we swapped the horses back.' Rick poured himself a glass of water from the jug.

'Where do you guys come into it?' Oscar not stupid, guessing there had to be some cut of the action for them. Rick leaving that to Zeen.

'A friend of ours came into the information by accident and tried to cash in. We had to protect them. We're doing fine with coffee, we didn't need this shit, but we couldn't let them go down.'

Oscar trying to process this, careful not to fall for some bullshit a second time.

'How did this cop know what was going down?'

Zeen said, 'Somebody talked. Probably somebody from the crew who set it up. And Pendle obviously found out too, somehow, and tried to cash in, or he would have been howling that it was a ring-in.'

Oscar remembering now how Harris had told him not to place any pre-bets, thinking maybe *he* was how Pendle found out, but not willing to own up to that. Getting a feel now, though, how it played out.

'Good coffee,' he said.

Rick preoccupied, thinking. Monaghan said he hadn't given up Rick. The only other people who knew of his and Zeen's involvement were Goose, who was out of the picture, and Sandy who'd been shot before he could reveal anything. He and Zeen should be quarantined from whoever had gone after Monaghan. Assuming it wasn't Pendle. But there was no logic in Pendle going after the priest when Paul was trying to cash in on the ring-in same as Pendle. Still, that time in jail made you hyper-aware of any inbound dirty weather. You had to stay vigilant. Right now, Rick wanted to relax, but his gut wouldn't allow it.

Oscar said, 'You guys thought of turning this into a bar?'

Rick said, 'Too much red-tape to deal with. And me an ex-con. Makes it difficult.'

Zeen said, 'We prefer to specialise in coffee, and we have a direct line from Brazil. Who supplies the coffee in your venues?'

The hotel room had been booked in the name of George Tupounia. Liz had shot through a request to a couple of Queensland colleagues to check their criminal database for entries matching the deceased Mr Tupounia, but it was Saturday night, and even later over there so she wasn't expecting an answer anytime soon. She had also asked for a check on Crispin Davis, reckoning these guys were likely both involved in the horse scam. She had tried ringing the trainer, Langer, but he hadn't returned her calls.

Not being the sort of person to wait till Monday, she was spinning in her chair in her now-deserted office, running her mental fingers over her possible courses of action. She could try to locate Joe Harris, but to date all she'd acquired in attempting that had been a head injury. The major crime team were on it, anyway. And could Harris ever have come up with this kind of scam? She doubted it. The original bet had been made by Goose Gordon, a miner. Liz had looked him up on the WAPOL criminal database: he currently lived on William Street, Northbridge. She got on her Netscape and did a search for cafés in William Street.

Bingo.

Café Inside, *'Perth's best coffee in a prison-themed café.'* She searched some more, landed on a low-grade magazine feature on the café. Rick Boski was opining about how 'ordinary Joes don't want to go to prison but would like to get a glimpse of life on the inside.' Liz chuckling to herself, Boski would be getting a refresher course if she had her way. He had to be involved in the scam.

Time to get a taste of Boski's coffee. She wasn't taking any chances; she armed herself.

It took a lot longer for Lionel to find the café than he'd anticipated. Turned out this Northbridge area was a warren of coffee shops, bars, what to his trained eye seemed to be strip joints or massage parlours. In the old days what would have been called 'The Latin Quarter'. Finally, he found Café Inside, realised he'd passed it at least twice because it wasn't lit up for business. There were lights on upstairs, though, and there was muted glow on the lower floor where the café was, like somebody could be in there.

Lionel parked across the road in a No Standing area. He wouldn't be paying the fine. He stuck his sawn-off under his coat, thought about leaving the cash in the car, but so much had gone wrong today, he took the bag with him. Traffic was moderate. He crossed the street, pretty young things in short dresses passing around him the way stormwater diverts around a parked car. His mind snapping back a couple of nights, wondering if that girl he'd been supplied with by the local brothel crew might be free later. First things first, though. The front door locked up tight. He tried the handle slow and easy, but it didn't budge. Cruised up to the plate glass, snuck a look in. Shadows moving, people in there for sure.

He walked to the next street corner, passing a noodle restaurant and a store selling cheap Chinese shit—the stuff that needs batteries, breaks easy because it's nothing but plastic and ribbons—hit the corner and threw a right. No parking in this street either, but the rear lane he'd anticipated was just ten metres up. Excellent. He started up there. No lighting once he was ten paces off the street, the smell of drains, garbage from the noodle place. Lionel estimating the café was where a lopsided tin gate topped by rusty barbed wire was not quite closed. He squeezed in between the two sides of the gate, found himself in a small rear car park. An old van, a runabout that a woman would drive, and a Mercedes sports that looked like a mouth after Tongan George had landed a straight right. For the first time getting a smidge sentimental. Guy was a character in those thongs and shorts, loyal too. And not smart enough to know how to rip you off, though if he ever did try, would've been obvious. Lionel had preferred him over Kieran, who was a psycho. That could have its uses but also drawbacks. Tomorrow, assuming Kieran was still alive, he'd arrange a lawyer to visit, tell the lad exactly what was expected of him.

There were windows here, but they were barred, not to go with the prison theme, more because this area looked like the kind of place you'd be burglarised every month or so. Back door was wooden and locked tight too. But he knew there were people inside, and maybe they hadn't deadbolted it? Lionel knew how to pick a lock.

First, though, he'd try the iron staircase leading to an upstairs backdoor, careful to take it quiet. He arrived at a door similar to the one downstairs, found it locked as expected. No point walking back down the stairs. He put down the bag of money and the sawn-off and got to work on the lock.

Rick had topped up coffees, Zeen explaining to Cornelius how she'd worked with Harris for a few years but then he had double-crossed her.

Zeen said, 'Tony here knocked him out, fractured his skull.'

Tony pointing out Harris tried to get him first.

'I didn't want to mention this, Mr Cornelius, in case you get the wrong idea. I thought he might be some friend of yours.'

'No friend. Man came to me telling me he was going to hand me two hundred thousand, so naturally I listened.'

A voice sounded from the staircase behind them.

'Isn't this cosy?'

They turned and found themselves looking into the barrel of a sawn-off shotgun.

37

By the time Pendle saw it was the café he was looking for, he'd already passed it, and the street being one-way at this juncture, was forced to do another complete lap. His strategy was simple: first hunt down this Boski fellow and the girl, get back the twenty grand that she'd taken from him at the unit. Then stick a gun down their throats till they coughed on who it was who had hit his office and removed an additional hundred. The bookie starting to speculate that the guy who'd done the robbery could be this miner mate of Boski's.

Circling the block, what does he see but his bag disappearing down the lane that runs behind the café. It appears to be in the hands of a guy looks like the one who knocked off his office! He acted quickly, pulled into the lane, stopping the car ten metres short of the café's rear entrance. Not caring he was blocking anyone wanted to use the lane as a thoroughfare: he was a man on a recovery mission.

It wasn't the first time Rick had found himself staring into the barrel of a gun, and the experience lost none of its terror by him having previously survived. Even so, part of him thinking: if this guy does shoot, I can't have him damaging the Milano.

Rick said, 'Would you like a coffee? On the house.' The man was well dressed, sports jacket, tailored shirt, looked like he would appreciate the coffee and perhaps that might defuse the situation.

The muscles in the guy's neck bulged. He said, 'What I'd like is the money that I don't have because somebody fucked me over.' Some kind of English accent back there, not toffy though: street. 'Are you Boski?'

Zeen, who'd also had a little experience in the gun-pointing stakes, jumping in.

'It's impolite to enter an establishment pointing a gun, sir.' Lecturing the gunman like she was the perfect lady, and he was some inbred poacher. 'Especially when we don't know who the fuck you are.'

Stalling, Rick was thinking, but she was angry too. He was trying to calculate what options he had here, but the answer seemed to be only one.

'My name is Lionel Howard. That ring your bell, sweetie?'

It rang some kind of bell for Rick, and not the kind that tinkles over a bookshop. Lionel Howard a name he'd heard somewhere in prison. That didn't bode well. Howard turned and pointed both barrels at Rick's chest.

'You owe me, Boski.'

Rick hoping if he could lure Howard close enough Tony might be able to do some kick-boxing move, but Howard wary, keeping his distance.

Cornelius swivelled on his stool said, 'Why don't we just all calm down?'

Which Rick admired but suspected was not the best choice of advice to offer a man pointing a shotgun.

The barrels swung in Oscar's direction. Howard said, 'Why don't you shut the fuck up. Who are you?' But taking a step closer, Rick watching Tony out the corner of his eye, noting Tony's eyes locked in.

'Oscar Cornelius.' Oscar shaking a bit now the gun was pointed his way.

'You involved in this too, hey? Maybe you're the money guy?' Sneaking a glance at Tony. 'Triad money, maybe.'

Zeen saying, 'We have no idea what you're on about. We're just friends enjoying a coffee.'

Howard said, 'I'm talking about what took me near on six

months' planning that somebody fucked up. My ring-in at the races today. You've been there, I can see …' A mean edge, nodding at Oscar's member's badge on his lapel. His eyes panned over Zeen. 'And that outfit? A little smudged now, but darlin' I never forget a body that good. You were there too, near the stalls. Coincidence, eh? Bookie named Pendle stole my scam and then somebody double-crossed him. I'm thinking it's you lot.' His eyes finding the cash still strewn across the bar in front of Cornelius. 'I'm guessing this is your cut.' Then swinging back to Rick, raising the shotgun to his shoulder, ready to discharge it.

'Drop the gun and give me my money.'

Everything happening in a blink. Rick looking over to see Pendle behind Howard pointing a handgun at him, Howard swivelling towards the new threat, Pendle firing wild, Cornelius yelping in pain, his stool splintering, a boom from the shotgun, Pendle going down, Howard advancing, pointing the gun at the whimpering Pendle, obviously hit, Howard ready to put him away, Tony jumping from the stool to charge the occupied Howard—and then from the shadows of the staircase another voice. A woman's.

'Police. Drop the weapon and get on your knees.'

Tony skidding to a halt, saved from another Bruce Lee moment. Howard not budging, the weapon still on Pendle, who was moaning. Atwood stepping down into the light, hands extended, holding a gun of her own, Howard maybe calculating if he should take a shot at Atwood, but deciding otherwise, dropping the gun, kneeling as Cornelius was crying out, 'My foot, my foot,' and Pendle lying on the ground continued howling, 'The bastard shot me. He shot me!'

While everybody was entranced or screaming, Zeen soccered Pendle's bag of cash that Howard had brought, through the gap in the bar, so it slid snugly under the Milano. Tony taking the hint and pocketing Cornelius's twenty thou from the bar top, Atwood fully occupied behind the kneeling Howard.

'Someone call an ambulance!' she yelled.

38

Having polished off a bowl of flat noodles, the chips the only other food she'd had all day, Liz had been sitting across the road from the café sipping green tea in a Chinese restaurant, still trying to decide if she should crash Café Inside, same time as marking this restaurant down as a bit of a score: the chicken and almonds with the noodles delicious and the price cheap.

Why not go across? She was thinking, pressure Boski, tell him he'd be heading back to jail unless he talked. Big chance he'd crack. As she's weighing this, a middle-aged guy in a smart jacket crosses the road from her side and stands out front of the café trying to peer in, looks like he's got a leather holdall and something else under his jacket but she can't quite see what. He waits for a moment like he's trying to suss if anybody is in there, and she's pretty sure he tries the handle of the door, but he doesn't step back and knock like you would if you were expected. Then he starts down the road and turns at the corner of the next street, maybe looking to head down the rear lane and into the café via its back entrance. Curious, the guy being dressed up, not your usual Northbridge look. And older than you'd expect. And what was in that bag?

And then while she was turning this new development over in her brain, she sees a Jag go past the café and hit the brake lights. Not just any Jag: Dominic Pendle's.

That was what decided her, one last sip of her tea before she got up, exited and crossed to the café side of William Street. She stood in the shadows by the corner where the Jag had turned before entering the back lane.

She had decided to follow. Found the Jag abandoned, heard the creak of a gate further up. She followed, squeezed through the gate just in time to catch the silhouette of Pendle at the top of the rear stairs. She drew her pistol, pursued.

She had entered the café on the accommodation level and silently made her way along the hall to the landing, still in Pendle's wake. Coming down the stairs she'd heard someone threatening to blow Boski away and then Pendle shouting for him to drop his gun. Then bang, bang.

Her cue to enter. She'd been wetting herself, wondering if the gunman would try and blast her with his shotty, but he'd dropped it. A shit day was finally turning around.

She watched Oscar Cornelius being loaded into one ambulance. A bullet from Pendle's wild shot had hit his ankle but he had quietened down since the medics had shoved the green whistle in his mouth. Pendle himself was being loaded into the other ambulance. The shotgun blast had got him in the left side and hip, but no major damage though he was moaning and groaning.

McGlashen and Martinez had come down to take the gunman—the older guy she'd seen acting suspiciously—into custody, and he was sitting in the back of the police van.

McGlashen came over, bouncing on his toes.

'Fucking ace work, Hardwood. You know who this guy is?'

'Said his name's Howard.'

'Lionel Howard. Biggest crook on the Gold Coast, but they've never been able to get him on so much as a parking ticket. They're going to love you over there.'

Which made Liz feel good about herself.

'And what's this about you getting shot?' McGlashen looking her over.

She explained she thought it was only with a tranquilliser dart.

'Newman and Hanon are handling it,' she told him.

McGlashen laughed. 'Good luck.' Not rating his colleagues highly. 'Nice day's work. You'll sleep well tonight.'

Liz smiled, but she wasn't finished here yet.

'We don't know what it was about,' Rick Boski was saying. He was pretty damn cute, and his coffee was excellent. The crime science people were taking photos and measuring, but with a police detective witness they had a head start on what had gone down. When Liz had cornered Boski, he had suggested they go to the back of the café where there was this big cell with bars on a roller. Liz could see why people would like the place. It was fun. She was sitting on this bench, held there by chains, the Asian guy, the girl and Boski opposite. McGlashen and Martinez would interview them individually when they got back, but she didn't have to do that, her concern was the race scam. She couldn't make them talk to her, but they had agreed to it when she requested. Least they could do seeing as how she'd likely saved them all from an angry Lionel Howard.

'Your friend Mr Gordon placed a large bet on Hysterical.'

'And it lost, which kind of sums up Goose's punting,' said Zeen easily. She was no Melissa, but it was obvious why men would do crazy things for her.

'Where do you fit in?' Swinging her attention to the man who'd given his name as Tony, wondering if he could be some triad member.

'I drive Mr Cornelius.'

Maybe not. Back to Boski. Not the worst assignment.

'Why did Howard threaten you?'

'I was trying to find that out,' said Boski. He had pale blue eyes and they danced with amusement. If he was the one who shot her with a tranquilliser dart, she could almost forgive him. 'Honestly, we have no idea. We've never met the man before.'

'I think you all had something to do with swapping Hysterical.'

'That *is* hysterical,' said Zeen. 'We don't bet. You even sure the horses were swapped?'

She wasn't going to let Zeen ask the questions, turned it back on her.

'You and Joe Harris go back. Spent a lot of time on racetracks together.'

'We all do things we'd rather forget. I'm sorry I ever laid eyes on Joe Harris. I hadn't seen him for five years, then he turns up out of the blue here asking for money to pay off Pendle.'

What Liz had thought in the first place. Maybe that part of it was true.

'So what was Pendle doing here?'

Boski said, 'Pendle was still owed money by Harris. I went over to Harris's flat to tell him to stay away from us, and Pendle's guys jumped me, thinking I was Harris. Pendle decided we should be liable for Harris's debt.'

'You never reported any of this to the police.'

Zeen giving a snort. 'Come on, Pendle's probably got half the pollies in this town in his pocket, and plenty of cops I'm guessing. If he wants to make things difficult for us, he can.'

Liz's brain clicking back on what Boski had said a minute ago.

'Where were you last night?'

Boski saying they had been here, they'd closed up at six, put their feet up.

'Any witnesses?'

Looking at one another shrugging.

'No.'

So, no alibi. But—

'These guys you say jumped you ...'

'Don't know their names. Young guys, body-builder look. Not too bright. Drove me over to some industrial unit in East Perth. You know Doug Austin?'

She sure did. 'Guy they call Missouri.'

'Right. He's Pendle's main muscle. He gave them a clip over the ear, told them I wasn't Harris.'

'Missouri wasn't here tonight?'

Boski said there had been no sign of him. He was wondering himself where he might be. Liz starting to grow more convinced it was Pendle's guys who'd shot her and tied her up. Made sense they'd be waiting for Harris at his apartment. Boski and Zeen here seemed too cool for that kind of shit.

'You know where Harris is?'

Zeen said, 'No idea.'

'You happen to know a Tongan man—George Tupounia?'

They claimed they didn't. Hard to say. She warned them if there was anything they knew about the horse-swap, this was their last chance to talk. Boski said they were not aware of any horse-swap. Liz would like to have found an excuse to chat with him for another hour or so, but she was forced to wrap it up. On the way back to her car, her phone buzzed.

'Hello?'

'Hey, legend.'

Bender.

'I hear you nailed Lionel Howard.'

Word travelled fast.

'Who told you?'

'Everybody. My phone is hotter than you at that Christmas party when you came as Steffi Graf. They'll make you Super next.' She *had* looked way sexy in that little tennis skirt. 'Where are you celebrating?'

'I'm not.'

Bender snorted, 'You should be. I'm chilling a bottle of champagne right now in expectation of your arrival.'

She shouldn't ...

'Come on. You know you're dying to tell someone everything blow by blow ... and that is not sexual innuendo ... unless you want to take it that way.'

What the hell. Bender wasn't Rick Boski, but it had been a long time between drinks, and he was right. This was a night to celebrate.

By midnight the last of the cops had packed up and gone, and Rick had been given the all-clear to go on living—at least until the next day, when McGlashen and Martinez would be around to interview them, Rick figuring the cops were looking for free coffee. As celebrations were in order, Rick pulled out beers for Tony and himself from the upstairs fridge and brought the Vodka down for Zeen.

'You think Oscar's gonna be okay?' Tony holding the bottle daintily on the very tips of his fingers.

'Depends how badly the bullet smashed the ankle. One time during my stretch we were playing a softball game and one of the guys tripped on the base, like hardly anything, but he snapped his ankle and never walked properly again.'

Rick reflecting on the irony. You went inside expecting all these terrible things might happen to you, and it turns out you never walk properly again because of a game of softball.

'Oscar's going to have the best surgeons in the country,' said Zeen. 'He'll be okay.'

Rick asked if she still wanted to scratch Oscar's car. Tony looking over, curious, and Zeen saying, 'He has a bad habit of parking where he wants to, regardless of others.'

'Tell me about it,' said Tony, accepting a second beer.

Zeen said, 'I think his Mercedes is banged up enough,' and then she and Tony laughed and relived the moments of the ram-raid, while a sombre Rick was left pondering how Sandy was doing in the hospital.

Tony said he needed a slash and took himself off, Zeen picking up on Rick's mood then and asking him what was the matter? Her fingers stroking down from his forehead to his jaw.

'I was thinking about Sandy,' he said, 'wondering if he has any family.'

'He's never been married, and he has no kids.'

Which Rick knew but was surprised when Zeen added, 'He says that's the biggest regret of his life, man should have children's what Sandy reckons.' Meeting his eyes as she said it and Rick getting this weird feeling that maybe she was asking the question of him: would he be interested in that step?

But before he could answer, he heard footsteps. It was a shame Tony hadn't taken a bit longer to piss, because this was a critical juncture in the road of any relationship—the moment when you decide whether it's a humpy or a full-blown house.

Only when he looked over Zeen's shoulder it wasn't Tony standing there, but Joe Harris, and he was pointing a gun.

Joe had rocked up to the café at around 10.30 to find a uniformed cop out front diverting people. It wouldn't do, Joe being picked up carrying a gun, so he kept walking and took the next street, figuring to take a peek in the back lane, but that was blocked off too, and he could see a big van with what looked like crime scene cops scurrying to and fro. Nobody seemed on edge, so Joe was thinking whatever had gone down wasn't homicide. All the same it was no place for him, so he kept walking, found a kebab shop a few doors along, ordered a bucket of chips and asked what was going down.

'You don't want kebab, mate? Best in Perth.' One of those Middle Eastern types with a lot of body hair, expertly using the electric knife. Getting Joe's juices flowing but he was running out of cash.

'Okay, but hold on the chips.'

He ordered the doner with the basic salad. The kebab guy saying he heard a couple of guys had been shot but he didn't think killed. Joe's brain whirring as fast as the knife, guessing Pendle must have come there to sort things out, hoping Boski and Pendle had shot one another. Only when he started eating what turned out to be a delicious kebab realising how hungry he had been.

He'd dawdled for nearly an hour, the early shift of pubgoers grabbing a bite before splitting for home, the next shift, clubbers just beginning their night, not wanting to stain their shirts and frocks yet. He'd thanked the kebab guy and wandered back towards William Street, taking a peek up the lane, noting the crime-scene van no longer there and the lane clear of cops. He did a full circuit, checking the uniform had gone from the front too, before doubling back down the lane. He slid through the part-open gate into the rear parking area where this whole adventure had begun with him overhearing the priest. The gun felt heavy in his pocket. It was a comforting feeling, even though he had never actually shot anyone. He'd pointed a gun before, though, and it sure helped make people do what you wanted. So far as he was aware Zeen and Boski didn't have weapons, so for once he would be the one calling the shots.

The back door was closed but not locked, and Joe had opened it a crack and heard voices in there. And then a laugh he knew well.

Zeen.

That's when he'd taken out the gun, counted to fifty, slow, keeping his heart rate steady, and walked in.

The disappointing thing was that prick Boski seemed to be alive and well and sitting at his bar, gazing into Zeen's eyes, really soggy romantic shit.

'Sorry to crash the lovefest,' Joe said, loving the way they jolted right apart when he put the gun on them, 'but I'm in a hurry and I need my money.'

'Your money?' Zeen giving him the twisted lip.

'Yeah. The twenty grand.'

'Oh, you mean the twenty grand you stole from me at the track.' Zeen doing that sarcastic thing of hers.

'If you like.'

Zeen said, 'I'm not giving you any money.'

Boski coming in hard on her heels, 'And Pendle's out of the picture, Harris, so you can scoot.'

'You shot him?' That had to be how it played out. Pendle must have turned up, walked into a trap.

'A guy name Lionel Howard shot him.'

'Vinyl Lionel?' Joe getting nervous tremors just at the name. He'd heard many rumours, told from sides of mouths between villains' furtive glances, about Lionel Howard.

'I believe that's his name.'

Zeen barking, 'Now get out of our café before I call the cops.'

The nerve of her. Him with a gun on her and all. Maybe he should plug Boski in the leg or something, just to teach these two some respect.

'The exit's that way,' Zeen pointing, Joe thinking she was angling her body weird. Trying to hide what? He changed his position. Saw a bag on the floor. Money!

'Give that here.'

'No.'

Zeen staring him down.

'Give it here or I'll shoot.'

'You're not going to shoot anyone, Joe.' Boski getting off his stool, playing the big man.

'I'd shoot you with great pleasure, Boski. Hand it over.'

'No.'

Zeen not budging, forcing Joe to choose.

'This is on you, Zeen,' aiming the gun at Boski's thigh.

Boski reaching down, tossing the sports bag at his feet.

'Here. Take it.'

Zeen shooting Boski a look, like that had been a stupid move.

Joe keeping one eye on them in case they tried to rush him. Unzipping ...

Holy Toledo!

'There's a lot more than twenty in here. This is my lucky day after all.'

'I don't think so.'

The voice coming from behind. Joe turning ...

Was this a fucking flashback? The same Asian dude who gave him the fractured skull. Joe raised his hand to shoot but the guy spun, and Joe's world snapped black before he could pull the trigger.

'You sure he's going to be okay?' Zeen wanting rid of Harris, but something short of death. It was close on two and she was in bed, been waiting for Boski to get his skinny arse in beside her.

'Harris was stirring when we dropped him off.'

'You don't think the concussion could be dangerous?'

'That's what I asked Tony, but he's seen it a hundred times in the ring. Said he only gave him a medium-size tap. Said he'll be okay in the morning. You see the way Tony spun?'

She had. It had been a blur, Tony's foot coming up and knocking Harris out cold.

'How much did we have to pay?'

'Six grand.'

She would have been happy to pay twice that to get Harris out of their lives.

Rick nuzzling her. 'What are we going to do with the rest?'

Close on a hundred grand, Zeen had counted. Zeen told him her idea, and he approved.

'I want to see Sandy tomorrow,' he said.

'It's already tomorrow,' she pointed out and he said, yeah, well in a few hours.

She told him she wanted to come see Sandy too. Sunday was quiet anyway, once the breakfast rush was over. Rick didn't see a problem: Kevin, who was rostered on tomorrow, could handle it. Rick was perched up on an elbow, looking at her weird now.

'What?'

'Before Harris turned up, we were talking about family. About how kids fulfil your life.'

They'd never discussed this before.

'What's your question?'

'Where do you stand on it?'

She was thinking the coffee business was just starting to really take off. She was thinking this wasn't a good time to be thinking about kids when she and Boski weren't even married, and though Zeen wasn't one of those women who hungered for the big wedding or the overseas service where you made your friends cough up to join you on your big day, there was something inside her she knew wouldn't be satisfied with a casual arrangement. Not if kids were involved. Sooner or later, you needed to piss or get off the pot, and all those couples she knew who were saying they didn't need to get married, didn't need an institution, she also thought deep down were cowards. Just like she'd been a coward up till now. Because essentially, we all want to bet on a sure thing.

So, when you rolled Boski's question over and took a real good look, wriggling underneath were a whole heap of worms that had been biding their sweet time getting fat in the shadows.

Finally, she said, 'I tell you where I stand on that,' and pulled him over and felt his body heat going through her as they started kissing.

Joe Harris regained consciousness the way a stage set rises, steadily but slowly. He wasn't sure where he was, but the thrumming beside his head convinced him for a moment he was still by the bins at the Malaysian restaurant after he'd fled the Apostrophe, time not synching yet. His head hurt, too. Not from drinking, not that kind of hurt, more like that other time when that Asian guy had fractured his skull. Seemed like yesterday. Speaking of yesterday, time seemed very fluid, inexact. He had a vague sense that something major might have happened, but what exactly he wasn't sure. What he was thinking was he had been lucky to get away from the Apostrophe, but that wouldn't stop Missouri hunting him.

He raised himself up and looked around. Where the fuck was he? A small narrow bed, steel walls. Jail? The little room was furnished with this low bed and a small desk. No window. Shit, maybe he'd fallen asleep behind the garbage bins and the cops had stuck him in some remand cell. Or worse, this was some place Pendle kept. In which case, would he ever be allowed out, or would he end up cold and dead under pine needles in a state forest?

Panicky, Joe swung around to the side of the bed that wasn't against the steel wall. He could smell diesel. He got up, unsteady on his feet, opened the door. A low-lit corridor. The thrum louder here. No sign of anybody. He was about to call out but thought better of it. If this was Pendle's joint, it might be Joe's only chance to escape.

His brain was all over the shop, flashing what must have been dreams posing as memories, fictional scenes that seemed very real but can't have been: Zeen taking a bagful of money off him, the Asian dude who gave him a fractured skull sailing through the air to smash him again but dressed differently this time.

He shook his head, tried to clear it, started along the corridor, steel doors with handles like they have in industrial freezers. He didn't like to think about what might be behind them. His legs wobbly. Maybe Missouri had beaten the crap out of him, what with his head being so sore and the earth moving beneath him.

Joe finally came to a door that didn't look like a freezer, pulled it open, nearly tripping on a weirdly jutting metal seam as he stepped through.

Outdoors. Blue sky above him, rusted metal and thick paint, the smell of diesel mingling with ... what?

Joe advancing slowly, puzzled, wondering if there might be a car he could steal ... Something wasn't right. That other smell, salt air? He gazed around him, shuffled as far as a railing, looked out. Nothing but ocean as far as he could see. He was on a fucking cargo ship!

How the f—?

He didn't need to finish the thought. Though his brain was ripped and logic a loose thread, he knew intuitively that whatever had happened to him could be boiled down to two words.

Rick Boski.

AND A FEW WEEKS ON

It was three weeks and then some on from the ill-fated race day, and Liz and Bender were lunching in the courtyard of a pub down the Causeway end of town, one favoured by cops on account of it was near headquarters. Sometimes the racing fraternity ate here too, but they tended to frequent the pub over the other side of Hay Street near the WACA. Bender had been away on a fishing trip to Albany the last two weeks. He and Liz had only reprised their late-night liaison once before he'd left, but it had been good.

'The DNA matched?' Bender shaking the saltshaker like it had a winning ticket stuck down the bottom, one of those guys sported short-sleeved shirts with palm trees and pineapples even though it was still officially winter. This was their first daytime date, though neither had acknowledged that. They'd not had a chance to talk beyond a quick hello goodbye while he'd been away. Liz had only got the DNA results on Hysterical the day before.

'Yeah, it was Hysterical who ran.' She didn't think her disappointment was why the pasta didn't taste that good today, but it might have been.

'So, the horses weren't switched?'

'That's the only explanation. It must have been a double con. Somebody set up the idea that there was going to be a ring-in, got all the money flowing on Hysterical, but they were really betting against her.'

'You got any idea who?'

Liz pushing the bowl away from her, this very question one that had occupied her ever since she'd stared disbelieving at the DNA results.

'The eastern state SP bookies were the big winners. Looking back now, Rapanaro was confident when I took that sample, so either he never knew there was going to be a swap, or more likely, he was in on the double con.' Having an identical horse at his property meant he was involved in something. 'Perhaps he was in on it but got cold feet.'

'Was Pendle behind it?'

'You'd think so, but no, seems like he got stung. He actually lost money betting on Hysterical.'

'But you think it was his guys played zookeeper with you?'

She'd confided that much to him the night of the café shooting. Since then, a tranquilliser gun had been confirmed as the weapon.

'Yeah, but Pendle and Doug Austin, aka Missouri, are playing dumb.'

Bender said of course they were. If they were shown to be involved, they would be in deep shit.

Liz said, 'I know Austin didn't do it personally, because I've got eyes at the Apostrophe who assure me he was there at the time.'

'They must have been real amateurs. Leaving a key under the mat, though.'

Bender laying it on, letting her know his suspicions she'd broken in.

'I guess that's where Harris left it, and I got lucky.' Not going to admit she broke in.

'You did get lucky. Moron could have had a real gun. Then I'd be denied the pleasure of your company. That would break my heart.'

She liked when he said things like that.

Bender was weighing the knife now like a surgeon might a scalpel. Dining some kind of sacred ritual with him.

'And the gunfight at Café Inside, still no idea what that was about?'

Didn't she wish she knew the answer. 'From what I heard when I was coming down the staircase, Pendle was saying Howard had a bag of his money. That he stole it. I doubt he means literally. More like Howard scammed him.'

'So, Howard was behind it?'

'Way it looks, yes. Double Volley, the other horse, was bought in Singapore last year by a company in the Virgin Islands. They sold it on to a group of pensioners in an old people's home in Queensland—for one dollar. We're still trying to work out the money trail, but my guess is it ends with Vinyl Lionel.'

'And Howard's not talking?'

'Not a word. And Pendle claims he just happened by, wanted to have a word with Boski about Joe Harris. Says Boski being an ex-con, he took the gun for protection, but when he saw Howard pointing his gun at Boski and the others, he stepped in.'

'Making himself the hero? Smart ploy, play well with a jury if it gets that far.'

'Except Oscar Cornelius, the one actually got shot by Pendle, claims that Pendle was only interested in having it out with Howard over some money he claimed Howard stole. But if Howard was pointing the gun at Boski, maybe Howard got stung too and blamed them.'

Bender twirled his spaghetti over and over.

'So, maybe Boski was behind it?'

Liz remembering those quiet blue eyes, not able to believe bad of Rick Boski.

'I doubt it, though Zeen could be. I wouldn't trust her. In fact, I think Joe Harris is probably the kingpin and somehow or other he got his old pal Zeen to help out. Maybe they scammed everyone. Harris has disappeared.'

Waldron wasn't talking, claiming he knew nothing and was getting out of the racing game, so she'd stop hassling him.

'And the guy got killed by the horse? Where does he fit in?'

'He was one of Howard's, I'm pretty sure. He was a boxer, had a criminal record in Queensland and was a KA of Vinyl Lionel. I'm thinking maybe he was sent to check on which horse was there. The trainer, Langer, parroted Davis's story about a horse syndicate. Which I believe, frankly, is horseshit.'

A couple of familiar faces entered, McGlashen and Martinez. They'd been lumbered with the shootout case at Café Inside.

'I'm going to transfer to Liquor and Gaming,' said Martinez, pulling up a seat. 'You get all the glory, Liz. We're stuck with our thumbs up our arses trying to make a case.'

McGlashen checked on who wanted drinks. A light round, only he and Martinez participating with alcohol. Martinez slumped on his spine.

'You'll get Howard. At the very least—intent to cause serious injury,' Liz trying to sound encouraging.

'Hopefully. Pendle's more iffy.'

Liz explained they had just been talking about that. She said, 'Cornelius's testimony will sink Pendle, and the best thing is, he'll probably lose his bookmaking licence for good.'

Martinez said, 'Maybe, but he's still got juice, don't forget.'

Bender interjected, 'Not as much juice as Cornelius's old man. You can't shoot the son of the most powerful man in the country and expect to get away with it.'

McGlashen came back with their drinks, white wine for Martinez and a lager for himself.

'But we've also got this attempted homicide thing,' McGlashen making sure not to spill a drop as he placed the glasses down.

Liz remembering now, they'd been called onto that while she was dealing with the dead Tongan not that far up the road.

Martinez said, 'The accused guy who wound up with the slashed throat is not talking, literally. But his mother told us he has a thing against priests after he was abused at school.'

McGlashen said, 'Though this guy Nettle isn't even a Catholic.'

'Kieran sounds Catholic,' said Bender still twirling pasta.

'But he's not.' Martinez gulping his drink. 'And only went to state schools. We don't know what mum's game is.'

McGlashen elaborated. 'The guy he shot is an ex-con who claims he did nothing but drop in on his old prison chaplain and finds Nettle beating the shit out of him. He tells Nettle to stop, Nettle shoots him. This guy says Nettle slashed his own throat, and the evidence supports that. Nettle claims to remember nothing after he walked into the house.'

Liz said, 'You think the priest could be involved in something? Two crims meet at his place?'

The cops said that had occurred to them, but there was no evidence to support it. The prison authorities were glowing in their references to the good Samaritan, guy named Sandy Hearne.

'And the parish loves Father Monaghan. No hint of abuse, just a regular guy.'

'But what's weird,' Martinez was saying, 'is that we can't place how Nettle actually got there. He had no vehicle, and you don't just hitch a ride or catch a bus to Helena Valley.'

Liz speculated he'd got a lift with the other guy, the one he'd shot.

Martinez said, 'Except the priest denies it, and the way he and the other guy say it happened fits all the science.'

'Plus,' Martinez adding, 'We had witnesses who swear they saw Hearne arrive by himself with his car and a horse float in the car park—fifteen minutes after the assault started.'

Liz's ears pricked up. 'A horse float?' She was thinking this was Helena Valley, the same area, the same day that the ring-in was going down.

'What's this guy's name again?'

'Sandy Hearne. Went down for a manslaughter thirty years back, been out of jail for fifteen years, no trouble of any kind.'

'Still,' Bender said, 'the guy is shot, and going back in history he killed somebody. Maybe it was payback?'

McGlashen and Martinez looking at one another like that was an angle had promise.

'Suppose,' McGlashen vibing on this new idea, 'Nettle is a hired hand by somebody associated with this historic manslaughter. He knows the priest is close to Hearne, so he goes there and starts beating him up, get him to tell when Hearne will be there?'

Liz could see a hundred holes in this theory but didn't want to get involved. All she asked was, 'Did he say why he had a horse trailer?'

McGlashen brushing that off, 'He's an odd-jobs guy. He said he got a call from a mate who owns the trailer saying somebody had asked for it to be delivered to Helena Valley, but the address was bogus.' McGlashen lighting up, 'But that could have been the set-up!'

Bender animated, too, 'Sure. It's a bogus job but they figure when he realises that he'll drop in on the priest and that's where Nettle will take him.'

Liz interrupting their flow, 'The guy who owns the trailer, you confirm this with him?'

'Of course.' Martinez leaned forward in his seat, enthusiastic. 'I reckon this might have legs.'

'Okay, I'm going to leave you guys while you're running hot.'

Bender looked torn. 'You want to go?'

'Things to do, but you stay, finish your meal.'

Bender smiled, gave her a thumbs up, motioned a phone call.

Back in her car Liz checked the correspondence she'd got that morning from the insurance company of the priest who'd collided with her. Looked for his name, found it: Monaghan. So, this ex-con has a horse float the day that the Hysterical ring-in doesn't eventuate. And he happens to drop in on his former prison chaplain—and Liz is certain if she were to check she'd find this guy was likely ministering at the prison same time as Rick Boski and his mate Goose Gordon were inmates. She's also thinking that Enzo Rapanaro, being Italian is Catholic, probably goes to Monaghan's church, and that this guy Nettle arrived at Monaghan's out of thin air, when not ten minutes' drive away at Rapanaro's there was a dead guy. And a car. She's thinking too that if Boski and his old chaplain got talking, he might have told Boski about an accident he had with a Detective from Liquor and Gaming just up the road. Zeen being on the spot and being sharp, would have guessed Liz had been up there spying on the doppelganger horse. Maybe that caused a change of plans, the ring-in too risky, so why not run the real Hysterical? Still plenty of ways for them to clean up.

Liz knew she could look into it further, but wasn't it sometimes better to let things go?

The bad guys were either in hospital or jail or both for some considerable time. You didn't want to muddy the waters, give judges and juries alternative theories that may lessen the chance of a conviction.

Right now, she was a hero, with a promotion on the cards. The near homicide at the priest's wasn't her case. And Bender was enjoying himself, feeling like he was useful again.

No, best she let sleeping dogs lie, enjoy the good times. They didn't come all that frequently. But one day it might be fun getting Boski on his own, asking what really went down. She was killing it at work and the thing with Bender was going okay. That probably wouldn't last, but for right now, it was enough.

41

He found Sandy in the church, fastidiously sanding down the confessional box by hand.

'I thought I might do us a roast for dinner.'

'You're already putting me up, Father, you don't have to feed me too.'

'I enjoy it, Sandy. I haven't had company for a long time. How's the side?'

'Better each day.'

'They're starting work on the toilet block during the holidays,' Paul said by way of making Sandy feel part of things, but proud of it too, although wary this time around, careful to ascribe all this good fortune to the Lord and not to himself.

'That's okay, I can be going back to my digs.'

Sandy getting the wrong end of it, thinking it was a hint to end his stay in the valley.

'I'm not asking you to leave, Sandy,' he said. 'Quite the opposite. I've seen how useful a handyman would be around here and I'm hoping you might stay. Proper weekly pay too, that we can fund out of the budget.'

Sandy stopping work, embarrassed.

'I'd like that, Father, but I can't let Rick down.'

Paul explained that he and Rick had already discussed the situation, and that Rick and Zeen both thought it would be a good thing for Sandy.

'There's a train runs from near my place in Maylands ...' Sandy working it out, Paul thinking no way in hell he would leave Sandy to see out his last year or so in that hostel where he dossed.

Paul said, 'I've got a parishioner, Gloria, she has a really nice room, and she'd take you in for minimal board.' It warmed his heart to see Sandy smiling. 'Deal?'

'I guess so.' Only an *aw shucks* missing from the moment.

Paul headed back to get the chicken prepared, first cleared the table that was littered with plans from his talk earlier with the builder and plumber. They were giving him a twenty-percent discount, both eager to help because their kids went to school here, both keen for Paul to drop a hint over who the anonymous donor was who had put a hundred thousand into the parish coffers, Paul saying he didn't know, he'd got a call to check his back step and the money was sitting there in a basket, all cash.

He opened the oven, wiped down the baking tray—a few filo crumbs from the apple turnovers he'd cooked last night—got the chicken in, and brushed on the basting liquid. Though you could never be sure, he felt almost certain that he had the answer to that question he'd posed back when all this was going awry: whether it was the Lord or the serpent leading him down the path.

At one point it had looked for sure to be the serpent calling the shots. Paul had seemingly lost all the parish funds as well as every cent he had to his own name. His reputation was going to be soiled for ever more and there would be no hope of rehabilitation because he was about to be killed by Kieran Nettle. And yet what had transpired had shown him the goodness and decency in the kind of people who, back in the time of the gospel, would never have been allowed into the temple. Rick and Zeen doing everything to help him, nothing in it for them but that he was a friend. Same with Sandy, the criminal, the Barabbas, taking a bullet for him. If old Satan had been behind it, he probably would have let Paul win that bet, made it easy, but the way it had gone had been anything but easy, forcing him to confront all his weaknesses. And yes, he was very proud, but not of himself, no, nothing to be proud of there. It was Zeen, and Rick and Sandy, he was proud of.

He'd been given the chance to save Kieran Nettle, and he had. Sure, he'd removed the weapon, the sharpened plastic card, put it in Kieran's hands, but he remained convinced that had been the right thing to do. He knew that Sandy had acted honourably, but the police might have got confused. And Paul had lied too, but not so much, the guts of everything he'd said was true.

At the end of the day the correct horse had run in the race and come where it should have. The people who had sought to profit from dishonesty had lost money, reputation or both, or had suffered injury. A hundred grand had found its way to Rick and Zeen, money that could never be claimed, and they had in turn passed it all onto him for the school and the parish. There had been a guiding hand after all.

Paul slid the bird into the oven. He no longer felt the need to go back to prison to be of use. He could do a lot of good right here.

42

MEANWHILE SOMEWHERE NORTH

Dry heat Missouri could take, but not humidity. He'd gone to Sydney once as a younger man, thought of working in Kings Cross, testing himself against the tough guys over there, but the humidity had drained him, so he'd scuttled back to Perth. And up here, oh, it was far worse than Sydney had ever been.

Kuta hadn't been so bad, at least there had been a pool he could sit around, but Lombok was a different story. And the ferry ride was something else. He knew a few guys who had moved up here from Perth. Most lived around Seminyak. He'd toyed with the idea, if Pendle didn't get his licence back, maybe moving to Bali, but realised now the climate would kill him.

He wasn't getting paid for this, but he couldn't just let it go, had a reputation to uphold. He'd found a shady spot at a table under a tree where he could sip 7-Up and watch. The guy was walking up the little dusty street now, big cardboard box on a handcart. Missouri drained the can and crushed it, flexed his shoulders. He dropped the empty can in a bin because in his job it was important to respect people's customs, leave everything neat.

'You think it's safe to go back home?' Scooter sitting on one of those little Indonesian stools about the only furnishing in the place, no proper chairs.

'Probably. Nobody stopped us anywhere.'

Colby drinking lukewarm beer. There was no fridge, but you could get ice from the iceman up the road, stick it in a bucket. It was his turn to go get it, and he was stalling. This the cheapest accommodation they'd been able to find with their savings nearly done, concrete walls and floor with a couple of mats, skinny beds with mattresses thin as the patience of a doctor's receptionist. They had return air tickets from Denpasar but would need funds to get back to there from here, so they were living off the smell of an oily rag to preserve what was left. Didn't want to be stuck here on Lombok.

'I don't think the cop had any idea who we were.' Wondering if he could bluff Scooter into thinking it was his turn to get the ice.

'You don't think Pendle would have told them?'

'No, only get himself in the shit.'

'And Missouri?' Scooter looking scared just saying the name.

Colby drained his beer, inclined his head.

'Best we avoid him. I can borrow some money from my sister. I think we go back to Darwin, work there for a bit.'

They'd spent a week in Darwin right after the incident. Good place but their money had been running out quickly and Colby thought it best they keep moving for the time being, so it was a return ticked to Bali and Kuta for a week.

What a week it had been. Party central, a great time with 'shrooms and German chicks, but by then their dollars were screaming. They'd heard about cheap places in Lombok. This was as cheap as it got but no fridge, no aircon, just an old electric fan.

There was a knock on their flimsy door. Probably the young kid they paid a couple of rupiah to fetch ice for them until yesterday, when they'd had to tighten the budget and start doing that themselves.

Colby opening the door. Not the kid, a skinny Indo guy with that leathery skin they all got up here. He had a cart with him, a big cardboard box on it.

'What do you want, sport?'

Colby was thinking like he was pretty sure Scooter would be too: some scam.

'For you,' the guy tapping the box.

Yep, scam all right. 'Not for us, mate, we never ordered anything.'

The man confused. Checked a paper note in his hand.

'Mr Colby? Mr Scooter?'

Saying it with a weird accent, the dude's English making Colby giggle.

'Yep, Mr Colby and Mr Scooter, that's us,' Colby looking over at his mate, raising an eyebrow.

'We're not paying you anything, mate.'

'No pay me, all paid.'

That changed things. The dude was small and skinny but wiry and strong. He hauled the box off his trolley and Scooter got up and helped bring it inside. It took up almost the whole floor of their place. The Indo guy waved and left, dragging his little cart behind him.

'It's heavy.' Scooter wondering what it could be and who could have sent it.

'A bar fridge, maybe?' Colby looking for the only knife they had and then settling in to attack the cardboard, ripping it open, building up a sweat quickly.

'Yeah, probably. I complained to the dude yesterday, but thought he ignored me.'

Scooter helping, tearing it away with his fingers. The outside cardboard came away finally, revealing two separate packages also tightly boxed in cardboard. Nothing written on them, but a paper note attached with sticky tape. Colby ripped that off, opened it. Scooter could see it was some kind of instruction like came with some made-in-China shit you get at Bunnings, diagrams and Chinese writing.

Colby was frowning.

'What is it?' Scooter coming closer for a look.

'It looks like a ... wheelchair.'

Two of them to be precise, Scooter was thinking as he looked at the diagram.

Another tap on the door. What they figured, the guy had got it wrong and was coming to get his package back. As if a couple of fit young guys like them needed wheelchairs.

AUTHOR'S NOTE

Back in the late 90s I created a film script full of crazy, fun characters in a wild ride involving death, coffee and romance. Though the movie remains unmade, eventually I adapted this movie script into my 2000 novel *Exxxpresso*.

It is a favourite of the books I've written, and I've wanted to bring back that cast of crazy characters ever since. Now thanks to Matt Rubinstein, my publisher at Ligature, we have *Double Exxxpresso*.

Much appreciation to Wendy James who got the editor's halter over this unruly beast, and to my gorgeous wife Nicole for her perpetual support.

Whereas *Exxxpresso* dealt with gold and the rogues who populate that world, *Double Exxxpresso*, in the spirit of Damon Runyon, doffs its hat to the racing industry.

If you've not read any of my books prior to this, I hope you might take a punt on one or two more. And by the way, any similarity to people (or horses) living or dead is coincidental. These characters were born in my imagination and hopefully now reside in your memory.

Good luck and good punting as they say on the track—
Dave Warner author.